PRAISE FOR THE COLL

"[A] gripping novel of suspense from E._____, ...ravels layers of intersecting stories, each one ____ ..o the overall story of the Mills family and their small-town secrets. Readers will want to see more from this author."

—*Publishers Weekly*

"Elliot succeeds in creating both a thrilling mystery and a fascinating character study of the people inhabiting these pages."

—Bookreporter

"With her riveting, narrative-driven, deftly crafted storytelling style as a novelist, Kendra Elliot's *The Last Sister* will prove to be a welcome and enduringly popular addition to community library Mystery/Suspense/Thriller collections."

—*Midwest Book Review*

"Suspense on top of suspense. This one will keep you guessing until the final page and shows Elliot at her very best."

—The Real Book Spy

"Every family has skeletons. Kendra Elliot's tale of the Mills family's dark secrets is first-rate suspense. Dark and gripping, *The Last Sister* crescendos to knock-out, edge-of-your seat tension."

—Robert Dugoni, bestselling author of *My Sister's Grave*

"*The Last Sister* is exciting and suspenseful! Engaging characters and a complex plot kept me on the edge of my seat until the very last page."

—T.R. Ragan, bestselling author of the Jessie Cole series

"Thriller Award finalist Elliot's well-paced sequel to *The Last Sister* opens at the home of fifty-two-year-old Reuben Braswell, a devotee of conspiracy theories, who's lying dead in his bathtub . . . The twist ending will catch most readers by surprise . . . [and] fans will look forward to seeing characters from the author's other series take the lead in future installments."

—*Publishers Weekly*

"Elliot skillfully interweaves the various plot threads, and credible, mostly sympathetic characters match the lovingly described locale. Fans of contemporary regional mysteries will be rewarded."

—*Publishers Weekly*

THE FIRST
DEATH

ALSO BY KENDRA ELLIOT

COLUMBIA RIVER NOVELS

The Last Sister
The Silence
In the Pines

MERCY KILPATRICK NOVELS

A Merciful Death
A Merciful Truth
A Merciful Secret
A Merciful Silence
A Merciful Fate
A Merciful Promise

BONE SECRETS NOVELS

Hidden
Chilled
Buried
Alone
Known

BONE SECRETS NOVELLAS

Veiled

CALLAHAN & MCLANE NOVELS
PART OF THE BONE SECRETS WORLD

Vanished
Bridged
Spiraled
Targeted

ROGUE RIVER NOVELLAS

On Her Father's Grave (Rogue River)
Her Grave Secrets (Rogue River)
Dead in Her Tracks (Rogue Winter)
Death and Her Devotion (Rogue Vows)
Truth Be Told (Rogue Justice)

WIDOW'S ISLAND NOVELLAS

Close to the Bone
Bred in the Bone
Below the Bones
The Lost Bones
Bone Deep

THE FIRST
DEATH

KENDRA
ELLIOT

 Montlake

Published by Montlake, Seattle

www.apub.com

Amazon, the Amazon logo, and Montlake are trademarks of Amazon.com, Inc., or its affiliates.

ISBN-13: 9781542006842 (hardcover)
ISBN-13: 9781542006828 (paperback)
ISBN-13: 9781542009973 (digital)

Cover design by Caroline Teagle Johnson
Cover image: © Joana Kruse / ArcAngel; © Aaro Keipi / ArcAngel; © wingmar / Getty; © Aaron Foster / Getty

Printed in the United States of America
First edition

For my girls

1

Don't say a word.

Be quiet.

Don't move. Don't move. Don't move.

Five-year-old Rowan held her breath and tightened herself into the smallest ball possible, her head hidden in her arms. Her leg hurt so bad. But that was normal now. It had hurt for days. She'd cried nonstop as it bounced and jerked while she rode on Malcolm's back.

Malcolm will be here soon.

She simply had to wait. Her brother would never leave her for long.

I'm so cold.

She shuddered and pressed closer to the trunk of the big bush. Malcolm had chosen the hiding place because of its low branches and big leaves. Dirt tickled her nose. Its scent of dampness and decay.

He was looking for them. She had heard his faint shouts as he called her name and Malcolm's.

Be quiet.

Malcolm had stashed her under the bush when he couldn't carry her anymore. He'd tried to keep going, but he was only seven, and he wasn't that strong. Now she wanted to sleep. Sleep and sleep. Her eyelids wouldn't stay open, and her limbs were deadweight, but her brain kept listening, waiting to hear Malcolm return and fearful that *his* calls would get closer.

She pushed up the sleeve of Malcolm's sweatshirt and scratched her arm, feeling the scab release and then wedge under her fingernail.

So itchy.

Bugbites. Dozens of them. Up and down her arms and legs. Many she'd scratched until they bled. The constant itch and sting made her cry. Something in the locked shed had thought she was delicious. Malcolm had a few bites but nothing like the number of hers. The only good thing about the itch was that it temporarily made her forget the pain in her leg.

Until she moved it. And then hot fire shot up her nerves into her brain.

She wiped her cheek with a filthy hand. Being dirty no longer bothered her. Her empty stomach bothered her. The cold and bugbites bothered her. Being alone and hearing shouts in the distance bothered her.

What if he finds Malcolm?

He wouldn't. Malcolm was smart and sneaky. He would get help and be back soon.

Rowan didn't know how many days had gone by since they'd escaped. She thought they had been in the woods for two nights, but her memory was fuzzy. It'd been dark when they left, and they'd stopped several times, when she'd dozed off. She was so very thirsty. And cold. And tired.

So tired.

She jerked awake. The shadows had changed, the green of the leaves was brighter, and she had a sense that she'd slept through a large part of the day. A few yards away, rustling and panting noises sounded, and she knew that was what had disturbed her sleep.

Malcolm?

He didn't breathe like that.

It must be *him.*

She scrunched herself small again, listening hard for a voice, grinding her teeth to keep from crying at the fresh pain in her leg. The rustling grew louder, and branches crackled as they were pushed aside. Rowan covered her ears and squeezed her lids tight.

He can't see me. He can't see me.

Something stopped and then pushed through the leaves of her bush. She heard a snort, and then breath huffed against her cheek.

A bear? A wolf?

Her eyes flew open, terror freezing her in place.

A dog.

The big yellow dog abruptly sat down outside her bush. He sniffed and whooshed air at her again. Then he smiled at her, teeth showing as his tail whipped back and forth in the dirt.

He's happy.

Rowan blinked several times. "Hi," she whispered. His tail beat faster and his smile widened.

Dogs don't smile.

But it was the only way to describe his expression. His dark doggy eyes held her gaze, and Rowan's own smile made her cheeks hurt. They were stiff and cold. They felt as if she hadn't smiled in weeks.

She hadn't.

"Good dog," she said quietly, suddenly desperate to keep him close. If he ran away, she'd be alone, and it felt as if she'd been abandoned for days. She sat up and stretched a hand out of her hiding spot toward the dog, her frozen muscles jerking with the movement.

Someone pushed through nearby bushes, and Rowan yanked her hand back under her bush, glimpsing a tall man in a dark cap.

He saw me.

Tears streamed. She'd been caught. He'd take her back to that horrible place.

"Great job, Colin!" he said. "Who's the best dog?" The branches parted.

Rowan pressed her palms into her eyes and curled into the smallest ball possible.

"Rowan? Don't be scared."

It's not him. That's not his voice.

"We've been searching for you, Rowan, and I'm so glad Colin found you," he said kindly. "Your parents are waiting for you a few miles from here."

Rowan moved her hands and squinted at the stranger through the leaves. He knelt in the dirt while he scratched Colin's ear. Both the dog and the man grinned at her, and she noticed the dog wore an official-looking red harness with words on it.

"And Malcolm? Is he there too?" she asked. "He said he'd come back for me."

The man's smile faltered. "We're still looking for him. We found you, so we'll find him too." He held out a gloved hand.

Rowan shook her head. "I can't move. It hurts too bad."

"What hurts?"

"My leg."

The man inched closer and pushed a few branches out of the way to see her leg. He caught his breath and then pressed his lips together as he studied it. Rowan kept her gaze on the man, refusing to peek. She knew her leg was hideous. Below her knee the skin had a huge, weird lump. The tissue was black and blue and an ugly yellow brown. It'd been turning different colors for days. Malcolm had said it was broken.

"I'm going to lift you as carefully as I can," the man said. "Wrap your arms around my neck, and we'll get you to a doctor."

Rowan nodded, steeling herself for the pain. Malcolm had said almost the exact same words.

He came close and gently scooped her up. She yelped as pain shot through her, making stars flash in her eyes. Rowan wrapped her arms around his neck and buried her face in his shoulder, breathing hard. He stood and held perfectly still until she caught her breath. "Ready?"

She nodded, unable to speak. Her cheeks wet with tears.

"Let's go see your parents." He turned smoothly and set off through the brush, Colin darting before him.

Rowan looked over his shoulder and watched her hiding spot vanish, blending into the greens and browns of the woods.

Malcolm was never found.

2

Deschutes County detective Evan Bolton stepped into the small home in Bend, Oregon, and smelled death. Outside the house he'd passed four patrol units, ducked under crime scene tape, signed the log, and then slipped blue protective booties onto his feet before entering the murder scene. The distinctive scent made him pause, swallow hard, and tuck away his emotions so he could focus on his job.

An hour ago a neighbor had walked into twenty-four-year-old Summer Jensen's home and found the young mother brutally beaten and dead on her kitchen floor.

Why are they always in the kitchen?

"First officer on scene had just cleared the home when the husband pulled up and parked in the driveway," said the sergeant as he escorted Evan inside.

Evan had seen the husband sitting on the back seat of a patrol vehicle, the door open, his feet on the concrete and his head in his hands. Despair surrounded him. An officer stood close, one hand on the man's shoulder as he comforted him in low tones. Evan hadn't talked to the husband; he wanted to see the victim and scene.

First suspect to eliminate is always the spouse.

"Husband seemed genuinely freaked out," the sergeant continued. "Took two officers to contain him. And once he realized his son was missing, he went ballistic."

Evan would have done the same. "The boy is five, right?"

"Yeah. We've got a neighborhood door-to-door search going on, checking for the boy and asking who has camera views of the street."

"K9s?"

"Our officer and his K9 are on their way, but he suggested we contact the local canine search and rescue to check the area for the boy. They train specifically for this sort of thing. Someone was available to come immediately."

"They're excellent at what they do," Evan agreed. "We can't have too many hands on deck with a kid missing. FBI been notified?"

"Yes. They're sending an agent."

"Good. What's the boy's name?"

"Wyatt."

In the kitchen Evan found medical examiner Natasha Lockhart standing next to the body, writing on a clipboard. He studied the victim's battered face and fought back a surge of emotion. The victim looked younger than he'd expected. Too young to have her life brutally taken away. A pair of medical gloves lay on the victim's torso, and a forensic tech slowly paced around the kitchen, taking photographs. Natasha looked up from her clipboard. "Good morning, Detective."

"What can you tell me, Natasha?" he asked. The gloves on the body indicated she'd finished her preliminary examination.

"First tell me what you see, Evan," she said with an inquisitive raise of one eyebrow.

He studied the blonde mother, who lay on her back, arms and legs spread-eagled. "Looks like she was hit in the mouth and left eye. Several times." He crouched beside the body. "Hands and nails don't show blood or contusions, so either she didn't fight back or couldn't. I don't see the beginning of any bruising on her arms." He took a pen out of his pocket and pushed Summer Jensen's hair off her neck. Faint marks. "He choked her?"

"I strongly suspect that's what I'll find when I get her on my table," said Natasha.

This can't be related.

Evan had two other murders on his desk. Both of young women who had been strangled during the past two months. But their remains had been abandoned in rural areas. They'd come from bad situations. One was from Portland and had been living on the street. The other was a runaway from Idaho. This death didn't feel like the others.

But the other murdered women were in the forefront of his mind as he studied the body. He'd gotten to know them through photos and interviews with their families. Summer Jensen's life experience was still present in the small house. And in her son.

"Her death was recent," added Natasha. "Within the last four hours."

"Our suspect can't be too far away, then. Maybe he has the boy with him." Evan noted that Summer was barefoot. She wore midcalf yoga pants and a thin T-shirt with the Nike logo. Evan stood and glanced around the kitchen. It had older black appliances and was neat and clean. It was very homey. An open box of Lucky Charms and a milk jug sat near the sink. An empty bowl featuring Thomas the Tank Engine waited nearby.

Making breakfast for Wyatt.

Slipping on gloves, Evan strode to the slider that led to the back patio and pulled on the handle. It slid open. "Was this unlocked when they cleared the house?" he asked.

"Yes. And the front door was ajar when the neighbor arrived," said the sergeant, who'd been silently watching and listening.

"Why did the neighbor come over?"

"She and Summer always run together a few days a week at this time. She entered the house because the door was ajar and called 911 when she found the body. She lives two doors down. Good witness.

Relatively calm. I sent an officer home with her, and she knows you'll want to speak with her later."

Evan nodded. "Where was the dad this morning?"

"At the gym."

Evan made a mental note to check whether the gym had scanned a membership card and whether it had any video feeds. He stepped through the slider to the patio and took a deep breath of fresh air. The backyard was small and mostly lawn with a thin border of bark dust along the chain-link fence. The grass needed to be mowed. Evan let his gaze wander the yard, not liking that he could easily see into several neighbors' yards through the fencing. He preferred a tall wood fence and privacy. A subtle shadow in the grass near the house caught his eye, and he squatted for a better angle.

From this lower perspective, he saw footprints had bent the tall blades of grass.

Wyatt.

The prints were too small and too close together to be an adult's. They made a path that ran close to the house and disappeared around a corner. Careful not to damage the prints, Evan followed the faint path around the house and found a small gate with an easy latch. On the other side of the gate, the ground was covered in bark dust, and it was impossible to see prints in the rough pieces of wood.

Did the boy get away while his mother was being beaten?

Worst-case scenario was that whoever had killed Summer had taken the boy; best-case scenario was that the boy had hidden somewhere in the neighborhood, traumatized by what he'd seen. Evan refused to make any assumptions but knew that the footprints would make an excellent starting point for the search dog.

"Hey, Detective Bolton."

Evan returned to the back of the house and saw the sergeant at the sliding door.

"Search dog is here. The handler wants some used clothing or a pillowcase or maybe a stuffed animal that the kid slept with for a scent article." He held out a large plastic bag. "She said to put it in this but try not to touch it."

"Got it." Evan took the bag and followed the sergeant back into the house. He wandered down the only hall in the home, passing a small bathroom and a home office. He stopped at the doorway of what was clearly a young boy's room. There were *Star Wars* sheets on the bed, with matching curtains, and toys were scattered across the floor. Evan spotted a pajama top and bottoms crumpled on the rug next to the bed. He pinched a corner of the bottoms with a gloved hand, dropped them in the bag, and sealed it.

That should work.

He took one last glance around the room and pushed the closet door farther open.

No boy.

He did a quick check of the parents' bedroom, a guest bedroom, and another bathroom. Everything looked normal. The parents' bed was unmade and the bathroom counter crowded with products. The guest bedroom looked as if it hadn't been used in weeks. All the closets in every room were open. Probably opened by the officers as they cleared the house. Nothing indicated a struggle had taken place.

Except the body in the kitchen.

He clenched the bag and headed back down the hall and out the front door. On the sidewalk in front of the home, he spotted Rowan Wolff and her black German shepherd, Thor, as she spoke with one of the officers. The tall woman did a double take at the sight of Evan and then waved. Rowan had a stellar reputation for finding lost people. Evan had worked with her a few times, and there was no one he'd rather have on the case.

He joined her and the officer, holding out the bag. "Good to see you, Rowan."

Her intense brown eyes were in work mode. "You too, Detective." She immediately focused on the bag. "What did you choose?"

"Pajama bottoms from the floor near his bed."

"Perfect." She took the bag. "That the dad?" She nodded at the man still sitting in the back seat of the car. Now two officers were speaking with him, one crouched in front at eye level.

"Yes," said Evan, taking a long look at the upset father. Geoff Jensen had salt-and-pepper hair and lines around his mouth. He looked at least twenty years older than the murdered young woman in the house. Once Rowan started her search, he planned to talk to the man. "There's a path of child-sized footprints that lead from the back door of the home around to the gate on that side," he told Rowan as he pointed to a corner of the garage. "Should be a good place to start." He glanced up and down the street. Some neighbors were in their driveways, watching the scene. "I'm hoping Wyatt is somewhere in the neighborhood. The medical examiner says his mother has been dead less than four hours. I can't see a five-year-old getting too far away."

"You'd be surprised at the distance they can cover," said Rowan. "But if he's still close by, he's most likely found a hidey-hole of some sort. All these strangers and police cars could be terrifying and stopping him from coming out." A shadow crossed her eyes, disappearing as quickly as it appeared.

Evan nodded. She was the expert, and he had full faith in her skills. Beside her, Thor sat at attention, his calm black gaze taking in the activity, his tongue hanging out one side of his mouth. He wore a red harness that said SEARCH AND RESCUE on each side. In the past Rowan had told Evan that when this harness was put on, the dog knew it was time to work.

A commotion pulled their attention. The father had stood and was trying to approach, but the two officers had each grabbed an arm.

"If that dog is going to look for Wyatt, I'm coming too!" Geoff yanked his arm out of an officer's grip. "I need to search for my boy!"

Evan strode to intercept Geoff and held up a hand. "Don't interfere with the dog and handler," he ordered. "They need space to search."

Geoff's reddened gaze pleaded with Evan. "I've got to look. I can't just sit here. My son is *missing*."

"I know," said Evan. "But unless you can tell us a spot where you know he would hide, you need to leave the search to us."

The stricken man looked blankly around the neighborhood. "I have no idea," he whispered.

"Does he have a friend that lives on your street? A home he'd go to where he'd feel safe?"

"No kids his age around here," said the father. "We've only been here a few months . . . I can't say that Wyatt would associate a particular home with safety."

"Then sit tight." Evan knew his words weren't helpful. "We've got several officers knocking on doors, and someone from the FBI should be here soon."

"FBI?" Geoff appeared stunned. "They'll help look?"

"Missing children are an FBI priority."

"Thank God." His face crumpled. "Summer is gone. I can't lose Wyatt too." An officer gave his arm a gentle tug and led him back to the car.

Evan watched him for a moment and then went back to Rowan. She opened the plastic bag, and Thor plunged his nose inside, inhaling and snorting at the blue pajamas.

The dog clearly knows it's work time.

"Find it," Rowan ordered, removing the leash. Thor lifted his head, and his nostrils widened, his mouth opening slightly as he breathed in. He was still for a moment and then turned and led Rowan to the side of the home where the little footprints vanished.

Incredible.

Evan watched the dog circle around in the small bark dust area and stick his nose into the wire of the gate, then spin and trot to the street, where he stopped and sniffed the air again.

Evan stiffened, hoping Thor hadn't already lost the scent. That could indicate Wyatt had been put in a vehicle. Thor made sweeps, swiftly going back and forth in the street in front of the house. Evan glanced at Rowan, hoping to gain some insight from her expression. Her gaze was locked on the dog. She didn't look concerned or optimistic. A calmness surrounded her. A deep focus.

The officers and neighbors all watched Thor's movements, and the dog ignored them, completely intent on his job. Wyatt's dad stood by the police car, observing, hope in his countenance.

Thor did two more sweeps of the street and then stopped, his muzzle lifting. Then he darted to the house. Evan's heart sank. Of course the dog would locate Wyatt's scent in the home. The child lived there. The dog stopped at the closed front door and sat, looking over his shoulder at Rowan as he mouthed a quiet doggy sound.

Rowan frowned. "The house was searched?" she asked, looking from officer to officer.

"Yes," answered two of them at once.

"Searched for a suspect or a small boy?" she asked.

"Shit," said one of the officers as they exchanged glances. "I had an adult in mind as I looked."

"Thor thinks he's inside," said Rowan.

"The whole house probably smells like Wyatt," said the sergeant.

"He can pinpoint the strongest scent, which will be the most recent. I believe at one point he walked along that side of the house and into the street," said Rowan. "But I'd like to take Thor through the home."

"Do it," said Evan. "The front door was open when his mother was discovered. Maybe Wyatt went out the back door and came in the front after the attacker left." He and Rowan approached the door, and Rowan snapped her leash to Thor's harness.

"The mother is in the kitchen," Evan said in a low voice. "It's not a good sight."

"Got it," replied Rowan, opening the door and allowing Thor inside.

Kendra Elliot

Evan followed them into the home after a look back at Geoff. Wyatt's father was still by the police car, watching them enter. He hadn't said a word since Thor had started working. An odd prickle went up Evan's spine.

Something is up with Geoff.

Thor trotted through the house. After a pause and a snort in the direction of the kitchen, he immediately turned down the hallway to the bedrooms. The dog wasn't the least bit interested in the smell of blood and worse from the murder. Thor was solely focused on Wyatt's scent.

Amazing.

Thor stopped in the doorway to Wyatt's room and huffed out two breaths. Then he continued down the hall and trotted into the guest room. He went to the head of the bed and sat, looking up at Rowan, making that soft doggy chatter sound again.

"Good boy." She scratched his head. "Wyatt?" she asked quietly. "It's safe to come out now. Nothing is going to hurt you."

Evan dropped to his knees and looked under the bed just as Rowan did the same.

No one was there.

Silence.

"What the . . . ," Evan muttered. "Let's look inside the box spring." He wanted to slide under the bed to look, but he was too large.

"Wait," said Rowan. She turned to the nightstand and opened one of its cupboard-style doors. Thor tried to stick his head inside, but she held him back. "Hi, Wyatt," she said kindly, peering into the dark, low cupboard. "I'm Rowan, and this is Thor. I'm so glad we found you."

Over Rowan's shoulder, Evan saw the small boy curled up into the smallest ball possible in the nightstand. Evan wouldn't have guessed a child could fit inside.

The officers cleared the house for an adult intruder. No one would have looked in there.

14

Rowan shifted out of the way, and Evan moved to make eye contact with Wyatt. The boy hadn't moved a muscle, but he met Evan's gaze.

He's terrified.

"Hi, Wyatt," Evan said. "Can you come out?"

The boy didn't budge.

Rowan and Evan exchanged a glance.

"You're safe now," Rowan told him. "You know your mother . . . was hurt, right?"

The tiniest of nods answered her.

"Whoever did it isn't in the house anymore," Evan told him. "I'm a police officer, and we're here to protect you."

Wyatt somehow made himself smaller.

Scared of the police?

Or . . .

"Wyatt, did you see who hurt your mother?" Evan asked.

Another infinitesimal nod.

"Who was it?" asked Evan. "No one will hurt you with us here."

Wyatt's gaze moved to Thor. The dog had lowered himself to his belly a few feet away and focused alert eyes on the boy in the nightstand, his ears cocked in Wyatt's direction. Rowan sat beside the dog, stroking his back.

Evan had been about to ask Rowan to take Thor out of the room, but Wyatt's terror seemed to abate a bit as he looked at the dog.

"Who hurt your mom?" Evan asked again.

"Will you put him in jail?" whispered Wyatt, still staring at Thor.

Evan had to bend forward to catch the almost-silent words. "Yes. I promise."

Wyatt's numb gaze turned to Evan. "Daddy did it. He pushed her to the floor and made her scream." He put his hands over his ears and started to cry.

Evan closed his eyes.

I knew it.

3

Standing in a dusty clearing in the middle of nowhere, Evan listened to the rattled young man who had found a dead body in the woods.

"It was his dog, dude," Jason stated.

Evan nodded encouragingly at Jason as the man ran his hand through his hair for the tenth time, his arms shaking. The twentysomething's gaze darted in every direction, and he nervously dug into the dirt with one hiking boot.

"I've never seen a dead body before," Jason stated, watching the activity around the blue tent behind Evan. "And I still wouldn't have seen one if it wasn't for his dog."

"Most people haven't seen a dead body," Evan told him. "It's not like on TV."

"Fuck no, it's not. I would have camped here for another five days not knowing there was a dead guy less than a hundred yards away if his dog hadn't come."

Evan thought that Jason would have noticed during those five days. The daily temperatures had been in the nineties. Unless Jason's nose didn't work, he would have smelled something.

The campground where they stood wasn't monitored by a state or federal agency. It was a deserted spot far off a little-used Forest Service road in the Cascade mountains where campers sometimes pitched their tents. Evan knew there was a makeshift shooting range in a canyon a mile away where people liked to practice.

Jason had called 911 after finding the body in the tent. The victim had two shots in the head and one in the heart. There was no ID with the body and no vehicle near the tent. The killer had picked up their shells before they left. Easy to find in the tent.

But we'll have the bullets.

Forensics was accustomed to digging bullets out of the ground.

"What did his dog do?" Evan asked. By the time he'd arrived at the scene, animal control had already taken away the black Lab.

Jason frowned. "I know dogs are smart, but I'd never seen one do this. He came to my camp at breakfast and kept circling around, just out of reach. He didn't look skinny, but I figured he was hungry, so I put out a couple slices of bread and poured water in a bowl. The Lab sniffed both and simply sat, staring at me. I picked up the bread and held it out to him, but he backed away. He wouldn't leave and he wouldn't eat. I finally noticed he'd walk away a few steps and look over his shoulder at me like he wanted me to follow. Full-on Lassie behavior, you know?

"I felt like an idiot, but I followed him, and he kept doing the same thing. Moving away and looking back. When he saw the tent, he ran and sat in front of the flap. It was unzipped about two feet. I announced myself and waited. Said something again and waited. The dog kept shifting closer to the tent flap and looking at me. I didn't want to snoop. For all I knew someone in there had a gun . . . or someone would walk out of the woods and get pissed that I was in his stuff. But I finally looked." Jason shook his head, looking pale under his numerous freckles. "Don't ever want to see that again."

"Did you touch anything?" asked Evan.

"Just the tent zipper. I didn't touch the body." Jason swallowed audibly. "Fucking holes in the face, man. And smelled like shit in there. I knew he was dead. That's when I called 911."

"You didn't hear or see any vehicles in the last few days?"

"Nah. Been quiet up here. Usually there's a few groups in the area, but not this week."

A faint odor of weed hung around the young man. He was alert at the moment, but the marijuana could have numbed him to any activity in the woods overnight.

Evan wanted to know how long the man had been dead, but all the medical examiners were busy at other scenes, and he didn't have an estimate as to how soon one could arrive. A county forensics tech had arrived before Evan and was currently documenting the scene in the tent. A forest ranger had been the first on the scene and had cordoned off a generous area to search. Two county deputies were currently doing a slow walk and scan through the area, looking for any evidence.

"Okay, Jason. You sticking around up here for a few days?" Evan asked.

The young man scrunched up his face. "*Fuck no.* It feels as creepy as hell here now, and if someone is shooting people in the head, I'd be dumb to stay." His gaze darted around the woods, as if he expected the shooter to appear. "Don't know how you're going to find the guy who did it. It's a big forest."

"We'll figure it out," Evan said noncommittally. "I've got your contact info. You'll probably hear from me again."

And I have your driver's license, license plate, and VIN.

If Jason tried to disappear, Evan could track him down. His gut told him the young man wasn't involved, but he wouldn't make any assumptions.

"Good luck, man. Hope you catch him."

"Hey, Detective Bolton?" The forensics tech had stuck her head out of the tent. "Can you come here for a minute?"

Evan nodded at Jason, ducked under the crime scene tape, and headed to the tent, watching where he stepped. "What is it?"

"A cell phone. Was tucked in one of his boots. Still haven't found any of his ID, but maybe this will help." She handed Evan a phone in a baggie.

He touched the screen through the plastic, and the phone lit up. Its lock screen was an image of a half dozen people posing outdoors near a creek. A cheerful group. Their arms around one another.

The phone was too old to unlock with facial recognition or a fingerprint—features Evan had used a few times when the body was nearby. This phone needed a code.

"Dammit," he muttered. He wanted to identify the body quickly.

"Yeah," said the tech. "Sorry about that. I haven't found anything else to help us figure out his identity. Might have to wait on fingerprints or for someone to come looking for him."

Evan studied the photo on the lock screen, easily picking out the victim in the center of the happy group. He was tall and appeared to be in his fifties, looking fit and healthy, with a graying beard.

It would be a good photo to release to the public if Evan hit a dead end with identification. Clearly the man had friends, and the background appeared distinctly Pacific Northwest. Evan squinted at the other faces and zeroed in on one of the women. She was peeking over the shoulder of one of the other men in the group. She wore a baseball cap, but her smile and eyes were quite clear.

"I'll be damned," he said. It was Rowan Wolff.

4

"Find it," ordered Rowan.

Thor turned away from the stuffed animal and shot across the front yard. Rowan jogged after him, her gaze locked on the black dog, observing his tail and head movements. At the corner of the house, he paused and looked back at her, a black void against the bricks of their home, but the language in his shiny eyes was clear.

/hurry up/

"I'm coming," she muttered. Thor liked her in sight. It was rare for him to vanish for very long. He'd always reappear, his ears twitching, eager to get back to the search but also wanting her nearby. Rowan tried to stay close because she didn't want the lack of her presence to distract him. He had a job, and it required 100 percent of his focus. But he didn't like leaving her behind.

He knows I can't move as fast.

When she reached him, Thor sped around the corner of the house, shot across the backyard, and started a wide sweep of the field behind her home, trotting back and forth, his mouth slightly open, his tongue visible. Thor abruptly stopped, lifted his nose a long moment, and froze. Then he made a beeline for the little playhouse under the firs.

Rowan smiled as Thor circled the plastic building, his wagging tail a blur. He stopped at the little door and shoved his nose into the crack between the door and the wall. And then he sat. He looked back at Rowan and made a soft *roo roo roo* sound. She'd taught him not to bark when he found his quarry, but she couldn't train away his discovery chatter.

/found her found her found her/

Rowan thought it was adorable.

The sounds weren't threatening, so she allowed it. Barking upon discovery wasn't acceptable because it could scare a lost child.

"Lily," Rowan called, "you can come out now."

The door opened. Rowan's nine-year-old neighbor appeared and gave Thor a big hug. The dog was ecstatic, wiggling and pressing against the girl, trying to get as much of the hug as possible. Then he looked back at Rowan, his ears directed at her, his tongue hanging.

/I did good/

Rowan's heart swelled with pride and love. A normal occurrence whenever she looked at her four-legged big ball of fur. She rubbed his head, relishing the velvet softness of his furry black ears. "Good boy, Thor. Such a good boy."

"He's the best," agreed Lily. "Can we do it again?" She gave Rowan a pleading look, her eyes eager.

Finding the girl wasn't much of a challenge for Thor. They'd been playing the game for more than a year, and there'd been numerous discoveries at the playhouse, under piles of leaves, in Lily's garage, and in her parents' camper. Lily liked to zigzag through the field or run in circles around the house before hiding, always amazed that Thor could filter out where her scent was the strongest.

Rowan enjoyed the games as much as her dog and Lily. It was good practice for Thor and always ended on a positive note, boosting the dog's confidence.

Thor looked at Rowan and uttered a long string of doggy chat.

/more more more/

As if Rowan didn't know that the dog would happily continue the game for hours. A movement out of the corner of her eye pulled

Rowan's attention back toward her house. A man stood next to her home, his hands shoved in his pockets.

Startled, Rowan froze and felt Thor do the same under her fingers.

Then she relaxed, recognizing the silhouette and stance of Detective Evan Bolton. She hadn't talked to him since they'd found Wyatt a few days ago. She'd been scanning the news but hadn't seen any updates on the case.

She'd known Evan for a couple of years. Last winter he'd hired her and Thor to find a close friend of his, an FBI agent who'd vanished during an undercover assignment. The snowy search had been a success, and Rowan still kept in touch with the FBI agent, Mercy Kilpatrick.

Does he have another job for me?

She doubted it. He would have called, not shown up in person.

Every job she took was important. Rowan and Thor had built a reputation on her professionalism and success in finding lost people. She'd helped a dozen federal agencies and nearly fifty police and sheriff's departments across the country. She sometimes worked with a few different Oregon teams of search and rescue (SAR) canines but often took jobs on her own. Some clients wanted discretion for one reason or another.

Most search and rescue was done by volunteers. Law enforcement agencies paid when they could, but the cost of bringing in a team of dogs and handlers for weeks of SAR often fell to the volunteers. Because of a grateful private client a few years ago, Rowan had the financial freedom to travel the country, taking on cases that other search teams couldn't.

Rowan and Thor had found the missing daughter of a wealthy retail magnate. He'd given her an unexpected reward that had set her up for life—if she kept her living expenses within reason. Rowan would have searched for his daughter for no money. In fact she'd agreed to the job without having a financial discussion.

It was what her soul was meant to do: find lost people.

Sometimes living. Sometimes not.

Rowan pulled a rope chew toy out of her big pocket and held it out to Lily. Thor stood still, every one of his senses trained on the toy. "Would you play with Thor while I talk to that man?"

Lily didn't even glance at Evan. She grabbed the toy and darted away. Quivering with anticipation, Thor looked to Rowan, who gave a nod. "Go play." The dog leaped and spun in midair, landing in a full sprint after Lily, catching up within seconds. Rowan watched for a few seconds. Sometimes Thor didn't realize how powerful he was and would accidentally knock Lily aside. This time the dog gave her space, leaving several feet between them.

Rowan started toward the house, trying to remember the local law enforcement gossip she'd heard a few weeks before about Evan Bolton. Something about a fire at his sister's home and her husband being injured. Rowan rubbed shoulders with a lot of law enforcement, and they were bigger gossipers than her sisters' hair salon clientele. She and Evan hadn't had time for small talk after finding Wyatt Jensen. Evan had gotten right to work, building a case to charge the father with his wife's murder, and Rowan had returned home.

Evan stepped off the stone path and came down the gentle slope of grass to meet her.

Rowan loved her home, an inheritance from her grandfather. It was a small ranch-style house on a gigantic lot that backed up to acres and acres of . . . nothing. Scrubby bushes, tough tall grass, some patches of tall pines, and lava rocks. But beyond the acres of nothing, she could see the tall Cascade mountain range. There was little snow on the mountaintops. It'd been a hot, dry summer in Central Oregon, and she looked forward to a cooler September starting the following week.

"Detective Bolton," she said with a smile. He was a good-looking man, she acknowledged. Tall, fit, and his shirt gave a hint of well-formed shoulders and biceps. Strong arms were her weakness. She knew the detective was about her age, but he seemed older. He had the aura of someone who carried a big burden from his past, something that kept him from fully enjoying the present.

The nurturer in her had always wanted to fix it.

But she knew not to try to heal brooding men. They had to tackle it themselves.

"Hey, Rowan," he said. "Sorry to just show up unannounced, but I wasn't far away and thought you'd like to know that Geoff Jensen confessed to his wife's murder this morning."

Relief shot through her. "That's fantastic." Then anger took over. "That asshole," she spit out. "He tried to lie his way through it for a few days?"

"He did. Claimed he'd been at his gym when he was actually out driving around looking for Wyatt. He'd seen the boy dart out the back door but was too busy choking his wife to pursue him until later." Rage flared in Evan's eyes. "I don't know what he planned to do when he found the boy. I'm not sure I want to know."

"Where is Wyatt now?"

"He's staying with Summer's sister, who has two boys around his age. She and her husband will try to adopt the boy if it's legally possible because it's doubtful Jensen will get out of prison before Wyatt is an adult. They seem like a good family."

"A happy ending," said Rowan, immediately regretting her words. "Not happy," she revised, "but the outcome could have been much worse."

"Definitely." Evan shoved his hands in his pockets and looked past her. "Thor's looking good."

Rowan glanced back to see Lily and Thor in a rough game of tug-of-war, Lily shrieking with laughter.

"He's doing well. Happy and full of energy like always."

"I knew he'd find Wyatt."

Rowan smiled and met Evan's gaze. And blinked.

Something has changed.

His eyes were calm. No hints of brooding or painful baggage. Even the strain that had always been around his mouth was mostly gone.

Maybe he met someone. Good for him.

A tiny pang of regret echoed in her chest. It was her own fault. She should have asked the detective out when she had a chance. But the moments had always felt wrong. They worked together very well, and she had been hesitant to do something that could affect it.

I'm meant to be a woman who just has dogs.

The corner of her mouth quirked. She'd always suspected that would be her fate. A disastrous, brief marriage nearly a decade ago had kept her firmly in favor of being single.

But it didn't mean she didn't like to look. And date. And enjoy the men who came and went in her life.

Her life didn't suck. It was pretty damn good.

She turned to look at Thor, the only man in her life at the moment.

"When you watch your dog, you look like a proud parent," Evan said. "My sister looks at her kids the same way."

"I heard something about a fire at your sister's home recently?" Rowan asked.

"Yeah. Mainly ruined furniture and smoke damage."

"Her husband was hurt?"

Evan shifted uncomfortably. "It wasn't the fire that injured him, but he's home and doing really well. My niece and nephew stayed with me for a while. Great kids." His face lit up as he mentioned them. "The family is starting an animal rescue on their acreage."

"Good for them," said Rowan, enjoying the happiness on the detective's face. "I appreciate you stopping by to tell me about Geoff Jensen."

Evan grew serious. "I had another reason."

Rowan waited. The detective appeared to be putting his thoughts in order, and her curiosity grew.

"I was called to a scene this morning, and there was no ID with the body, but the lock screen on the victim's cell phone is a group picture." He paused, a sympathetic look on his face. "I think you're in the picture."

Her lungs stopped.

Who is it?

Her mind raced through a dozen people, her anxiety growing as friends' faces streamed through her mind. "Let me see it."

Evan pulled a phone out of his pocket. "I took my own photo of the lock screen." He touched the face of his phone, dragged his finger to enlarge something, and handed her the device.

She took it with damp, unsteady hands. She instantly recognized the photo. It'd been taken after a canine search and rescue training session the summer before. These people were her close friends.

Who died?

"The victim is the guy with the gray beard in the center."

Rowan shut her eyes.

Ken. No!

Her heart cracked into a dozen pieces. Ken had found her when she and her brother had been kidnapped twenty-five years before. It was because of him that she worked in search and rescue. He'd been her mentor and close friend.

This isn't happening.

She opened her eyes, blinking away the instant tears. "His name is Ken Steward." Her voice shook, and she took several deep breaths. "He was a good man. The absolute best. What happened to him?"

"All you need to know is that he probably died instantly. No pain."

Fury made her vision narrow. "Don't give me that mitigated informing-the-friends-and-family shit. *Tell me what happened.*"

Evan looked away, a struggle on his face. "He was shot. Two in the head, one in the chest. He was found in a camping tent off a Forest Service road."

Rowan stared at Evan, horror flooding her. "That sounds like something you see on a TV show. An assassination." She wished she hadn't asked. Her brain was graphically filling in details.

"It does. I suspect he was asleep. There are no defensive wounds as if he'd held up a hand to block a shot, and he appeared undisturbed in his sleeping bag."

She tried to take comfort in Evan's description.

I can't believe he's gone.

A black hole formed in her chest. Ken had been an anchor, a confidant. His death would leave a gaping empty space in her life.

But their last encounter had not gone well. Ken had been short-tempered and snapped at her during a training exercise, calling her incompetent. Rowan had immediately whirled in his direction and ordered him not to disrespect her. He'd never spoken like that to her. Ever.

And she'd never spoken to him like that either. But Ken had triggered her. Few things did. But she'd suddenly heard her ex-husband's voice in her head. His constant criticisms that had contributed to the end of their short marriage.

But worse to Rowan was that neither she nor Ken had apologized. They'd ended the training day in silence, each going their own way.

I should have called him.

Now it was too late.

Tears burned again.

"Is he married? Have kids?" asked Evan.

"No. Neither. Three ex-wives. The last divorce was a year ago. I know all of the women. I can put you in touch."

Evan frowned. "You know all of them? Then the two of you have been close for a long time."

Rowan's throat seemed to close. "Very close. He saved my life a long time ago." A thought struck her. "Where's his dog? A black Lab."

"County animal control has the dog. Ken's body was found because the dog led a camper to your friend's tent."

Tears threatened again. "Of course she did. Juno is the best dog. The two of them were inseparable."

How is Juno going to get through this?

Her mind immediately weighed the best options for Juno. She was the love of Ken's life, and their teamwork had been perfection. "The best place for Juno right now is with Ken's third wife. Her dog and Juno are best buds. I'll give you her contact information. She's the other woman in this picture."

"Thank you." Evan held out his hand, waiting for her to return the phone.

Rowan took one last look at the photo, thankful she had the same image stored on her computer because it was a good picture of everyone. They were a close group, but Ken had been the glue that held them together, and she knew it'd never be the same. She gave Evan the phone.

"I'm sorry, Rowan. I can tell you were close to him." Compassion filled his tone.

"Yes." She couldn't say anything more. Her lips quivered as she tried to smile.

Reluctance crossed his face. "Do you know anyone who would want to hurt him?" he asked, his tone hesitant.

Rowan understood the question was part of his job. It felt abrupt and wrong immediately after she'd received devastating news, but Evan needed to collect information as rapidly as possible to find Ken's killer.

She exhaled and considered the question. "I don't. It sounds cliché, but everyone liked him. He was generous and kind. I can't think of a cross word anyone has ever said about him. And if he had conflicts in his life, I'm unaware of them. Shannon—his most recent ex—would be the best person to ask. They're still close." She paused. "Were close."

"That will be my first stop." He touched her upper arm and gave a light squeeze. "I'm really sorry, Rowan."

The sincerity in his eyes calmed her. "Thank you."

"Text me Shannon's full name and contact info," he said. "I'll want to talk to you again in a day or two."

"I can stop by."

"I'll let you know when." His gaze went to Thor, who'd abruptly stopped in the field and turned his head their way, his ears forward, as if he knew something had happened with his owner. "I know you have a good comforter."

Rowan smiled at the dog. "I have the best."

5

Evan liked Shannon Steward. The woman gave off a bustling energy that spoke of efficiency and directness. Ken Steward's third wife had been on her way to a doctor's appointment when Evan called her about Ken's death, but she'd immediately turned her car around and headed to the county shelter. As with Rowan, one of Shannon's initial questions had been about Juno's location.

SAR people love their dogs.

He'd seen it in Rowan's words and actions with Thor. The comfort and care of the dog always came first.

Shannon had taken Ken's dog home and then met Evan at the sheriff's department that evening. They were in the detectives' small break room. It was more welcoming than the department's stark interview rooms, and they often used it when they needed to speak with families. It had a microwave, small fridge, and coffee maker along with a round table and half a dozen mismatched chairs. The other detectives knew not to come in to refill their coffee mugs when the door was closed.

Shannon wiped her eyes as she faced Evan at the table. He knew she was in her late fifties. Her hair was a pale red, worn in shoulder-length curls, and he would have guessed she was ten years younger. She was well freckled and wore shorts and hiking boots, clearly someone who loved to be outdoors. "He was such a good man," she said, echoing Rowan's opinion. "He loved to help people."

Evan thought about how many times he'd heard that during past cases only to discover dozens of secrets held by the victim. Secrets about crimes committed, other relationships, or financial problems. He never made an assumption based on other people's opinions; he had to experience it for himself.

"Were you married long?" Evan asked.

"Only two years, but I've known Ken for at least twenty. I was friends with his second wife. We all ran in the same circles." She gave a weak smile. "The SAR community is small and tight. People come and go, but there has been a core group of us forever, and Ken was always at the center of that core. A good man," she repeated. "He had his idiosyncrasies like everyone does. I know these quirks added to his divorces. He couldn't help it; it's just how he was. He wasn't malicious or anything. He just . . ." She paused. "I don't want to speak ill of him."

"I understand," said Evan. "No one wants to do that. But getting a good picture of his relationships with other people can possibly help pinpoint a motive."

Shannon grimaced. "I don't want to believe that Ken was murdered because he had quirks. Everyone has things that they like a certain way."

"Give me an example of one of his," Evan said encouragingly.

"Well, sometimes he needed to sleep outside."

Evan raised a brow. "As in . . . needed some time to himself?"

"No, he needed to be outdoors. Sometimes the house was too confining."

Claustrophobic.

"I see," said Evan. "I don't think someone would be murdered for that, but maybe it was hard on a marriage sometimes."

"In our case, we just couldn't live together. I'd been divorced for ten years when we married and couldn't adjust to having someone in my space."

Evan had often wondered if he'd have the same problem now. He'd lived with one woman in the past, but the two of them had been young

31

and eager to make things work. Until they didn't. "I've heard of married couples that live apart."

Shannon lifted one shoulder. "We discussed that. But it didn't feel right. We decided to legally separate things but we still . . . dated occasionally." She pulled up a photo on her phone and showed him. "Our wedding day three years ago."

Different strokes for different folks.

Evan tried to wrap his head around the facts that they still dated and that she carried their wedding photo. The photo showed a happy couple standing in the snow, a mountaintop sloping up behind them. She wore a dress in a loud Hawaiian print along with snow boots and held a bouquet of fir branches at her side, her mouth wide open in laughter. Ken was in jeans with his eyes trained on his new wife. They looked blissfully happy.

The image made Evan's throat tight. "Again . . . I'm sorry for your loss. It's great that you two were still close."

"Ken was one of those people that never met a stranger," Shannon said, wistfully eyeing the photo. "Everyone was immediately welcomed and made to feel special around him." She looked at Evan. "You said there was no ID with him. How did you identify him?"

"I recognized someone in the photo on his cell phone's lock screen. I went to her for identification."

"Rowan," Shannon said, nodding in understanding. "She was like a daughter to him. He was always concerned about her. He didn't think it was healthy that she'd go looking for her brother."

Evan was confused. "Looking for her brother?"

Shannon cocked her head, caution crossing her face. "How well do you know her?"

"Not that well, I guess," said Evan, wondering what Shannon was holding back. "We've worked together on a few cases."

The woman studied him. "It's her story. Not mine to tell."

"Of course." Evan respected the woman's protection of Rowan's privacy. Clearly Shannon Steward wasn't a gossip.

But I'm dying to know.

He shifted gears. "Juno had been picked up by animal control when I arrived at the scene, so I don't know what she was like, but I had a hard time imagining that a dog would allow someone into her owner's tent. Especially someone intent on violence."

Shannon had started nodding vehemently during Evan's statement. "I imagine most dogs wouldn't. But Juno is the biggest sweetheart and absolutely loves everyone. Gets excited to meet every stranger. She probably welcomed him into the tent." Fresh tears rolled down her cheeks. "Damned dog."

"Not a watchdog," Evan commented.

"Most definitely not. Even Ken joked that she'd probably give a robber the keys to his home."

"I know this next question is going to be tough, but—"

"Do I know of anyone who would hurt him."

"Yes." Evan picked up the pencil next to his yellow pad. "Don't let your feelings for him impact anything you want to say. Any help could point us in the right direction to start looking."

"Start looking?" Shannon paled under her freckles. "You have no leads?"

"We're still processing the evidence from the scene," Evan said smoothly. "While waiting for that, we interview the people closest to him. There were no witnesses."

"No leads," Shannon stated. "Well, shit." She looked out the window, twisting her lips as she thought. "Ken's been rather quiet lately. We usually meet for drinks every Thursday, but he had to cancel last week. Didn't say why, and I didn't ask."

"He doesn't ever cancel?"

"Never," she said emphatically. "He's always been annoyingly reliable." One side of her lips drew up in a half smile at her description, but sadness flashed in her eyes.

"Any arguments with his neighbors? Personality clashes with coworkers?"

Shannon exhaled as she thought, but after a long moment, she shook her head. "I'm trying to be objective, and I honestly can't think of anything."

"What did you mean when you said he'd been quiet?"

"I hadn't heard from him as much. Usually we text every other day or so. A long phone call once a week." She picked up her phone and scrolled. "I haven't heard from him since he canceled last Thursday."

"Was that a text?"

"Yes. And before that he hadn't texted for six days." Her eyebrows rose as she scrolled. "And then three days before that." She shook her head. "I hadn't really noticed until now."

"So something was occupying his time."

"Maybe he didn't have anything to say." She shrugged. "But that's not Ken. He was always the one with a story to tell and knew how to tactfully pry conversation out of the biggest introvert."

"That's a skill."

"He came by it naturally." She sucked in a shuddering breath. "Oh jeez. I'm going to lose it again. Excuse me, Detective." Shannon snatched two tissues out of the box on the table, bent her head, and pressed the tissues against her eyes.

Evan leaned back in his chair, giving her some space, mentally running through their conversation. Other than something *possibly* pre-occupying Ken over the last weeks, he hadn't gleaned anything to follow up on. He still needed to ask her who Ken's closest friends were, but Evan suspected his closest was sitting across from him.

"Excuse me, Shannon," Evan said quietly, hating to interrupt her moment of grief. "Can you tell me who Ken would consider his closest friends?" If Ken didn't have any known enemies, he'd start with the friends.

She lifted her head, sniffed, and wiped her eyes. "I'd say his cousin Eric Steward—he lives outside of town—and his friend Rees Womack. Rees is canine SAR too. He has a German shepherd. Gunnar."

Evan wrote down their names, smiling inwardly because she'd included the dog's. It appeared that in the close-knit SAR community, owner and dog were often seen as one unit.

Shannon's phone chimed, and she glanced at the screen. "It's Rowan. Checking up on me. She's a good kid."

Rowan had to be in her early thirties. That meant Evan also was a kid in Shannon's eyes.

"Is there anything else you think I should know about Ken?" Evan asked, prepared to end the interview.

Shannon scratched her neck as she thought. "I feel like I should have a secret to reveal to help find his killer, but I don't."

Evan stood, prompting Shannon to get to her feet. "You've been a big help. You have my number if you think of anything else."

After she left, Evan returned to his desk and pulled up his email, pleased to find two attachments from the forensics team. One was a list of every object recovered from the campsite. Multiple objects had been highlighted for testing, like Ken's clothing and sleeping bag. The other list was from Ken's home. The team had collected some finger-print evidence and looked for weapons. His desktop computer had been removed to be sent to the FBI's regional digital forensics lab in Portland along with the cell phone from the scene. Evan made a note to wait a few days and follow up on the electronics, hoping he wouldn't have to prod the lab to move his case up the priority list. Every investigator wanted their evidence to be highest priority, and the lab was overworked.

He'd already submitted a request to the wireless carrier for the last two months of Ken's cellular activity, and the medical examiner had planned Ken's autopsy for the next morning. She'd placed Ken's death at between midnight and 4:00 a.m. but warned Evan that the window of time was an estimate until she ran some labs from the autopsy.

A BOLO had been issued for Ken's SUV. A ten-year-old Ford Explorer.

Evan knew it was possible he was looking for two suspects. Somehow the killer had gotten to the camping location but also managed to take Ken's vehicle with him. It indicated two drivers.

He didn't feel the stolen vehicle was the killer's target. The deliberate shots to the head and torso didn't jibe with someone who simply wanted to steal an older SUV.

The killing felt personal.

A tour of Ken's home was next for Evan. The forensics team had found no evidence of a break-in or violence at the house.

Evan glanced out the window. The sun was moments away from setting.

Tomorrow.

He wanted to search Ken's house in natural light. He knew a patrol car had been parked in front of the home since Ken's identification, keeping watch until Evan could go through the house. He grimaced, hating to tie up a much-needed patrol unit overnight.

I should go through the home now.

He could always return in the daylight.

Evan shut down his computer and pushed in his chair, his gaze falling on his notes from the interview with Shannon.

Rowan's missing brother.

It had absolutely nothing to do with his investigation, but damn, he was curious. He could do a quick search, get an idea of what Shannon had meant when she said Rowan was looking for her brother.

He pushed the thought away.

I have a killer to focus on.

6

Rowan stared at her reflection in the salon mirror. No one looked good with their hair in foils.

No one.

Her younger sister Ivy deftly painted color on more strands and folded another foil, chatting with her identical twin, Iris, who swept the floor around the adjacent chair.

Rowan sighed. That evening she'd stopped by her sisters' salon, Dye Hard, for a quick discussion about an upcoming birthday party and had been cajoled into the chair. Ivy had started it. She'd wrinkled her nose as she eyed Rowan's wavy, long hair. "Your dirty blonde is looking flat and more dirty than usual. Let's punch it up."

"It's fine," Rowan had replied, inching backward toward the entrance, knowing what was next.

"Nope," said Iris, taking Ivy's side as usual. "Get in the chair. It won't take long."

Iris and Ivy's definition of *long* was much different from Rowan's.

Her twin sisters were like puppies. They surrounded and ganged up with sweetness and big brown eyes. Rowan knew not to be fooled. The two women were powerhouses of getting what they wanted while making people believe it had been their idea in the first place.

They were dangerous.

Rowan eyed the multiple bowls of color on the tray. As far as she could tell, Ivy was determined to add a half dozen shades to her hair. Rowan sat meekly, struggling to keep still. She hated the long process, but her sisters were wizards with color, and her hair always looked amazing when they finished.

The hair salon had originally been their mother's. It had started with the benign name of Main Street Salon, which it had kept for several decades before the twins had taken over eight years ago. As they did with every project, the twins entirely threw themselves into updating the salon and giving it a classy edge. The interior was stylish, with clean lines, huge mirrors, and elegant chairs in the waiting area. The decor was black and white except for the pop of rich green from the long plant wall. A row of heavy, intricate chandeliers hung from the high ceilings. Rowan knew they had cost more than the entire rest of the remodel.

A large photo of Bruce Willis with his arms around the seventeen-year-old starstruck twins was propped up on a delicate table in the waiting area. He'd been in town shooting a movie, and the encounter had influenced the salon's name.

The twins sparkled in their environment. Three years younger than Rowan, the girls were identical in their energy and drive but not in their individual styles. Single mom Ivy leaned toward the stylish elegance of the forties and fifties, her hair always elaborately coiffed and her lipstick bright red. Iris always dressed with a theme. One day she would look as if she'd been on a street corner in Haight-Ashbury in the sixties, and the next day she would be full goth or eighties Day-Glo, but always with impeccable hair and makeup. Photo ready. She managed the salon's Instagram account. The photos of the stylish twins were always more popular among their several hundred thousand followers than their clients' hair photos.

"I'm so sorry about Ken," Ivy murmured as she folded a foil that had been blocking Rowan's vision. "I know how close you were to him."

"Thanks." A raw pain blossomed, but it wasn't as overpowering as it had been earlier that day. Rowan suddenly realized that her sister was doing her hair because this was how the twins gave comfort. They thrived on providing services that made people feel good. "And thank you for doing my color," Rowan added. "I appreciate it."

Ivy beamed. "I love working on your hair."

The salon door opened, and Rowan's mother came in, holding West's hand. Ivy's eyes lit up at the sight of her seven-year-old son. She took a step back, and Iris smoothly moved in to take over Rowan's foils. Each of the twins always knew what the other needed. They often seamlessly switched between clients.

"We can postpone tomorrow's birthday party," said Iris as she dipped a brush in the color. Her outfit today was styled after Wednesday Addams, complete with braids. "You've got enough going on."

"No. It'll be a good distraction for me," stated Rowan. She wouldn't put off her missing brother's party. The family had been celebrating Malcolm's birthday without him for decades. Rowan wouldn't have it canceled out of pity for her.

Iris frowned. "You're not going to . . ." She let her sentence trail off.

"I am," Rowan said firmly.

"Are you sure that's a good idea right now? Ivy and I aren't so sure. Maybe go another day." Iris set her hand on Rowan's shoulder and met her gaze in the mirror. Concern filled her sister's eyes.

They don't understand.

The twins had been too young to remember when Rowan and Malcolm were kidnapped and missing for three weeks. They only knew their brother through photos.

Rowan remembered everything.

Every year on his birthday, Rowan returned to the woods where she had been found. She and Thor would search for a sign of Malcolm for several hours. Rowan didn't know exactly what she was looking for, but she'd know it when she saw it.

A small Nike tennis shoe. A silver belt buckle. Bones.

Something.

Rowan's family thought it was unhealthy, but she found it cleansing. She used to go several times a year—which she finally realized was a bit obsessive—so now she only went on his birthday.

"It's what I do," Rowan told Iris. "I need to do it."

Iris dropped her gaze. "We know." The twins often used *we* instead of *I*, even when they were far apart.

Rowan watched Ivy hug her son.

He's the same age Malcolm was when he disappeared.

In her memory, Malcolm was strong and confident and represented safety. Not a child. A result of her five-year-old perspective. Rowan couldn't see her nephew, West, in that way, even though the boy was quite mature for his age.

Her mother's gaze caught hers in the mirror, uncertainty in her smile. Malcolm's birthday was always hard for her, but she was the ringleader when it came to making the plans. Rowan suspected having the party comforted her mother the same way returning to the woods comforted Rowan.

Miriam rarely cut hair anymore. She had a few special clients she would make time for, and she still did the bookkeeping for the salon, but her primary profession was watching West while Ivy worked. And she absolutely loved it. Rowan suspected she'd love it even more with a few other grandchildren.

She'd be waiting awhile.

Rowan had no child plans on her current timeline. Iris and her boyfriend hadn't been together that long—although their relationship seemed quite serious to Rowan. The pair appeared genuinely in love. Ivy's two-month marriage at the age of twenty had made her extremely picky. Men swarmed, but Ivy was rarely interested.

"I'll know it when I meet him," she'd said a dozen times.

Her ex-husband was still in the area, but Ivy had full custody of West. Her ex had been arrested too many times for stupid crimes. Theft. DUI. Domestic assault. Rowan had disliked him on sight, but Ivy had been swept up in a whirlwind romance and dashed to Las Vegas to get married.

Ivy was more practical now—almost too practical and rigid in her life. A contrast to the fanciful Iris.

Miriam approached Rowan's chair, peered into the bowls of hair color, and then gave an approving nod. "That's going to look amazing." She and Iris launched into a detailed discussion about the process, and Rowan tuned them out. She was the only woman in the family not interested in hair.

Not that she didn't like her hair to look good. But most days it was simply pulled back in a ponytail or in a messy bun on top of her head. Her world revolved around her job and Thor. Her fashion choices were based on the weather. She dressed for heat, rain, or snow. Her closet looked like an REI outdoor store with a few nice dresses thrown in for the occasional date.

"Your dad will be there," Miriam said.

Rowan blinked, abruptly realizing her mother had addressed her. "Be where?"

Amusement crossed Miriam's face, making her resemble Rowan more than usual. If she hadn't looked so similar to her mother in height and coloring, Rowan would have wondered if she'd been adopted. The twins didn't look like Rowan at all, and their personalities were energetic and bubbly.

Rowan was her mother's daughter. The two of them were just as driven as the twins, but in a silent, unnoticeable way. They were the type of people who got things done under the radar. Steady. Dependable.

Her father was more like the twins. He'd built his landscaping business in record time during his twenties, accruing contracts with all the large businesses in town. His vibrant personality drew people to him.

He had a dozen crews, and he was often found working side by side with them. But he put family above all else, and he was deeply in love with his wife. His face lit up whenever she walked in the room, and his gaze followed her when she left.

Relationship goals.

"I said your father will be at the party. He'll be back in time," Miriam said.

"Good," said Rowan, clueless as to where her father was returning from, yet faintly remembering that there'd been talk of him not making the party. "We'll do the usual?"

"Of course," said Iris. "I've already shopped."

The usual was burgers and Tater Tots with strawberry shortcake for dessert. And orange soda. All Malcolm's favorites.

"How are you doing?" Miriam asked in a quieter voice.

A sharp pain stabbed Rowan in the stomach. "Better," she said as Ken's face flashed in her mind.

"And the investigation?" asked her mother.

"Detective Bolton is handling it."

"Oh, I like him," interjected Iris, nodding enthusiastically. "He's very sharp and gives a damn about his work. Attractive too." She eyed Rowan speculatively.

Rowan looked away. Attraction had pinged between her and the detective, but now he was in charge of finding Ken's killer. Nothing else mattered.

"Okay!" Iris folded the last foil and patted the top of Rowan's head. "Let's get you under the dryer for a bit."

"Not too long," advised Miriam. "She'll glow."

"What?" asked Rowan, not liking the word *glow*. She glared at Iris. "What did you two do to me?"

"Nothing. It's going to look great." She pointed at the dryer. "Go."

Rowan stood up. "It feels like I've got a hundred foils in my hair. That's not *nothing*."

Iris laughed. "It's not a hundred."

"It'll be fabulous," said Ivy, coming to join the conversation.

Standing beside his mom, West took a long look at Rowan's foils and said nothing. He was used to seeing women in the salon look like aliens.

"It better," grumbled Rowan, knowing full well her sisters knew exactly what they were doing.

An hour later she couldn't look away from her hair in the mirror. Her sisters had blended all different shades of blonde into her long waves, and even a few strands of red peeked out here and there. It was amazing.

Ivy and Iris stood behind her looking like proud parents. "A little more platinum next time," said Iris, and Ivy agreed.

"You're magicians," said Rowan. "No . . . you're witches, right?"

"We prefer the term *sorceresses*," said Ivy.

"It's stunning," said Miriam, touching Rowan's hair. "It suits you." Her lips quivered a little, and she forced a weak smile. "You'll be at the house by six tomorrow?"

Her mother was acknowledging that Rowan would be busy with her yearly search for Malcolm.

"Yes. I won't be late."

"Good."

The four of them exchanged hesitant smiles. Tomorrow was always a difficult day, but they attempted to make it a happy one.

I won't be happy until I know what happened to Malcolm.

7

"He's coming," whispered Malcolm. "I heard the door slam."

Rowan darted into her corner of the shed as Malcolm squatted in his. She could barely see an outline of her brother in the dim light. The shed didn't have any electricity. The only light came in through two windows that had been nailed shut. On the outside they were covered with chicken wire.

Malcolm had talked about breaking one of the windows to escape, but Rowan had begged him not to. If they couldn't get past the chicken wire, the man would be furious when he saw the broken glass.

They never wanted to make him angry.

But no matter how well they behaved, he was angry every day.

Rowan shivered as she wrapped her arms around her legs, pulling them tight to her chest. During the day the shed was stifling and hot from the summer sun beating on its roof, but at night she was cold no matter how close Malcolm hugged her as they tried to sleep. Her brother had asked for blankets but been told they didn't deserve blankets.

It made no sense to Rowan.

She wasn't bad. And neither was Malcolm. But the man told them over and over how bad they were.

Am I wrong?

"In the corners!" yelled the voice outside the shed.

The kids had learned to retreat to their corners and not say a word. On the second day, Malcolm had told him that they were in place, and it'd sent the man into a rage. So now they waited silently.

Squeaking and clanging noises sounded as he unlocked the door. Rowan covered her eyes even though she hadn't been ordered to yet. She lived in terror of accidentally seeing his face. At first she'd been curious to see the man who'd locked them in his shed. Now she believed he'd whip her if she saw him. She screwed her eyes shut tighter and hid her face in her knees.

A soft sound told her he'd tossed in the blindfolds, and the door slammed again. "Get them on. I'm counting to twenty."

They both darted to pick up the blindfolds. Her heart racing, Rowan held hers to her eyes and turned her back to Malcolm. She couldn't tie it herself. His fingers fumbled with the length.

". . . eight, nine . . ."

It finally tightened around her head, and she touched it around her eyes, making sure there was no place for light to creep in. And then crawled back to her corner, feeling her way across the concrete.

". . . fifteen, sixteen . . ."

"Did you get yours on?" she whispered, worrying her heart was beating so loud the man would hear it.

"Almost." Malcolm's voice was panicked.

". . . eighteen, nineteen, twenty! Face your corners."

Rowan was in place and prayed Malcolm was too. The door swung open, and a tiny bit of light crept under her blindfold. She gasped and squeezed her eyes as shut as possible.

"What the hell, boy! I gave you a full twenty seconds!"

Malcolm didn't get his on in time because he had to help me.

Rowan put her hands over her ears, guilt and fear freezing her in place. She flinched at the slaps sounding across the shed.

"Get it on!" The slaps continued.

She imagined her brother trying to tie the blindfold while being hit in the face.

"Tighter!"

Rowan held her breath.

"There. See? That wasn't hard." The man's voice was suddenly kind. "You'll do better next time, right?"

"Yes, sir," said Malcolm.

"You have to be punished now because you failed, you understand?" His tone was encouraging.

No! It wasn't his fault.

"Yes, sir," repeated Malcolm.

"Go over to your sister."

Rowan sat with her legs crossed, facing her corner and hunched over.

Not again.

She heard Malcolm crawl across the floor and felt his presence behind her a split second before his hand touched her back.

"Pinch her," the man ordered.

Rowan tensed. It'd been the same punishment yesterday.

"She didn't do anything," Malcolm said.

Don't say that!

The slap to the back of her head nearly knocked her over. Rowan's hands flew out to catch her as pain radiated from her scalp.

"Look what you made me do," the man said. "I told you what needed to be done. Are you going to make me hit your sister again?"

"No, sir."

"Then pinch her!"

Little pinches started on her shoulder blades. They didn't hurt. Yet.

"Harder!"

Rowan gasped as the pinches shot pain through her nerves. She pressed her palms against her mouth to stay silent.

"You enjoy pinching her, don't you? You secretly hate her. All brothers hate their sisters."

"Yes, sir." Malcolm continued to pinch Rowan's back.

"No food until you say you hate her."

"I hate her," said Malcolm, his tone flat.

"Okay," said the man. "Good job. Back to your corner."

Rowan sagged in relief.

We made it.

"Turn around, girl," the man told Rowan.

She slid on her bottom until she faced in his direction, her neck rigid, preparing for more slaps.

"Here." Something was forced into her hand. "Eat."

A sandwich. Her fingers recognized the bread and she smelled peanut butter. Starving, she immediately took a bite. No jam. The sandwich stuck to her tongue and the roof of her mouth, but it was delicious.

"Eat faster," the man ordered her.

She heard the plastic crackle and *thunk* as a water bottle was set near her knee. She placed her sandwich on her other knee and felt for the bottle. The water was warm and tasted like metal but she drank. She managed to finish the sandwich and drank as much of the water as possible because she had learned he'd take the bottle with him.

"Good." His footsteps headed to the door. "Set the blindfolds on the ground just inside the door." He stepped outside and closed the door as the children raced to obey. "Back to your corners." A moment later the door opened long enough for him to grab the blindfolds, and then the locks sounded again.

Rowan let out a big sigh but didn't move. The kids always waited a few minutes in case he came back.

"Are you okay?" Malcolm whispered. "I'm sorry he made me do that."

She turned around and crawled over to join him in his corner, tucking herself in tight next to him and leaning her head against his shoulder. "I know."

"I hate hurting you," he said. "But he'll hit you more if I don't do it."

"It's best if we do what he says," said Rowan. "Next time I'll act like it's really hurting so he won't tell you to pinch harder. At least the peanut butter sandwich was better than the crackers yesterday."

Malcolm was silent. She straightened and peered at his face in the poor light. "You got a sandwich, didn't you?"

"No."

Rowan wanted to cry. "Did he give you some water?"

"A little. There wasn't much in the bottle."

"You said you hated me like he told you to! He said he'd feed you for that. He's a liar!" Fury rocked through her. "I hate him."

"I hate him too," said Malcolm in a low voice. "I don't understand why we're here."

"Do you think Carissa got away?" asked Rowan, fully aware Malcolm didn't know the answer. They'd discussed their babysitter dozens of times. They hadn't seen or heard her since the bad man had brought them to this place.

She and Malcolm had been in the back seat of Carissa's car when the man wearing a mask forced himself into the car at an intersection. He'd pointed a gun at their babysitter and then at Rowan and Malcolm, threatening to shoot them if she didn't drive where he said.

Neither of them knew where they were. They'd driven for a long time down dirt and gravel roads. He'd made Rowan and Malcolm take off their shirts and tie them over their heads so they couldn't see where they were going. When they'd finally stopped, he'd told the kids he'd shoot Carissa if either of them tried to get out of the car. He'd gotten out and taken Carissa with him and vanished for a few minutes. Rowan and Malcolm had sat frozen in the car. Both too terrified to move. Malcolm had lifted his shirt and peeked. All he'd seen was big trees.

A few minutes later, the man led them to the shed. Rowan had asked about Carissa and been slapped, making her trip and fall. She'd been quiet after that.

Three nights had passed so far. Rowan wondered how many more there would be.

"I don't know what happened to Carissa," said Malcolm. "Maybe she got away and went for help."

Rowan nestled against her brother. "Someone will find us."

8

"I'll wait until you're done, Detective," the patrol officer told Evan. "This isn't the best neighborhood."

Evan looked around as he slipped booties over his shoes. Ken Steward's home was in an older subdivision; the homes were a little shabby and sat on large lots. He didn't see anything that signaled *bad neighborhood*. "Seems okay."

"We get calls all the time from this street. Big drug problem, which leads to all sorts of different crimes. Domestics. Break-ins. Car theft." The young officer scowled as he looked down the street.

"I won't be long," Evan promised. "Leave if you need to." He put on gloves, unlocked the door, and entered the quiet home. He shined his small flashlight at a wall, looking for a light switch, and turned it on.

A bachelor lived here. Evan recognized that fact immediately. Several women he'd dated had pointed out the bachelor-ish elements of his own home, and Ken had the same ones. Large overstuffed sectional. Big flat-screen TV. A coffee table with water rings. No rugs. No decorator pillows. Blank walls. Except for the flat-screen.

It felt comfortable but dull.

He stepped into the room and spotted two huge dog beds on the floor that had been blocked from his view by the sofa. One near where Evan assumed Ken liked to sit on the sofa, judging by the sagging cushion, and the other at the far end of the room, in front of a window, where it would catch the sun. There was also a folded blanket coated with black dog hair next to Ken's place.

Evan could picture Juno and Ken relaxing in front of the TV.

No more.

He was grateful that Shannon Steward had taken Juno. No doubt Shannon's home was also a place with multiple dog beds and a special spot on the couch. Even though Evan had never met the dog, the home felt as if a spirit were missing. There was a distinct loneliness that Evan suspected wasn't solely from Ken's absence.

Evan had thought about getting a dog after his niece and nephew moved out. The kids had stayed with him for a little while, and when they left, they'd taken Oreo, a tiny black-and-white dog Evan had found and adopted during an investigation. He still keenly felt the absence of all three of them. A dog would help fill that emptiness.

He shook his head. He'd had this argument with himself before. His work hours were too long. It would be unfair to the dog.

Evan sighed and moved into the kitchen. The cupboards had a brown wood finish and old corroding pulls, and the counters were cluttered with appliances and stacks of papers. There were three different coffee makers, an espresso machine, two blenders, and three toasters. Plus a toaster oven and several other kitchen gadgets.

Evan wondered why someone would need three toasters. Every appliance was plugged in, so he assumed they all worked. Maybe Ken had a fondness for kitchen electronics.

He sifted through the closest stack of papers. Utility bills. Months and months of them. Pay stubs. Bank statements going back a full year.

Don't most people use digital records now?

Some people didn't care to change. A system worked, so they kept it. Ken's system appeared to be to keep everything in mixed-up piles.

He stopped on a page. Ken had been working as an Uber driver in his spare time.

Another lead.

Evan would need to file a request for Uber to release all Ken's records. Maybe Ken had butted heads with a rider. He assumed there would be trip records of some sort in Ken's phone but didn't think they'd be comprehensive. Evan wanted every detail Uber could provide.

He went through the bills. No credit card bills. After Ken had been identified, Evan had sent a request to the major credit bureaus to find out which credit cards he'd used. With his wallet missing, there was a chance the killer had used them.

If he was stupid enough.

Evan had met plenty of stupid criminals. He returned the papers to their stack and looked around the cluttered kitchen again.

Two metal dog bowls sat on a floor mat. Another sign that the home would never be the same.

Who will clean out the house? Shannon?

Ken had never had kids, but Evan had learned the first two wives had both brought kids to the marriages, so he did have stepkids.

More people to interview.

Doesn't matter if he didn't have his own kids. Clearly he had people who loved him.

Evan's mother had hinted in the past that she wanted grandkids, and he'd told her she was putting the cart before the horse. At least she had his niece and nephew to dote on.

Evan moved down the hallway of the small ranch-style home. The first bedroom was used as an office. He glanced at the messy desk and tall filing cabinet and decided to come back after checking the rest of the home. In Ken's bedroom he went through the nightstands and poked around in a bookshelf.

What am I looking for?

Primarily he was trying to get a feel for the type of person Ken Steward had been. A large photo of Ken and Shannon hung on the bedroom wall. It was from their wedding day, but they were in a different pose than in the one Shannon had shown him. He wondered if Ken had not gotten around to taking the photo down, or if he liked looking at it.

Does Shannon know?

He peeked in both bathrooms and opened the door to the single-car garage. No room for a vehicle. It was packed with all sorts of camping gear, two kayaks, and three paddleboards. Several fishing rods. Backpacks of all shapes and sizes hung on one wall. Evan opened the drawers of a small workbench, expecting to see tools, but found more camping equipment.

No weapons.

Evan was a little surprised by the absence of guns. Most of the SAR people he knew usually carried something when working in the woods. Bears, cougars, and bobcats all lived in the Pacific Northwest. Usually the animals were apprehensive of humans and stayed away, but not always.

He returned to the small home office. A monitor sat on the desk, but the computer tower was missing, taken by forensics. Maps and SAR training guides cluttered the desk. File boxes were stacked in a corner of the room. Framed newspaper articles covered the walls, and Evan stopped to scan a few. Each was about a successful rescue. He smiled. Ken had had a lot to be proud of in his life; he'd helped many people. One article's photo was of Ken and a yellow Lab—not black Juno—and Evan realized the clipping was fifteen years old.

It must be devastating when a dog passes.

He wondered how many dogs Ken had worked with in his lifetime.

Evan moved along the wall, and the articles got older. Another photo caught his eye. Ken had a serious expression on his face and a young girl in his arms. The child was reaching down to Ken's dog, straining to touch its nose. Evan read the caption and froze.

The little girl was Rowan.

Surprise made his heart speed up as he scanned the article. Rowan and her seven-year-old brother had disappeared, but she had been found in the forest several weeks later.

Weeks?

He read to the end, learning that the search for her brother had been still ongoing when the article was published.

Shannon Steward's words about Rowan's brother echoed in his head: "He didn't think it was healthy that she'd go looking for her brother."

Was her brother never found?

The article was twenty-five years old.

Evan pulled out his phone to search for more information and abruptly realized that was not his job at the moment. He shoved the phone back in his pocket and turned away from the article, seeking to refocus. He yanked on a drawer of the filing cabinet.

Locked.

He eyed the desk and opened the top drawer, immediately spotting a wimpy-looking key. It fit. He opened a file drawer and found the gun he'd expected. It wasn't primarily for home protection; otherwise it would have been in a nightstand or maybe in the kitchen. It was locked in a filing cabinet in his office. It was clearly a SAR tool. A necessity.

The next drawer held files. Each was labeled with a date and location and held paperwork from a particular search. The files were tightly packed together. A lifetime of work.

The other two drawers had information on Ken's dogs, past and present, and more general household paperwork. Evan closed the drawers, finding himself drawn back to the photo of Ken and Rowan on the wall. He couldn't see her face, but his mind pictured her as a child with lively brown eyes and a wide grin.

She probably hadn't been smiling, he realized. Rowan had been lost for weeks.

Evan wanted to know the rest of the story.

He took a last look around the office and headed to the front door. Nothing in the home had jumped out at him, pointing at someone who would want to murder Ken Steward. He mentally crossed his fingers for results from the phone or computer, but at least he'd found a few new avenues to pursue for leads.

Evan locked the house door and waved at the patrol officer in his car at the curb. The officer gave a casual salute and pulled away. Evan got in his SUV, his mind spinning with next steps in the investigation. It would be hard to sleep. In each case, he pushed and pushed, exhausting every possible element of the investigation.

In the back of his mind, curiosity about Rowan's past kept bubbling up, and he continued to shove it away. He'd look for answers another time.

Home. Sleep. And start again tomorrow.

9

The sun was barely up when Rowan stepped out of her vehicle. She'd left home in the dark and driven for almost two hours. The location wasn't that far from her Bend home, but getting there took time. Back roads, Forest Service roads, and a long detour because of a washed-out road. Beside her in the passenger seat, Thor had watched the scenery with interest. He loved car rides.

She let the dog out, and immediately he trotted in small circles, sniffing the ground, his ears swiveling in all directions. Today he wore a normal harness. Even though Rowan was searching for signs of her brother, it wasn't a work assignment for Thor. She had no scent articles for him to work from. There was no point in attempting to use Thor's skills after twenty-five years.

For Thor it was simply a glorious walk in the woods.

For Rowan it was a day for reflecting.

To remember her brother and their last days together. To remember the good days before they were kidnapped. Truthfully, she didn't recall much of her childhood before the kidnapping. Old photos helped, but she often wondered if the memories were refreshed by the photos or had been created by the photos.

Ken was on her mind too.

He was intertwined with her thoughts of her brother. The traumatic event that had taken Malcolm had brought Ken into her life. Her parents had been uncertain about whether to encourage the attachment she felt toward the man who had saved her. A child psychologist had evaluated Rowan and given the go-ahead as long as Ken was willing. He was. Ken had attended her high school graduation, her college graduation, and all her SAR certification tests. He'd gone on camping trips with her family. He'd attended picnics and her soccer games.

He had been her favorite unofficial uncle.

She and Thor left the old logging road and moved into the forest, inhaling the scent of fir needles and earth. The morning air was chilly, but she knew it would quickly warm. There wasn't a cloud in sight.

The location where Ken had found her was a mile into the woods. Rowan knew the way by heart after having returned for the last ten years. Ken had brought her a few times as a teenager after she begged and begged. Eventually she'd returned on her own, wanting to spend as much time as she could combing the area. She'd never been able to pinpoint the bush she'd hidden under. Too many years had passed.

But she still looked, convinced she'd instinctively recognize it.

Thor was off leash, constantly running ahead, circling back, and stopping to investigate fascinating smells. Every few minutes he'd halt and look for Rowan, checking to see that she was keeping up. She grinned, amused at her dog's protectiveness. She spotted a stick, picked it up, and called him. He instantly changed direction, bounding toward her over rocks and downed trees, his gaze locked on the stick.

She threw it, and the stick bounced off a tree and went careening in a different direction. Thor altered course on a dime and rocketed after it. The game continued for several minutes as they continued their trek.

When her GPS showed she'd reached the location, she stopped the game, to Thor's great disappointment. The air always felt different in that area. More somber and heavy. In her gut she was convinced that Malcolm's last hours had been spent nearby.

Jerry Chiavo had confessed to Malcolm's kidnapping and death, calling her brother's death an accident, but had claimed he couldn't find the spot in the woods where he'd buried the boy's body in a panic. Several times Jerry had returned to the woods with detectives near where Rowan had been found, trying to locate Malcolm's grave, but he'd only led them in circles.

Rowan knew it was unlikely that she'd ever find anything of Malcolm's in the forest. But she had to try. The act of looking appeased her soul and lessened her survivor's guilt.

If Malcolm hadn't left me to find help, Ken would have found both of us.

Malcolm had tried to help her and died for his efforts.

The least she could do was search for him.

Ken had been uncomfortable with her constant searches as she grew older. Several times he'd pleaded with her to let it go, convinced it was an unhealthy mental process. Rowan disagreed. It brought her peace. The search was cathartic. Her expectations were low; she understood the odds. But going through the movements was a balm for her heart. The pain would slowly build throughout the year, and on Malcolm's birthday, the search would take it away.

She wouldn't give up.

Rowan and Thor spent several hours trekking through the area, working a grid pattern. Five years ago she'd started using colored ribbon, marking the areas she'd searched. Every year she used a different color. This year was blue. That morning she passed weathered yellow, lime-green, orange, and red ribbons tied to various trees.

What if Jerry Chiavo lied about not remembering the location of Malcolm's grave?

It was very possible. Exhuming Malcolm's remains might reveal indications of murder, not an accident. Jerry didn't need another murder sentence. He'd already received three.

Jerry had killed their babysitter, Carissa, and two other young women.

Carissa's vehicle and his own greed had led to his arrest.

Jerry hadn't been able to make himself abandon Carissa's Nissan. It'd belonged to her parents, but she had used it while babysitting Malcolm and Rowan. The car had been only two years old, and Jerry had believed he could eventually sell it. He'd hidden the vehicle in a shed on his property, hoping to wait out the vehicle's BOLO. Instead, five years later, a neighbor he was feuding with had reported the vehicle he'd found while covertly searching Jerry's property for his missing chain saw. The neighbor had thought it suspicious that Jerry never used the new-looking car under the tarp and checked the VIN, assuming it was stolen.

The county sheriff had taken Jerry into custody the next day.

Inside the vehicle had been the backpack Rowan's mother had filled with activity books, crayons, and paints. Jerry had never disposed of it.

Rowan finished searching the grid and moved to stage two of her yearly expedition.

Stage two was returning to the area where Carissa's body had been found three days after the kidnapping. Hikers had discovered her on the banks of a small river. Nude and strangled.

The location at the stream was another mile from Rowan's grid.

Rowan visited the site to remember Carissa. When the carjacking happened, Carissa had begged several times for Jerry to let Rowan and Malcolm out. Not once had she asked for mercy for herself. Rowan's memories of their babysitter were good ones. She'd loved to entertain the kids. She hadn't been the type who spent the entire time on the phone while making the kids watch TV. Board games and outdoor projects had been Carissa's loves. Rowan's too.

The thought of the young woman's body carelessly abandoned hurt Rowan deep inside. But Rowan had found that sitting for a few minutes beside the river and remembering Carissa was always a soothing end to her yearly quest.

She and Thor made their way through the woods, following the guidance of her GPS, and her thoughts strayed to Jerry.

She'd been ten when Jerry Chiavo was arrested. Her parents had tried to keep the news from her, worried it would stir up bad memories, but classmates found out and told her. Rowan confronted her parents after verifying the story of his arrest in the local newspaper, worried she'd have to testify in a trial. She couldn't stand the thought of being forced to recount those days in the shed. The games. The cruelty. The pain. Her last days with Malcolm.

Her parents explained that Jerry Chiavo would be tried for Carissa's murder, but they were hesitant to have him tried for kidnapping—they didn't want to put Rowan through a trial. Detectives were working to discover what Jerry knew about Malcolm's disappearance. They hoped he'd share information if they agreed not to prosecute him for the kidnapping.

It was a gamble. Jerry Chiavo could possibly be acquitted of Carissa's murder and then never be prosecuted for what he'd done to Malcolm and Rowan.

But then he'd been connected to the murders of two other young women that had happened around the same time as Carissa's, and the odds he would go to prison increased. Rowan's parents agreed to accept whatever sentence he received for the murders of the three young women, desperate to keep Rowan away from a trial.

Three life sentences had been the result. Along with Jerry admitting to the kidnapping of Rowan and Malcolm and the accidental death of her brother.

Accidental, my ass.

All through her teens she had refused to think about the man who had mentally tortured the two of them and broken her leg. She'd erected a wall in her brain and hidden him behind it. Later several therapists had helped her deal with the guilt and the memories, and then, in her twenties, she'd grown curious and read everything she could find about the man.

In one way, the information was healing. But it fueled her obsession to find where he'd buried her brother.

The trial had been heavily covered in the media. The murders of three young women had created a sensationalized story of which the public couldn't get enough. She and Malcolm were often mentioned, but most reporters had tried to honor her family's wishes that the children's privacy be respected.

Jerry Chiavo had been fifty-five when he was arrested. He'd been married for thirty-five years but never had children. He'd been a deacon in his church, and he and his wife had fostered dozens of children. No one had a bad word to say about the man. His foster kids had adored him, and his church considered him a pillar of the congregation.

But clearly he had another side.

Rowan had pored over the photos of him and his wife, Suzanne. They looked so normal. Slightly overweight, perfect smiles. They were a solid middle-class couple with lots of friends. They lived on a few acres just outside Eagle's Nest, a tiny town a half hour from Bend.

When the property had been searched, investigators found jewelry from all three young women in Jerry's vehicle, tucked away in a tiny box in his glove compartment. Neighbors came forward, claiming Jerry had been framed.

Jerry had pleaded not guilty to the murders of the young women. He refused to talk to the investigators about the women, but admitted that Malcolm had died in exchange for not being prosecuted for the kidnappings or Malcolm's death.

It didn't make sense to Rowan, but she'd come to the conclusion that Jerry must have thought he'd be found not guilty of the women's deaths and still be protected from being tried for what he'd done to her and Malcolm.

As she studied the reports of the trial, Rowan saw that Jerry Chiavo believed he could talk his way out of a guilty verdict. He was overly cocky and confident that everyone would take his word as fact.

He was delusional. There was plenty of evidence that tied him to the young women.

One of the investigators had become close with her family. For years Detective Sam Durette had kept her family updated on the cases. Rowan had been immediately drawn to him as a child. He gave her a sense of security and talked gently with her while listening to her stories of what had happened in the woods. Between Detective Durette and Ken with his search dog, Rowan felt safe. She might have never mentally healed as well if those men hadn't stayed in her life.

Detective Durette had retired about ten years ago. He now lived on a big ranch outside Bend and often had Rowan over for dinner with him and his wife. He'd worked tirelessly to solve her case. The arrest of Jerry Chiavo wasn't the end of his work, and he'd continued to search for her brother too. He'd accompanied her for a few years in the woods until his hip couldn't handle the trek. But she would call him after every search, and even though she never had any results to share, the detective was encouraging. The call was another part of her routine for the day.

The forest opened up, and Rowan smelled the fresh, damp odor of the small river. It fed into the Deschutes River, which wound its way to the Columbia River and then to the Pacific Ocean. Rowan carefully crossed the big, slick rocks to the river, fascinated that the water passing by could eventually travel hundreds of miles to the ocean. She picked a large rock and sat, watching Thor, who took a tentative lap of the water and snorted at a spider-looking bug skimming along the surface.

The sun was mostly blocked by the tall firs, but here and there its light sparkled on the water. Rowan pulled a protein bar and some dog treats from her day pack, amused that Thor had returned to her side the moment she touched the pack's zipper. "Good boy," she said, offering him the treats one at a time. "Another birthday under our belts," she continued. "We just have to get through the party at Mom's tonight." Thor swallowed the last treat and his ears twitched, his eyes begging.

/treats treats treats/

"That's all."

The dog huffed and set his chin on her thigh.

She stroked his head, enjoying the companionship of her dog and the quiet of the woods. After a few long moments, Thor returned to his exploration of the stream. When he'd gone quite far upriver, Rowan stood up from her perch, stretched, and made her way upstream, following the black shadow and his wet paws.

He's scented something.

Thor barely glanced back at her and continued to steadily make his way along the riverbank.

Please don't be a bear.

She swung the day pack off her shoulders and took out her bear spray. She never entered the woods without the pack. A small medical kit, her GPS, protein bars, dog treats, water, and a Leatherman tool were also in it. The bare necessities for her short hike.

Ahead Thor sat down and looked back, waiting for her to catch up. A large rock wobbled under Rowan's foot, and she caught her balance with her weaker leg but nearly tumbled into the water.

"Shit."

Her leg had been badly broken while she was kidnapped. Four surgeries later, it was pretty good, but never quite right. No matter how much she worked it, the leg didn't have the full strength for certain movements.

Like catching her balance when her good leg was compromised.

It'd taken Rowan years to accept her subtle limp. She could mask it if she concentrated, but ten years ago had given up hiding it. There was no point. This was how she was. She'd learned to give no fucks about what other people thought.

If the worst thing in her life was that she limped a bit, she was grateful.

When people asked, she simply smiled and said, "A bad break when I was a kid." And changed the subject. The surgical scars weren't attractive, but she'd accepted those too.

They were who she was. A road map of her life.

Rowan pushed forward, choosing more cautiously where she placed her feet.

She froze as a sound reached her over the noise of the river.

Oh no.

It was Thor's discovery chatter. He'd found something.

She shaded her eyes and squinted. One of the sun's rays highlighted bare flesh on the river's rocky bank. The body didn't move.

"Thor! Come here."

Her dog swiveled his ears, confused that he was being told to leave his discovery. Thor paused for a second but then obediently trotted back to Rowan, meeting her halfway. "Who's the best boy?" She scratched his ears, her gaze locked on the body partially in the water.

It was a woman. And she'd been dead for some time.

10

From fifty feet away, Evan saw the frown on Rowan's face.

He followed the deputy along the river toward the crime scene. He'd been warned before he left Bend that it would be a long hike. He'd put on hiking boots and appropriate clothing and then added more layers and some supplies to a small backpack. In the past, he'd learned anything could happen at a crime scene in the forest and tried to be prepared.

Evan knew that Rowan had discovered the body, but she wouldn't have known he'd caught the case.

He had a good idea why she was frowning.

It wasn't Evan's turn for a new case, but there were too many similarities to two investigations already on his desk. His supervisor had heard "abandoned nude female body" and immediately assigned it to Evan.

Is it related?

So far only basic commonalities tied his other two women's cases together. Age of victim. Strangulation. Nude. Body dumped. He had no evidence the crimes were related, but his gut told him they were. The other bodies had been left in quiet semiremote areas where someone would eventually find them.

He wondered if Rowan had been working a training exercise for Thor or just been out for a random hike.

Our paths are crossing a lot lately.

Usually he saw her a few times a year. Now it'd been three times within a week.

She sat on a large rock in the shade, several yards from the crime scene tape, facing away from the water. A breeze moved some fir branches and the sunshine touched her, lighting up her hair in its long, wavy ponytail.

Evan liked her. He'd always thought she was the total package. Intelligence, personality, looks. He'd been tempted to ask her out in the past, but the situation had never been right. Like now. A crime scene wasn't the place to suggest a date.

Inside the large taped-off area, pale limbs were draped over the rocks on the riverbank. Her legs were in the water. A forensic tech slowly circled just inside the tape, photographing every square foot of the scene. She wore tall rubber boots, shooting some of her photos while standing in the water. Evan knew she'd move closer and closer to the body, documenting everything.

"Rowan, Thor." Evan greeted both of them, and Thor's black, bushy tail wagged against the ground as he sat, clearing a triangle in the fir needles and small rocks.

"Why are you on this case?" asked Rowan as a greeting. "Isn't your plate rather full?"

I knew it. She wants me focused on the Ken Steward murder.

"No more full than usual," he said. "I'm not ignoring Ken's case," he added gently. "I always balance a few." He turned to glance at the body near the river. "I was assigned this one because it's similar to two others I have." He met her brown gaze.

Her face cleared. "I read about those murdered young women. They're connected?" She frowned. "And this one could be too?"

"Maybe."

"This woman might not have been found for weeks," said Rowan. "Only serious hikers come up here."

"Like you," said Evan. "What brought you here?"

66

Rowan looked away. "I hike around here occasionally. I don't usually come this far up the river, but Thor led me to this spot. He knew."

"You don't have to stick around," Evan told her. "I'll take a statement and you can go." He pulled out a tiny notepad and pen. "Did you notice anyone else in the area while you were hiking?"

"No. Nothing," she said. "Besides . . . she's been here for a while."

Evan nodded. Even at this distance he could tell decomposition had started to take a toll. "The medical examiner shouldn't be far behind me. She can give an estimate of how long she thinks she's been dead."

"I really have nothing to report except that we found her," said Rowan. "But I'd like to stick around for a while."

"No problem." Evan put the pad and pen back in his pocket.

Voices sounded, and a group of the sheriff's department's teenage explorers headed their way. At a scene like this, Evan needed a dozen sets of eyes combing the surrounding area for evidence. One of the deputies who had been talking to the forensic tech immediately strode toward the new group. "I'll get them organized, Detective," he told Evan.

"Appreciate it." Evan didn't want them staring at the corpse.

"The ME's with them," added the deputy.

Evan spotted Dr. Natasha Lockhart bringing up the rear of the group.

"It's Dr. Lockhart. Good," said Rowan. "She knows her shit."

Evan agreed. Dr. Lockhart was his favorite of the medical examiners who covered his territory. The ME was petite with long, dark hair. She looked like a college student, not a pathologist.

The explorers swarmed around the deputy, and Dr. Lockhart approached Evan and Rowan.

"Hey, Thor." The doctor addressed the dog first. Thor stood and pushed his nose into her outstretched hand, his tail a blur with its rapid wagging. "How's my favorite boy?" She squatted next to the dog and gave him a hug, making Thor squirm with joy.

Evan met Rowan's gaze. She smiled, apparently used to people greeting her dog before her. Evan realized he sometimes did the same with other dogs and owners.

"Hello also to you two," said Dr. Lockhart, standing back up. "Beautiful day. I appreciate working outdoors on days like these."

Her words sounded a bit callous considering a dead woman was nearby, but Evan completely understood. When you worked with death every day, you acknowledged the good things wherever you found them.

Dr. Lockhart looked toward the crime scene. "Looks like Jenna will be taking photos for a bit longer." She met Rowan's gaze. "I understand you found her?"

"Yes."

The doctor paused. When Rowan didn't expand, she locked eyes with Evan. "Have you taken a look?"

"Not yet. I just got here too."

"Let's go." Dr. Lockhart headed toward the crime scene tape.

Evan checked the explorers. The deputy had them in a line and moving into the woods a step at a time, an arm's length apart on either side, gazes scanning the ground. "I'll be back in a bit," he told Rowan, and he followed the doctor. They both stopped to sign the scene log.

The dead woman lay on her back on the rocks. Her discolored abdomen was severely swollen with gases from decomposition. The current of the river made her lower legs seem to undulate, appearing gelatinous. Small animals had been at her eyes, mouth, and fingers. She had long, dark-blonde hair, and Evan couldn't guess her age; her body had swollen too much. There was some sort of flower tattooed on one ankle, and her toenail polish was hot pink.

She's younger. I can feel it.

She was looking more and more similar to his other two victims. Dr. Lockhart held a small flashlight next to the woman's neck, examining the mottling. Evan couldn't distinguish strangulation bruises from the rest of the discolorations, but the doctor was nodding.

"Strangled?" Evan asked.

"It's a possibility." The doctor did a quick visual scan of the woman's body and then palpated the skull, checking for depressions or injuries. "All clear so far. Help me roll her over." Evan stepped into a few inches of water, trusting his boots to keep his feet dry. He rolled the woman on her side, and the doctor scanned her back with the flashlight. Her skin was dark purple. "Looks like this is the location where she died. You must be wondering if it's related to the other two strangled young women," Dr. Lockhart said quietly.

"That's my job," answered Evan.

"You haven't found a concrete link between the other two?"

"No. Just that the situations and victims were similar. No physical evidence."

"I remember one was from Portland . . . where was the other from?"

"Idaho," said Evan.

"Both far from home," said the doctor.

"Bend is a vacation destination," said Evan.

"But neither young woman was on vacation."

"True." The first young woman had been living on the Portland streets in a homeless camp. No one had noticed when she vanished. The other had been living with her boyfriend when they got in a fight and she stormed off. He hadn't been surprised not to hear from her for several days.

"Something or someone brought them here," Dr. Lockhart said quietly.

Evan was silent. He didn't like to speculate on how the women had arrived in Central Oregon; there were dozens of possibilities, and nothing indicated they'd arrived under the same circumstances. One woman had been found six weeks ago and the other four weeks ago.

The doctor hummed to herself as she continued her rapid examination.

"How long ago did she die?" asked Evan.

"Somewhere between five and ten days," said the doctor. "I'll try to get a tighter timeline after I run some labs. Lot of factors to consider. The sun speeds things up, but the cold water might have slowed them down." She stood and looked up and down the river. "At least it's a peaceful place."

Evan didn't care. There was no mitigating the circumstances of the woman's murder. Someone had brutally taken her life. It made no difference to him whether the location was peaceful.

It could be suicide. She might have poisoned herself.

And removed her clothing?

No clothing had turned up yet. No indication of how she'd arrived in the middle of nowhere.

Someone undressed and killed her here.

So far everything pointed at a murder.

"Hey, Detective Bolton."

Evan turned to see the deputy who'd taken charge of the explorers. Evan's jaw tensed at the concern on the deputy's face. "What'd they find?" he asked.

The deputy stopped and looked at Dr. Lockhart, who was watching with interest. "You might want to come take a look at this too, Doc. One of the kids found a lot of bones."

"Human?" asked Evan, already sure of the answer.

The deputy grimaced. "Can't vouch that all of them are human, but I know a human skull when I see it."

"Let's take a look," said Dr. Lockhart, already heading toward the explorers.

Rowan had stood up from her seat on the rock, concern wrinkling her forehead. "What's going on?" she asked as they approached.

"Explorers found something," said Evan.

Rowan joined their group without asking permission, Thor at her side. The deputy glanced at Evan as if expecting him to protest, but

Evan ignored him. Finding things was what Rowan and Thor did best. The group tramped into the woods. Ahead, the explorers were spread out in formation but standing still, watching the four of them. The deputy must have told them to hold their positions.

Evan and the others followed the deputy to an explorer at the far end of the line. The teenager's eyes sparkled with excitement about her discovery.

"I saw something pale," she said as they moved closer. "I thought it was a rock and simply pushed it with my boot. Then I saw the teeth." She gave a small shiver, but the animation didn't leave her eyes.

"Good work," said Evan. "Would you mind joining your teammate over there?" Disappointment crossed her face, but she moved.

Evan watched where he stepped. The skull was just visible under a scrubby-looking bush, the teeth of its upper jaw visible. He squatted with Dr. Lockhart, and Rowan peered over his shoulder. Gloved, he picked up a stick and gently moved some of the dirt next to the skull.

More bones appeared.

"That's a female skull," said Dr. Lockhart. "There's some more bones over there too," she added, pointing a few feet away. "Looks like a humerus and radius."

"There's a second skull," whispered Rowan. She had one hand on Thor's harness. Evan followed her gaze.

"Yes," said Dr. Lockhart. She took Evan's stick and dug away the dirt from the other skull. "It's smaller. Might be male."

A sharp intake of breath from Rowan made Evan stand. "Are you okay?" He put a hand on her shoulder, noticing she'd gone pale.

Her brother.

Shannon Steward had said Rowan still searched for her brother.

Is this where he went missing? Is that why she's here?

He looked back to the second skull. "Are you sure about the sex, Doc?"

The doctor took a closer look. "Well, I take that back. With younger skulls it's more difficult to tell," said Dr. Lockhart. "We need an anthropologist and recovery team up here."

Rowan's gaze moved from the second skull to Evan, and he swallowed hard at the pain in her eyes. "I know what you're thinking," he said in a quiet voice. "We'll find out."

She nodded.

"Find out what?" the doctor asked sharply, her gaze bouncing between the two of them.

Evan lifted a brow at Rowan, asking permission to share. Her nod was infinitesimal. Either she couldn't speak or she didn't want to.

"Rowan's brother went missing in the woods," Evan said. "He was seven."

The doctor's eyes widened, and she immediately returned her focus to the skull, speculating.

Evan eyed the bones.

Could this be her brother?

11

Malcolm, twenty-five years ago

"Hit her, boy! Pinch her hard!"

Malcolm hated him, but he did as he was told.

Rowan whimpered although Malcolm had barely touched her, making him proud. She was so little, but she got it. She had learned to act, pretended to give the man what he wanted. He wanted to see them hurt each other. He liked it. They'd gotten good at pretending they'd hurt each other worse than they had.

Malcolm hated him.

But he obeyed.

That night his reward for making her cry was a warm can of soda, and the man made Rowan watch him drink it. It was diet soda and tasted of sickly-sweet chemicals. He'd always hated the flavor. The two of them hadn't eaten since early morning, and the gross drink hurt Malcolm's gut, making him worry he'd vomit. He held the can several inches from his lips, breathing deep, trying to calm his stomach.

I can't imagine what he'll do if I throw up.

Malcolm felt his silent rage at his disobedience even though he couldn't see the man because of the blindfold. The hairs on Malcolm's arms rose as the man's breaths sped up, and he sensed the man move closer.

"Drink it! Finish it up! Ungrateful brat! I give you an entire can of soda, and you act like you're too good for it!"

His breath touched Malcolm's cheek, but Malcolm knew if he moved away, he'd be punished. Determined, he drank as fast as he could, ignoring the awful taste, and soda spilled out the corners of his mouth.

"Slob!" He wrenched the can out of Malcolm's hand and slapped his face. "Ungrateful child! I do everything for you two, and this is how you treat my gifts!"

Malcolm's face stung but he held still, terrified that if he moved, the man would hit him again.

"Finish this!"

His voice was farther away, and Malcolm knew he'd given the can to Rowan. He thought he had drunk two-thirds of it, so Rowan should be able to finish it. She suddenly coughed and hiccuped at the same time, and the man laughed.

"Good girl. See, boy? Even your sister could finish it, you worthless piece of garbage." He chuckled as he left, and Malcolm stayed frozen in place until he heard the last lock click into place.

Malcolm ripped off his blindfold and blinked in the poor light. "Are you okay?" he whispered. Rowan's blindfold was already off, and she set it close to the door in case he returned to retrieve it. Malcolm added his.

"It wasn't bad. It was sweet."

"It's disgusting." His stomach churned, and he pressed his lips together.

"Do you think we'll get anything else for dinner?" she asked in a small voice.

Rowan might get more, but Malcolm doubted he would, since he'd screwed up. "Don't know."

"At least he was laughing."

"Yeah, it's always better when he's happy. Maybe he'll bring something else," Malcolm said, trying to be optimistic for her.

Rowan was thin. Her elbows were more pointed than usual, and her face was skinny. Shame swept through Malcolm because he knew she needed more food, and he had made the man mad today.

I'll be okay, but she needs to eat. I need to sneak her more of my portions.

"I'm cold." Rowan sat in a ball on the floor, their blanket wrapped around her shoulders. Malcolm sat beside her and got as close as he could, hugging her through the blanket. She kept shaking. He pulled off his coat and tucked it around her over the blanket.

"You need your coat," she said.

"Nah. I don't feel cold right now. Maybe later."

She laid her head on his shoulder as they huddled together. Malcolm fought to hold still through his shivers, not wanting her to feel them. It was more important that she was warm.

I don't know what I'll do if she gets sick.

They needed to get out of there. He'd thought the police would have found them by now, but he didn't think they were coming.

We're on our own in the hands of the devil.

12

As she drove to her parents' home, Rowan waited for her call to be answered.

"Rowan? I was wondering when I'd hear from you today." Sam Durette's deep voice filled her vehicle and made her smile. The retired detective was always a ray of light. He had seen the worst of what people did to one another, yet his positivity and humor were always present.

"I'm on my way to the birthday party," Rowan said. "It turned out to be a long day in the woods."

"Sounds like something happened."

"It did." She told him about the body of the woman she'd found and then about the cache of bones. "The medical examiner thinks one of the skulls is young. Possibly male. A forensic anthropologist will remove them tomorrow."

There was a long moment of silence.

"There are two sets of bones?" Sam asked.

"At least," said Rowan. "We didn't want to disturb a crime scene."

"I don't need to tell you not to get your hopes up."

"You don't," she said. "Even if it has nothing to do with Malcolm, hopefully the bones will be identified and provide answers to other families who are missing loved ones."

"Tell me about the woman in the river."

Rowan gave a brief description. "Detective Bolton caught the case because it's similar to two others he is handling."

"What is similar?" Sam asked sharply.

"Nude female. Dumped somewhere. Strangled. Although that hasn't been confirmed as the cause of death for this victim. The other two were in their early twenties, and we don't know the age of this one yet. So I guess there aren't that many confirmed commonalities."

"I hadn't heard about the other two women," said Sam. "Usually I notice that sort of thing in the news."

"I saw an article about it," said Rowan. "I think it was bigger news in their hometowns than here."

"Could be." He cleared his throat. "Sorry I can't be there tonight. I need to stay with Grace. She keeps telling me to go, but I know she's not feeling well."

Sam's wife was doing chemotherapy.

"The party will be different this year," Rowan said softly, thinking of Ken. Both he and Sam had always attended Malcolm's birthday parties.

"I'm so sorry about Ken," said Sam. "He was one of the good ones."

"He was. Just like you are."

She ended the call a few moments later, her mind full of past parties to which Ken and Sam had brought their wives. The parties were always upbeat and social. Music. Laughter. Food. Everyone would have a good time.

It was always the day after the party that Rowan would be hit with heaviness and a deep sorrow about what could have been.

She parked at the curb in front of her parents' home.

Don't mention the bones.

Rowan had argued with herself for the entire drive about whether to mention the bones discovered near the river. The family's hopes had been dashed too many times over the years. Chances were that this report would do the same.

But it'd been so long since there had been any news or hope of any kind. The discovery today was the first in many years.

If I say nothing, then tonight will be as wonderful as always.
Say nothing.

It was doubtful there would be questions about the body she had found. She hadn't told anyone besides Sam Durette.

Rowan grabbed the gift and bottle of prosecco from the passenger seat and headed toward the front door. Prosecco had been added to the celebration when the twins turned twenty-one. It worked quite well with Malcolm's favorite orange soda, creating a twisted version of a mimosa that was extra fizzy.

She was late. Rowan walked right in the front door, and her stress from the day melted away. She loved her parents' home. Giggling came from the kitchen, and music sounded from multiple speakers. She heard her father's deep laugh, and it warmed her heart. He was the type who always had a smile and a word of encouragement for everyone.

Would Malcolm have been the same way?

In her heart she knew he would. He'd always cheered her on and had been infatuated with the twins, delighted by their pudgy cuteness.

Some acquaintances judged the family for celebrating Malcolm's birthday, claiming it was unhealthy to hold on to the past. That was why they were acquaintances, not friends. Her parents had stopped defending the gathering years ago, letting the busybodies wallow in their own nosy concern.

Fuck them all.

"Aunt Rowan!" West charged her from the family room and wrapped his arms around her waist. "What's in the present?" He lowered his voice. "I won't tell anyone," he said in a conspiratorial tone.

She laughed. "Nice try." The white elephant gift swap was always a highlight of the evening. "Where's your mom?"

West led her around the corner to the kitchen, which was part of a huge great room with high ceilings and an eye-catching fireplace. The other four adults were at the island, champagne glasses of fizzy bright-orange mimosas already in their hands. Two empty prosecco bottles stood in the sink.

"Good thing I brought another bottle," said Rowan as she hugged her father. "I'm glad you made it, Dad."

"Wouldn't miss it." He took a step back and studied her. "Girls, her hair looks amazing," he said to the twins.

"Told you so, Dad," said Iris as she finished her drink. "I've already put the before and after photos up on Instagram."

"Do they show my face?" asked Rowan. The twins had once featured her as one of their amazing hair makeovers, and Rowan's friends had teased her unmercifully.

"No. Just the back of your head," said Iris, rolling her eyes. "You made it clear last time not to do that again."

"Good." Rowan set down the present and took the drink her mother offered. "Let's do this."

Two hours later Rowan was exhausted.

But in a good way. She'd kept the news of the bones and murdered woman to herself. It'd been the right decision. Wearing the sparkly pink cowboy hat she'd stolen from her father in the gift exchange, she kissed her parents goodbye and hugged her sisters. West was sound asleep on the sofa, his stomach full of an impressive number of Tater Tots.

Outside she headed to her SUV, her step light and her heart content. It'd been a perfect evening even though their number was smaller than usual. She opened the passenger door and set the hat carefully on the seat, grinning as she recalled her father's glee when he opened the white elephant gift from Ivy. He'd immediately put it on his head, and it had rocked, too small to sit correctly.

Rowan's girly side had craved the hat, loving the pink sparkles. Even though they didn't appear in her wardrobe, she had a weakness for things that glittered.

It'd been a long, emotional day. She knew the heaviness that always came after Malcolm's party was about to start.

It was best to go home, hug her dog, and go to bed.

13

"Find your brother and you can split a candy bar."

He pulled the blindfold from five-year-old Rowan's eyes. She covered her eyes, the sunlight too bright.

"You've got five minutes."

Rowan removed her hands and squinted, letting her eyes adjust. It wasn't that bright. The man had brought her deeper into the woods, and the trees gently filtered the light.

"Get searching! Move!"

She broke into a run, not knowing where to go. The man had pulled Malcolm out of their shed early that morning, and she'd been panicking for hours, pacing and crying, wondering what he was doing to her brother. She rounded a tall pine. No Malcolm. And then shoved aside branches to peer under a thick bush.

Rowan didn't dare call out Malcolm's name, terrified the man would hit her for speaking or take it out on Malcolm. She doubted Malcolm would have answered anyway, scared of the same results. She glanced at the man. He wore his usual black mask that covered his entire head. His gaze met hers, his eyes angry in the mask's holes.

"You're getting colder!"

She reversed direction and sprinted to look behind more thick tree trunks.

What had he done to Malcolm?

Rowan continued to scramble and search. She tripped over roots and sliced a hand on a sharp branch. She and Malcolm were like the Hungry Hungry Hippos. Trapped in a game where the man pounded on their levers, making them snatch as many stupid marbles as possible. No skill involved. Simply a minute of frantic free-for-all to briefly entertain him.

And then do it over again.

But the find-your-brother game was new. Usually he brought them out at the same time to play his sick games. Rowan pushed her hair out of her eyes, sweat running down her forehead.

Where is he?

She just wanted the game to end.

"If you don't find him, I'm not sure what you deserve. Maybe the hose."

Rowan ran faster. She feared the hose. He'd used it on them several times, claiming they stank and needed to bathe. He forced them to stand still and soaked them in their clothes. If they moved, he'd swing the end of the hose at them. The metal tip had hit Rowan in the temple when she shuffled her feet to keep her balance in the spray. She'd bitten her tongue to not cry out.

Afterward she'd had soaked clothes, a cut on her head, and a deep sore on her tongue.

Malcolm had made her take off the wet clothes. At least the man had finally given them two thin blankets. He'd draped the clothes in the shed and wrapped her up in a blanket and then done the same for himself. At least it hadn't been cold that night.

Would he still spray them when it started to snow?

Would he give them more blankets when it got really cold?

Rowan stopped, overwhelmed by the thought that she and Malcolm would still be suffering from this man when winter arrived.

"You don't want me to hurt him, do you? You're not trying very hard, so that means you do want me to punish him. I know you hate your brother."

She didn't reply and ran around the closest tree, not caring that she'd already checked it.

"You're forcing my hand, girl. This is all your fault."

Rowan dashed around more trees, hate and fear driving her legs.

"Maybe you should look under that pile of rocks." He pointed at a clump of a few dozen rocks. It hardly could be called a pile. Nothing larger than a frog could hide under them.

But she dropped to her knees and started hurling rocks to the side. When there was nothing but dirt and fir needles left, she risked glancing at the man.

"Dig," he ordered. "Maybe he's under the dirt."

Rowan dug. The earth was packed and dry. Dirt wedged itself under her fingernails. She scratched hard, trying to make a dent in the solid ground.

Did he kill Malcolm and bury him here?

"Stupid girl. He can't hide under there. Maybe he went that way." The man gestured to her left.

She scrambled to her feet and ran, brushing her hands against her pants, trying to relieve the pressure of the dirt under her nails. Rowan wove between trees, no longer looking, just running.

Maybe I can get away from him.

But what about Malcolm?

She couldn't leave her brother behind. Her pace slowed, and she worried she was about to get lost. The woods suddenly opened up and a river appeared. Surprised, she slammed to a halt. She hadn't known there was a river near their prison shed.

Rowan stepped onto the river rocks and froze. Her brother lay on his back, his feet in the river. Slowly moving closer, she saw his eyes were gone.

Rowan shot up out of bed, her heart pounding, terror shooting through her limbs. She swung her legs over the edge of the bed and sat there, trying to catch her breath. Thor pressed against her leg, and her hand sank into his fur.

It's a fucking dream.

That never happened.

Or did it?

She strode out of her bedroom and into the kitchen, blindly grabbed a bottled water from the fridge, and drank. She wasn't thirsty. She needed the shock of the cold. Rowan wiped her mouth, took several deep breaths, and ordered her heart to slow down.

"I shouldn't have used a sleeping pill," she muttered. After getting home from the party, she'd taken the pill because in the past she'd struggled to sleep the night of Malcolm's birthday. It'd seemed like a good solution, but combined with alcohol from last night, the pill had created a very vivid dream. Clearly influenced by the dead body she'd found in the river the day before.

Her subconscious had combined the dead woman with the memories of her brother.

But it seemed so real.

She flexed her fingers, still feeling as if she had dirt under her nails.

Am I blocking something?

Rowan had met with therapists for years, working through the trauma Jerry Chiavo had forced on her and her brother. She'd been home for months before she told a therapist about the games Jerry had made them play. Sibling against sibling. Pain. Punishment. Guilt.

So many horrific memories.

Some she'd waited years to share. Rowan couldn't recall if she hadn't wanted to talk about them or if she had suppressed them. The therapist had always claimed they were suppressed, but Rowan remembered the guilt she'd felt because she'd been hesitant to share.

Which could mean I remembered . . . I just didn't want to talk about it.

It was 4:30 a.m., and she didn't see the point in trying to sleep anymore. Rowan sighed and started her coffee maker, knowing what she needed to do. Her favorite therapist had taught her how to work through bad dreams, pick them apart, study each piece from a distance.

It took away the fear and broke them into manageable pieces.

Thor sat by his bowl, his black eyes locked on her every movement. /food/

"It's too early, Thor. You'll pester me for dinner at two o'clock." /food/

"How about a snack instead?" She got his canister of snacks out of a cupboard. The rapid wag of his tail told her he approved.

Thor never refused snacks.

He gently took the dried meat from her hand and trotted away to chew it in the dog bed near her sofa.

Rowan watched the coffee stream into the glass carafe. "I can't wait." She pulled out the pot and stuck her mug under the stream. Her cup full, she slid out a chair at the table in her kitchen nook and caught her reflection in the windows, her yard impossible to see in the black night.

I look like I haven't slept.

I don't think I did.

As she sipped her potent coffee, she let her mind carefully wander through what she could recall of the dream. Running through the trees. Searching for Malcolm. Jerry threatening to hurt them.

Her hand tightened on the mug as she remembered throwing the rocks aside, simply doing as Jerry said, knowing it was pointless.

I can still feel the rocks.

"Jesus Christ." She took a big gulp of coffee and welcomed the startling burn in her mouth and down her throat. Her brain had cooked up quite the dream, combining elements from her past and her present. "No more sleeping pills."

She allowed the image of her brother at the creek to skim across her mind. It had never happened. Malcolm had been alive the last time she'd seen him. The creek image was from the day before. She made herself remember the woman, replacing the image of Malcolm with the right one.

It's still horrible to see.

Rowan had seen many dead people in her lifetime; it came with SAR. Each one was branded into her memory.

14

Evan was in his office early the next morning. He'd gotten little sleep the night before, his mind bouncing between Ken Steward's case and those of the three murdered women. He had a list of follow-up items from all the cases, and the earlier he started, the better.

Who needs sleep?

Today's schedule was busy with the autopsy of the river woman later this morning and a meeting with the forensic anthropologist in the afternoon. He didn't like calling the victim "the river woman." It felt impersonal; he wanted her name. She was a human, not a location. He knew the medical examiner would have assigned her a moniker consisting of "Jane Doe" and a number, and he pledged to replace that impersonal identifier too.

Forensic anthropologist Dr. Victoria Peres had been assigned to remove the bones. Evan had wanted to speak with her at the site but knew from previous cases that it was best to wait until she'd organized the excavation and made a little progress. The doctor ran a tight ship during her investigations. If she wanted you off her dig, you were gone. No questions, no excuses.

Evan had watched her kick a burly deputy off a scene after she spotted him taking pictures. She hadn't gone to the deputy's sergeant to request the deputy leave; she'd walked right up to the picture taker and ordered him off with language that had made Evan blush. The rest of the crew had immediately gone silent. And made certain their phones were tucked away. Dr. Peres was intimidating. Tall, direct, and intense.

And one of the best in her field.

Evan checked his email and found a preliminary autopsy report on Ken Steward, noting that Dr. Lockhart had sent it after one in the morning. Apparently the medical examiner didn't need sleep either. The immediate blood labs showed a low blood alcohol and the presence of marijuana. The doctor had requested more labs, which Evan knew would take several more days, possibly weeks. He felt guilty about missing Ken's autopsy, but he'd been called to the river woman crime scene. Dr. Lockhart verified that there had been two gunshots to the head and one to the heart. No other wounds.

Death had been nearly instant.

The one consolation.

Ken Steward probably hadn't known what had happened. Evan imagined the man had fallen asleep a little drunk and a little high. It was doubtful he'd heard anyone enter the tent.

"Morning, Evan." Detective Noelle Marshall strolled into his office. "I knew you'd be here bright and early, so I figured I should be too."

Last night Noelle had been assigned to help Evan with the Steward murder and the three female homicides. She'd cleared a big robbery case just as Evan's boss had decided Evan needed more hands and eyes. Evan suspected the publicity of Ken Steward's death had prompted Noelle's assignment. There had been a big outcry for results from the local community.

But there hadn't been much talk about the murdered women. Often the public seemed to simply accept that it happened: young women got killed. But the murder of a beloved, generous longtime community member got press. Evan didn't like the unfairness of it, but it didn't affect how he worked. Every case got his full attention.

Maybe the women will get more press with the news of a third death.

"I'm glad it's you," Evan said to Noelle with a grin. "If Hickson had been assigned, I'd have to wear earplugs." The young detective never stopped talking.

"I promise not to talk about my cats' litter box habits while you're eating," said Noelle. "Or give an in-depth rundown of every volleyball game I played in college."

Detective Hickson had a three-month-old and would enthusiastically describe every exploding diaper and projectile vomit, ruining his colleagues' lunches. Before the baby was born, he'd enjoyed reliving his college football games play by play with anyone unlucky enough to be nearby.

"He means well," said Evan. "Just doesn't know when to stop."

"He's a good guy," agreed Noelle. "Has a lot of potential." She pulled a chair closer to Evan's desk, where she could see his computer. "I spent last evening reviewing what you have on the Ken Steward case so far. I really hope those bullets they dug out of the dirt give us a good lead. Anything new on him today?"

Evan gave her a recap of the Steward autopsy. "I just got his cell phone report from his carrier. Can you take care of that?"

"Absolutely. What else?"

"Waiting on forensic results from his computer. I still need to interview his first two wives, his cousin, and a couple of close friends. Maybe his stepkids." He frowned.

"What is it?" asked Noelle.

"I keep coming back to his SUV." He pulled up the registration for Ken's Explorer. "Where's his SUV? Someone took it. Are we looking at two suspects? It seems logical that someone drove the killer to the location. It was too remote to get to on foot."

Noelle nodded, a furrow forming between her eyebrows. "What if the killer had ridden in on a bike? It could have been put in the back or on top of the Explorer."

"Good point. I think there are mountain bike trails not too far from there. It would still be a long ride to get there from any town, though. Even if he was dropped off near the trails, we're still looking at more than one suspect."

"Assuming whoever dropped him off was involved. He could have asked an innocent friend to drop him off so he could go mountain biking."

This was why he liked working with Noelle. Her sharp brain went in different directions from his, so they complemented each other well. Noelle Marshall was in her early forties, and Evan knew the outgoing, tall, blonde woman had been divorced twice, didn't have kids, and had a huge circle of friends. Confidence surrounded Noelle, and she always strode with purpose. People made fun of the TV show *CSI*, claiming detectives and forensic specialists didn't run around in high heels.

Noelle did.

One time when Noelle was investigating a break-in, she had run down a nineteen-year-old suspect and tackled him when the idiot returned to the scene. She'd been furious that the tackle had ruined a shoe. One of the deputies who'd witnessed her sprint had told Evan his wife claimed Noelle wore $500 heels.

Evan's good suit didn't cost that much.

He glanced at Noelle's feet, noting the bright-blue sandals that she wore with her slacks had a moderate heel. "Can you go with me to talk to the forensic anthropologist at the river woman scene this afternoon?"

"I'll make time. Is Victoria doing the excavation?"

"Yes."

"Good. I like her. Takes crap from no one." She grinned at Evan. "And yes, I'll change my shoes before that hike. Clothes too."

"I will too," said Evan. "It's going to be a hot one today. It's a couple miles' hike to the site and mostly uphill."

"Then how did the body get there?" asked Noelle. "That's a long way to carry deadweight."

"She was killed there," said Evan. "Lividity matched the position we found her in." He remembered the deep color he'd seen on the victim's back when he'd helped Dr. Lockhart roll the body. There had been a few blanched spots that lined up with large rocks that had pressed against her back. The description had also been noted in the preliminary autopsy report.

Noelle tapped her fingers on the desk as she thought, her large rings catching the light. "Did he come across her in the woods or convince her to go on a hike with him? Or force her into the woods?"

"One of those," said Evan.

"He'd risk meeting other hikers who'd become suspicious if it appeared she was being forced," said Noelle. "Is he overconfident?"

"I hope so," answered Evan. "He'll trip up and make a mistake somewhere."

"Preferably a mistake before another victim."

"Assuming these three cases are related."

Noelle's dark-blue gaze probed him. "You think they are."

"My gut says they are, but I don't have any physical evidence to back it up."

"Maybe we'll get lucky with the forensics on this one and we'll find some links. Do you want me to focus on the women's cases or Ken Steward?"

Evan had already decided where he wanted help. "I need you on both. It'll take some juggling."

"I'm a fantastic juggler. It's part of the job." Her eyes gleamed as she considered the challenge.

Evan approved of her reaction. Some of the detectives grew tired of dealing with the nonstop questions and setbacks that naturally came with an investigation. Not Noelle. She thrived on a puzzle. Evan did too.

She looked at the vehicle registration on Evan's screen. "I read Steward was an Uber driver. You've requested records from Uber?"

"Yes. I've never had to do that before."

"Same here. I suspect we'll be doing it frequently in the future. Rideshare is a common part of our society now. Did Steward do anything else besides Uber and the SAR?"

"The SAR aspect of his life had a lot of facets," said Evan. "He worked with several local SAR groups, and he was involved with many dog trainers across the States."

"Shit. A lot of spread-out people."

"My first thought too. But the dog trainers seem to be a pretty tight-knit group considering how they're scattered. Everyone knows everyone else, and Ken had an excellent reputation with them."

"Lots of interviews to do."

"Maybe," said Evan. "I'm crossing my fingers that forensics points us in a solid direction first."

Noelle laughed. "You're hoping for the smoking gun? We all wish to find that in every case. How often has that worked out for you?"

"Rarely," Evan admitted. Most of his investigations consisted of hours of phone calls, research, interviews, and legwork. It wasn't glamorous. He checked the time. "I'm headed to the medical examiner's now. You want to come?"

Her nostrils widened slightly, as if she'd suddenly smelled something foul, and she gave a small shake of her head. "I'll get started here. Cell phone. Uber. Computer forensics. I'll make some pushy phone calls and light some fires under people. And do it all with a big smile. I'm good at that."

They all had their strengths, and attending autopsies didn't appear to be on Noelle's list. Most likely they made her squeamish. Evan had attended several where a law enforcement member had had to suddenly leave the room or vomit into the handy trash can. A tech always pointed out the location of the can to visitors before the autopsy started. Evan had even seen one detective crumple to the floor in a dead faint.

It wasn't for everyone.

"Thanks." Evan trusted her. It was good to work with someone who pulled her weight. "I'd like to head up to the river woman site around noon."

"I'll be ready," Noelle promised. She stood and grabbed the binder for Ken Steward's murder. "I'll focus on Steward this morning and the women later this afternoon." She strode out of Evan's office, her heels clicking on the tile floor.

Autopsy time.

15

Dr. Natasha Lockhart had already opened the torso of the river woman by the time Evan showed up.

Evan had run a search for Oregon women with blonde hair who were missing, keeping the search to a one-year window simply because his victim hadn't been dead for long. He had a short list of names of women of all ages and hoped Dr. Lockhart would determine the age range today. He'd also made a separate list for other hair colors, knowing the victim could have colored her hair. His lists were a shot in the dark. The woman could be from out of state or outside the country. She might have gone missing years before and just died. But the lists were a start.

The autopsy suite was cold. Evan had pulled a sweatshirt over his collared work shirt before going in, remembering how many times in the past he'd stood shivering as he observed a procedure. The thin, papery gowns provided by the ME didn't add warmth. Evan put on a mask, a face shield, booties, and gloves even though he planned to keep his distance.

The medical examiner stood on a low platform next to the table. Dr. Lockhart was petite, and the tables didn't lower enough for her. An assistant held a clipboard, making notes as the doctor removed and weighed various organs. Fleetwood Mac played in the background. Over the years Evan had learned he liked her taste in music.

"Good morning, Detective," Dr. Lockhart said as Evan approached.

"Good morning. Anything new so far?"

"No time for small talk?" the doctor said, the corners of her eyes crinkling behind her shield.

"Not today, no. I have a lot to do."

"Her hyoid bone is broken, and she has petechiae," Dr. Lockhart told him, following his request to get to business. "Strong signs that she was strangled. I haven't found any other physical injuries, but there is adhesive on her wrists. I suspect it will come back as duct tape. There is also a faint pattern in her flesh that duct tape often leaves behind."

"Labs?"

"Her initial blood labs showed nothing of interest, but I will run more."

Evan stared at the victim's feet. The flesh was pale, and a thick outer layer had detached, making it look as if her feet had been dipped in wax and it could easily slip off. Being submerged in the water had created the effect.

He'd seen floaters before. Bodies that had been found in water after being missing for days or weeks. Swollen, misshapen, chewed on by underwater scavengers. The sight was horrible. This woman had been only partially submerged and was still difficult to look at, but full floaters were worse.

"I ran her fingerprints and didn't get a hit," said Dr. Lockhart. "But I know you have other databases to try."

"Age?"

"Between eighteen and twenty-five," said the doctor. "She still has her third molars—wisdom teeth—and they've erupted into the jaw and show full root development. She could be as young as sixteen, but usually the roots haven't fully formed at that age. Films of her skull also guide me to that age range."

The closest age on his missing-blonde list was thirty-five. On the other list in the right age range were two brunettes. "Can you tell if she colored her hair? Could she be a brunette?"

"She's a blonde."

His lists were suddenly useless. "Eye color?"

"Green. She's five foot five. About a hundred and twenty pounds. I've tightened the time of death down to five to seven days . . . give or take a day or two." She met Evan's gaze. "Does that line up with any of your missing women?"

"Not yet," said Evan. "I'll expand my parameters. It's possible she hasn't been reported missing yet."

"Didn't two of your other recent victims have long blonde hair? And were about the same age and size?"

Dr. Lockhart had done both their autopsies.

"You have a good memory."

"After we left the crime scene yesterday, I looked them up. It was seeing you that prompted my memory. You always show up for the autopsies—unlike some other detectives—and I knew you'd been here for young women recently."

"Attending autopsies isn't for everyone," Evan said, thinking of Noelle Marshall.

"I know. I don't judge."

"Anything else you've come across that can help me out?" he asked.

Dr. Lockhart straightened her back and twisted her shoulders. "She has two tattoos. They're hard to see with the discoloration. I'll include photos in my report, but there's one on the inside of her right ankle and another just below her hair on her neck."

Evan stepped closer, remembering he'd noticed the ankle tattoo the day before. "Looks like a tiny daisy." The loosened flesh had distorted it.

"The one on her neck is a yin and yang symbol. It's also small. About two centimeters. Do you want to see?"

He studied the victim's head. It would be awkward to move the body for him to view it at that moment. "I'll wait and look at the photos. Anything unusual about the neck one?"

"Nope. Looks like the dozens of other yin and yang tattoos I've seen."

"Any other distinguishing marks or scars?"

"I didn't see any. We took thorough photos of everything before I started today. X-rays too."

"What about her dental charting?" he asked.

"You'll have her dental films and charting in my report. But I will say she's had good dental care. Straight teeth with only a few composite fillings. A perfect smile."

With the victim's face so disfigured, Evan struggled to imagine a perfect smile. He could see some of her teeth because her mouth hung open. But even his imagination couldn't see a young woman with a warm smile.

"Thanks for your help, Doctor," Evan said. "I'll keep you updated."

She met his gaze. "Like we discussed . . . this is similar to your other two cases."

"I know."

"Does the public need to be notified?" she asked softly.

Evan understood what she hadn't said: the ME was concerned a serial killer was in the area. "I've been weighing that," he told her. "But there's been no physical evidence to connect the three young women."

"Yet."

Evan nodded. "Yet."

Dr. Lockhart held his gaze for another long second and then turned her attention back to the victim. "Keep me updated," she said, repeating Evan's phrase.

He felt as if he'd been judged and found guilty.

Am I not being proactive?

Evan didn't want to jump to conclusions. He would continue to study all three cases from every angle. If there was a serial killer preying on young women, the public deserved to know. But he wasn't sure yet. And he didn't want to raise a false alarm.

"Have a good day, Natasha."

"You too, Evan."

He turned and walked to the door, where he stripped off his personal protective wear and tossed it in the bin. A minute later he was outside, pulling his sweatshirt over his head. The temperature had gone up at least ten degrees, and the welcome sun baked his head.

Is there a serial killer?

16

"This is an investigation—*my* investigation—and you have no business here," the doctor snapped, her dark eyes glaring lasers at Rowan.

Rowan stood her ground at the forensic anthropologist's order. "I know. And I do have business here. I found the victim yesterday, which led to the additional discovery of these bones." She gestured at the taped-off scene under the pines.

It was hot out. Much warmer than the day before. Six people were working in the area where the bones had been discovered. There were two deputies, a photographer, two techs working in the dirt, and the forensic anthropologist. They'd taped off a very large area to search because it was assumed bones had been scattered by wildlife. A grid of string and small stakes covered the immediate area of the remains they'd found the previous day.

Rowan had just arrived, unable to focus at home knowing a forensic anthropologist would look at the small skull that day.

I have to know.

And the person who could tell her stood right in front of her. Dr. Victoria Peres. Rowan couldn't wait for an official report including the sex of the skull.

The tall woman wasn't swayed by Rowan's answer. "Get lost. Or I'll have one of the deputies escort you out."

"I wasn't done speaking," Rowan said. "I do search and rescue full time. I know how this works. But . . ." She swallowed hard, holding the doctor's gaze. "My brother vanished in these woods more than two decades ago. I need to know if that smaller skull is male."

Surprise flashed in the doctor's eyes, and her face softened.

"My name is Rowan Wolff. I work with a lot of law enforcement." She raised a hand at the two deputies who were watching the conversation with interest. Both returned the gesture. Rowan racked her memory to come up with their names. "Nate and Chris will vouch that I'm not nuts."

Dr. Peres folded her arms across her chest and looked down at Thor, who sat close to Rowan's feet. "Is this Thor?"

Now it was Rowan's turn to look surprised. "Yes."

"I've heard of the two of you," admitted Dr. Peres. "Strange our paths haven't crossed."

"I've seen you in the field," said Rowan. "But we've not had an occasion to speak."

Dr. Peres held Rowan's gaze for a few long seconds, and Rowan struggled to not look away. The doctor had a posture of absolute authority, and her brown eyes scrutinized Rowan from head to toe. "I'm very sorry about your brother."

"Thank you," said Rowan. "It was a long time ago, but not knowing what happened is agonizing."

"I understand," said Dr. Peres. "I've dedicated my life to finding answers and bringing closure to people like you."

"That's my job too."

An affinity for the dark-haired woman sprang up in Rowan's chest, and she thought the doctor also felt it.

"I haven't examined the skulls yet. You can watch, but stay outside the tape." The doctor turned and started back to the site. Slightly shocked, Rowan followed. "And be careful where you step. More remains can turn up outside the tape."

Rowan fought back the "Yes, ma'am," that formed on her tongue. Dr. Peres pointed out a place for Rowan to stand next to one of the deputies and then entered the scene, walking a narrow, taped-off path that led to the remains. Use of the entry and path was strictly enforced to keep people from wandering through the scene.

"You friends now?" the deputy asked Rowan with a grin.

"I don't think *friends* is the right word, Nate," Rowan said in a whisper, hoping that Dr. Peres didn't have bionic hearing.

"You're still standing. That means the Ice Queen likes you," said Nate, a serious look on his face.

Rowan felt as if she'd won a lottery. She had been aware of the forensic anthropologist's tough reputation but hadn't known Dr. Peres was working the scene until she arrived. "She's doing her job," she told Nate, annoyed at his "Ice Queen" comment. "And she's good at it."

He looked past her, suddenly on alert. "More company." Nate squinted. "Detective Bolton and . . . Detective Marshall. Didn't know she was on this case."

Pleased that Evan had arrived, Rowan turned to see the pair approach. Thor stood, his tail going full speed and his ears trained toward the detectives. She studied the tall blonde woman next to Evan. Rowan had heard of Detective Marshall but never met her. "What's her first name?" she asked Nate.

"Noelle."

Statuesque was the adjective that popped into Rowan's head. The woman moved with confidence and power. Defined muscles moved in her thighs, and her chin was high, her eyes alert.

Rowan watched Evan laugh at something Noelle said and felt the smallest seed of jealousy sprout in her chest. "What the fuck," she muttered, annoyed at the emotion.

"What?" asked Nate.

"Nothing."

Rowan glanced over her shoulder. Dr. Peres was also watching the detectives approach.

"Rowan! I didn't expect you up here," said Evan. His eyes looked happy to see her, promptly eliminating her seed of jealousy. "But I'm not surprised. Do you know Detective Noelle Marshall?"

"I don't." Rowan shook the woman's hand, admiring her direct dark-blue eyes.

"Rowan is the SAR member I told you about," said Evan.

He told her about me?

"And this is Thor." Evan squatted to greet the dog and received a lick on the cheek.

"Nice to meet you, Rowan. And Thor is gorgeous." Noelle admired the dog.

Rowan liked her even more. No better way to her dog handler's heart than showing sincere admiration for her dog.

Evan stood and turned his attention to the scene. Dr. Peres gestured for him to come in. "Stay on the path," she told the detectives.

Rowan watched them enter, envious that they were getting up close. But she and Nate stood only twenty feet from where the work was happening, and they could hear pieces of the conversation.

Rowan frowned as Evan said something in a low voice to the doctor that she couldn't make out. The doctor's response was also quiet.

Dammit.

She had a feeling it concerned her. And Malcolm. Annoyance stirred in her belly. If the doctor had an idea about the sex and age of the skull, Rowan wanted to hear it. At that moment both Evan and Dr. Peres looked back at her, as if they had heard her thought.

"I'll get her," Rowan heard Noelle say before she headed out of the crime scene.

"Would you watch Thor?" she asked Nate, who immediately nodded. Heart pounding, Rowan rapidly walked to the entrance to meet the detective.

"What is it?" Rowan asked. "Is the skull a young boy?"

"She hasn't removed the skulls yet," Noelle told her. "Evan told her you should be in there."

Disappointment flared, but she was also pleased. Evan was on her side. "Thank you," she told Noelle, who indicated for her to follow.

Feeling as if she were walking on hallowed ground, she joined the two detectives and Dr. Peres.

"I prefer to work without an audience," the doctor said, holding Rowan's gaze. "But I'll give you a few minutes."

"I appreciate that." She truly did. Rowan studied the scene. One tech was carefully turning over dirt with a hand trowel near the larger skull while another sifted dirt with a large screen. The third tech, the one with the camera, hovered at the shoulder of the first. She also had a notepad with a rough sketch of the scene, and she constantly added more detail to it. When the skull was fully exposed, many photos were taken, and then Dr. Peres carefully lifted it.

"Hair," said the first tech. She grabbed a large, clear baggie from a kit and gingerly added long strands of dark hair that had been under the skull. The mandible still lay in the dirt. The remains were skeletal, and no soft tissue remained at all, so the mandible had detached from the skull.

How long did it take to become fully skeletal?

Rowan tried to remember what she'd read but only recalled that many factors influenced the time.

"Can you tell how long they've been here?" Evan asked.

The doctor grimaced. "No. I believe they were fully buried at one point, but the grave was quite shallow—which could speed up decomposition. Either animals have uncovered it or possibly the ridiculous amount of rain we had last winter did it." Dr. Peres studied the skull in her hands. "Definitely female. Caucasian." She wrote something on the skull in pencil and set it in a tub. Then she grabbed a trowel and helped the tech unearth what Rowan quickly identified as ribs and vertebrae.

"Anything?" Dr. Peres murmured to the tech.

"Nothing obvious," the woman said. "Maybe something will turn up in the filter."

"What will?" asked Noelle. She rested her hands on her knees, bending over as she intently studied the two women's actions.

"Buttons, zippers, belt buckles, jewelry," said the doctor. "Sometimes they're caked with dirt and hard to distinguish at first." Dr. Peres's tone was uncertain.

"You're not expecting to find any," Rowan said flatly. "You think she was naked."

Like the woman yesterday.

"It's too early to say that," said the doctor. "Way too early." She shot Rowan a sharp look.

Rowan wanted to ask her to start on the small skull but said nothing. She was on thin ice already. The doctor continued to dig and remove bones, writing on each one before she added it to a tub. "You good here?" she asked the tech, who nodded without looking up.

Dr. Peres moved to the smaller skull several feet away, and Rowan held her breath, suspecting the doctor had worked on the other skeleton for a while simply to teach Rowan some patience. Two-thirds of the second skull had been visible the day before, and the doctor removed more earth around it, adding the dirt to a bucket to be screened.

"Hello," the doctor said softly as she lifted the skull. It was clearly smaller than the first. Dr. Peres examined the face and the cranial sutures and turned it over to look at the teeth and other sutures. "Caucasian," she said, frowning. "That's the easy part. Young. The first molars are well established. No second molars yet, so most likely under twelve. I'll narrow it later when I can take some films, measurements, and examine it in better light."

Rowan couldn't breathe.

Dr. Peres ran fingers over the forehead and touched the upper parts of the orbital sockets and frowned again. "I think it's female . . . but it's hard at this age." She looked at Rowan, sincerity in her eyes. "I'm sorry I can't tell you for certain at the moment."

"Hair?" Rowan croaked.

Evan touched her arm. She'd forgotten he was even present. "You okay?"

"Yeah." As okay as one could be standing at the possible grave of a missing loved one.

Dr. Peres examined the dirt under the skull. "There's no hair immediately visible. We'll sift for it. But it's possible the skull was moved a bit from its original place. I'm glad we're on a flat piece of ground. Gravity and weather and animals can really spread out a scene when it's on a slope."

She moved some more dirt and nodded to herself. "This skull isn't where I'd expect it based on the position of the rest of the bones for these particular remains. The bones have been moved in some way. Animals maybe."

"Could a person have moved them?" asked Evan.

"Sure," the doctor said with a one-shoulder shrug. "I don't know why someone would, though."

"Dr. Peres." There was tension in the first tech's voice. "There's another skull under this one's ribs."

The doctor set the small skull back in the dirt and immediately joined the tech. "Photos," she ordered, taking the sketch pad from the photographer. Dr. Peres scowled at the new skull and added details to the sketch as the photographer's camera rapidly clicked. "It's another adult female."

Rowan and the two detectives exchanged glances.

There are more bodies?

"Is this a dumping ground?" Evan asked under his breath.

Rowan looked back at the small skull.

Malcolm?

17

Malcolm, twenty-five years ago

Rowan and Malcolm were in the shed when he shouted for them to put on the blindfolds. Unprepared, they scrambled to do as he said. "Why?" Rowan whispered.

Malcolm didn't reply because he was also confused, dread filling every muscle. The man had already run them around that day, and it wasn't time for dinner yet. The sun was high in the sky, and the shed was roasting. He usually left them alone at that time of day.

"I'm so tired."

"Shhhh," Malcolm told her, kneeling in his corner.

The locks rattled and clicked, and the hinges squeaked as he opened the door. "You. Boy. With me." He stepped inside, and Malcolm felt the floor dip.

Malcolm leaped to his feet, and the man grabbed his arm, leading him out of the shed. The door slammed, and he fastened the locks.

Malcolm was relieved Rowan was inside, because now he knew it wouldn't be a competition, and the man wouldn't make him hurt her.

But what will he do to me?

They walked for several minutes, the man's hand still on Malcolm's arm, and when Malcolm's blindfold shifted the tiniest bit, he didn't adjust it. Now he could see some of the ground and was less likely to trip.

Many minutes later, Malcolm stood silently inside another building. The temperature was comfortable, and he could see gold-and-orange linoleum. Anger flooded him. Their shed was too hot, and the floors gave them splinters, while this place was minutes away with normal floors and air-conditioning.

Why are we kept like animals?

Malcolm's legs ached, and he shifted his balance from foot to foot, wondering how long he'd been standing in the cool room. Too long. But the man had told him not to move, so he obeyed. He could hear the man walking around the room, occasionally muttering something.

Something scraped the floor—maybe a chair—and Malcolm had the impression the man had sat down directly in front of him. It was silent for a long moment, so Malcolm waited.

"How would you like it if your sister goes home?" the man asked.

Shock froze Malcolm's tongue. He hadn't expected the man to say that. His mind struggled to understand . . . he was going to free them?

But he'd said Rowan . . . not both of them.

"Answer me, boy. Do not disrespect me like this. Speak clearly and quickly when someone asks you a question."

"I would like that, sir." Malcolm didn't dare ask for clarification.

"I'm thinking about sending her home. But you would have to be a better boy. You need to listen better. Move faster."

Malcolm's heart sank, and he tried not to cry.

Rowan gets to go home. I have to stay.

But Rowan needed to leave. She should get out of there. Malcolm worried about her health.

"Or you both could stay," the man said. "I haven't made a decision. The problem is I don't really have enough food for both of you, so meals will have to be smaller if you both stay."

Malcolm caught his breath. Rowan and he could stay together.

I'm being selfish. She needs more food. She's not going to last on the little food he gives us.

"Take off your blindfold, boy."

Malcolm didn't move; was it a trick?

"I just said you need to be a better boy. Did you forget that already?" he snarled. "Take off the blindfold."

Malcolm ripped it off and blinked in the light.

And saw the man for the first time.

The man had a brown beard and sat six feet away, staring at him. Malcolm studied the face of the person who had made their lives hell for days. He was a large man, probably close to the age of their dad, and he wore a tank top and denim shorts with hiking boots. He studied Malcolm with direct, cold eyes.

I feel like a caged animal at the zoo.

They were in a small building, and it almost felt like a trailer, but it was wider and longer. There were a sink, cupboards, and a refrigerator on one side and a small table with chairs on the other. At the far end was a partially open door, and he saw a bed in the room beyond.

Malcolm's gaze returned to the table, and he was startled as he spotted a second man sitting there in the shadow. The second man remained motionless as he watched Malcolm. He wore jeans and hiking boots with red laces. Malcolm immediately looked at the floor, scared to look at either man.

The heavy-bearded man stood and took something out of the little fridge. He held a plastic bowl of macaroni and cheese in front of Malcolm, the kind his mother made from the blue box. The cheesy scent made his stomach rumble and his mouth water.

The man laughed. "Take it, boy."

Malcolm glanced up to see if he was serious and saw a gentle smile on his face.

"Yes, it's for you. Here's a fork."

Malcolm took both and clenched them tightly. But he didn't eat. It had to be a trick. The second man watched, not saying a word.

"Eat."

He took a bite and it reminded him of home. It was cold, but he didn't care. It was the best thing he'd eaten since he'd been there. Malcolm ate quickly, barely chewing the pasta, scared the man would take it away at any second.

"I see you like that," said the man with the beard. "That's how it can be for you every day if your sister goes back home."

The food dried up on Malcolm's tongue, and he struggled to swallow. He met the man's eyes, and they were still kind. Malcolm glanced at the second man. He hadn't moved.

"Would you like that, boy? Plenty of food for you every day?"

I can do it. If Rowan is safe and healthy, I could manage.

He tried to eat another bite, but his mouth was still dry, so he chewed and chewed.

"You don't need to answer yet," the man said. "Think about it." He held out his hand for the bowl, and Malcolm slowly handed it over. He'd eaten half of it. His stomach was uncomfortable, and he almost didn't recognize the sensation of a full belly.

The man replaced Malcolm's blindfold, tying it gently. He patted Malcolm's shoulder in an affectionate way. "I'll walk you back."

In the shed, Rowan launched herself at Malcolm after the man locked the door. Her face was wet.

"I was so scared you weren't coming back," she cried, hugging him. "I didn't know what to do." She wiped her nose on his shirt and hugged him tighter.

Malcolm patted her back, an echo of how the man had touched him. "I'm okay. Nothing happened. You're fine."

"What did he want?"

"The usual," he lied. "He had me move firewood from one pile to another. A useless chore." He hugged her, and they sat on the rough floor. She clasped both his hands, still needing to touch her brother. In the poor light, Malcolm saw her lips were cracked. He knew she was hungry and wondered if she could smell the mac and cheese on his breath. He closed his mouth and breathed through his nose.

Hours later Malcolm tried to sleep. Rowan had fallen asleep after crying because the man had never brought them dinner and moaning that her stomach hurt. Guilt racked Malcolm.

This is how it will be for her unless I let her go home.

Malcolm cried a little. He didn't want to be left alone with the bearded man or the other silent man. But in his heart he knew he needed to let her go.

It was the right thing to do.

In the morning the man yelled for them to put on the blindfolds. Instead of giving them breakfast, the man took Malcolm back to the other place, and he worried that Rowan wouldn't get any food again. It had been twenty-four hours since she'd eaten, and Malcolm didn't want to hear her cry again.

Soon he'll send her home.

Inside, the man took off Malcolm's blindfold and smiled at him. Malcolm looked away, quickly glancing at the second man, and noticed he was sitting in the exact same spot, wearing the same clothes, and Malcolm wondered if he'd moved since yesterday. He smelled cinnamon and sugar and scanned the small room for the source of the amazing scents.

Then the bearded man handed him a cinnamon roll. It was warm and the icing was melting. Malcolm swallowed hard and met his gaze.

"Eat."

Malcolm ripped off a piece and shoved it in his mouth. He nearly wept at the taste of sugar and butter and spice. He wanted to save some for Rowan but knew better than to ask. So he just ate, licking his fingers as he went, not caring that the two men watched his every move. After five bites he was mildly nauseated and felt guilty about eating while Rowan had nothing.

Surely he'll give me something for her.

"Did you think about my idea?" the man asked. "I'm sure your sister was excited by it."

"I would like her to go home, sir." Malcolm didn't mention that he hadn't told Rowan that she could go home. He didn't want her to know that he would stay behind. He knew she'd cry and refuse to leave. He couldn't deal with that.

Malcolm kept his gaze on the floor and saw round drips of icing from his roll. He shuddered, waiting for the man to yell about the mess.

"You want her to leave?"

"Yes, sir."

"And you'll try harder? Work faster? Listen better?"

"Yes, sir."

The man's laughter filled the room, and Malcolm's gaze flew up. The man had to sit down because he was laughing so hard. The second man was solemn, simply watching. He blinked, his eyes like an owl's, and Malcolm realized it was the first movement he'd seen. The second man's eyes were emotionless; they offered no explanation for the other man's laughter.

Malcolm didn't know what to do. He was terrified and hopeful and confused. He crushed the rest of the cinnamon roll in his grip, knowing something was very, very wrong.

"You should see your face!" The bearded man grinned at him as if Malcolm were his best friend.

I don't think I am.

"You must be the most stupid boy in the world." He coughed, and an evil gleam appeared in his eyes. "Did you really think I would send her home?"

Malcolm looked down again, fighting to keep the roll in his churning stomach. The strong cinnamon smell made it worse.

"There's no point in sending her home. Your parents aren't looking for you two anymore. They finished a while ago."

He's lying.

Malcolm met his gaze, searching for the truth. But he saw no hint that the man lied. The man actually looked sorry for him now. Hate flooded Malcolm, burning through his limbs. Lowering his head brought the linoleum back in his gaze, but he felt as if he were looking through a tube. His vision narrowed, and he felt light-headed. Malcolm abruptly sat on the floor and pulled up his knees, burying his face in them.

The only positive was that Rowan didn't expect to leave. Malcolm was thankful he hadn't told her.

"I know the news about your parents is a shock, boy. But I'm not surprised. It's very hard to keep searching for a missing child. It feels better to give up and move on. I heard your family is moving out of state. They don't want to keep living in the place their children vanished, and they want a fresh start."

He's lying. My parents would never give up.

Or would they?

His mom had been tired all the time from taking care of the twins. His and Rowan's absence must be causing her so much more stress.

Maybe the family needed to move on to protect his mom.

"I'll figure out something else to do with your sister. You win most of the competitions and are much stronger and faster. You've told me how much you hate her, so I'll think on it. I know you want her gone."

Malcolm's muscles went cold at his words. He couldn't move.

What will he do with Rowan?

"Unless she starts performing better. She's always so much slower than you."

Malcolm lifted his head, anger returning. "She's little. She's a girl. She can't help it," he said.

The bearded man turned around to look at the other man for the first time. "See," he told him. "I said he's not ready. Close, though. I can fix that."

I have no idea what he is talking about.

18

"Detective Bolton!"

Evan turned at the voice. He'd been crossing the parking lot, headed into the sheriff's department's building at the ass crack of dawn. He tensed when he saw a tall man thirty feet away but relaxed a bit as he noticed the pure-white hair under the cowboy hat and how the man lurched as he walked, favoring a hip. Something about him felt familiar.

The lanky man held out a hand, huffing slightly. "Sam Durette."

The name rang a bell, and Evan shook his hand. "You're a retired detective."

"I am," Sam said proudly. "I did twenty-five years in that building right there. I know every broken floor tile and stained ceiling square."

"Like above the fridge—"

"In the rear break room," Sam finished.

"Nice to meet you," Evan said, remembering he'd heard that Sam had been well respected. Sam Durette was tall, with wide shoulders that were now a bit hunched. His icy blue gaze skewered Evan, making him feel like a target. "Were you waiting for me?"

"I was. Been sitting in my car for a good half hour. I figured you for an early bird like me. Don't need as much sleep as I used to, and when something's on my mind, I gotta address it before it eats away at me."

"I know the feeling." Evan grimaced. He'd had about four hours of sleep the night before, autopsy and skeletal remains images appearing every time he closed his eyes. The best way to get rid of them was to solve the cases.

Which was why he was at work at 5:30 a.m.

"What can I do for you?" Evan asked, itching to get in the building, but making himself give the detective the respect he deserved.

"I heard about those young women's murders you've got on your desk." Sam's stare continued to bore through him. "Sound an awful lot like cases I had way back. Three young women. Blonde. Nude. Dumped. Strangled. Sound familiar?"

Sam now had Evan's full attention. "How long ago? Were the cases closed?"

"It's been about twenty-five years. We made an arrest. He's doing time in Salem."

Oregon State Penitentiary in Salem.

Sam scowled. "You weren't aware of those cases? They didn't come up in your research?"

"No," Evan said shortly. "I didn't look at closed cases from twenty-five years ago." He was ready to end the conversation.

"They were found in the same general area as the woman and skeletal remains you looked at yesterday."

Evan went still. "Your man could be responsible for the buried remains?"

"Could be."

"Let's move this inside." Evan's skin tingled, curiosity energizing his nerves.

Five minutes later each of them had a cup of scalding-hot department coffee and had taken a seat in Evan's office.

"How'd you hear about what was found yesterday?" Evan asked. He wasn't too surprised. Word traveled fast in law enforcement. Even reaching people who had been out of the office for ten years.

"Rowan Wolff."

Evan's hand tightened on his cup. "How do you know her?"

Sam's face softened. "I've known Rowan since she was found in the woods. Finding the asshole who kidnapped her and her brother, Malcolm, was one of my biggest cases. I grew tight with her family. I still see them a few times a year."

Again Rowan had appeared in Evan's work. The link was a bit indirect this time, but Evan couldn't ignore it. Coincidence no longer explained her ties to his cases.

What does?

"The man who murdered the young women back then was also those kids' kidnapper. Jerry Chiavo," said Sam. "Their babysitter was one of the murders."

Wheels and gears spun in Evan's brain.

But how can a man sitting in prison be related to what's happened in the last few weeks?

"Chiavo pled not guilty to the murders of the three women," Sam continued. "He still claims he didn't do it but wouldn't—or couldn't—tell us who did."

"Are you suggesting someone is killing again? That you put the wrong man in prison?"

Different emotions flickered across the retired detective's face. "He belongs in prison. He admitted to kidnapping those kids, and although he claims Malcolm died in an accident, I have my doubts. The mental and physical abuse those two kids suffered at his hands tells me he's right where he belongs." Anger and rage clipped his words.

"But maybe he wasn't responsible for the young women's deaths."

"Solid evidence was found on his property to connect him to them. I understand you know Rowan . . . she doesn't like to talk about her past, but I'm surprised you didn't do some digging into her background yourself."

Evan looked down at his coffee. "I only learned of her kidnapping three days ago. I was definitely curious and wanted to read up on it, but I decided to focus my energy on my cases. After learning that her brother had disappeared near where that cache of bones was found, their kidnapping was at the top of my list to familiarize myself with this morning."

"She's been searching for him for a long time," Sam said. "Not the healthiest habit."

A thought occurred to Evan. "If you were the detective assigned to the case, then you knew Ken Steward."

"I did! Good man. I knew him quite well. I was crushed to hear of his murder . . . wait . . . what the fuck." Sam's tone lifted as an odd expression flitted across his face, and he stared at Evan. "Is it related?"

The air in the office seemed to grow heavy.

"I'm investigating his murder," Evan stated, trying to make sense of Ken's murder and the fact that they were discussing a case in which Ken had played an integral part.

Both men were silent for a long moment.

"I can't connect the dots," Sam finally said after a long pause. "There's a thread here . . . but it's a coincidence?"

"I don't believe in coincidences when it comes to murder," Evan said softly.

"I don't either," said Sam, shaking his head. "I heard he was shot in his sleep while camping. Is that correct?"

"Yes."

"What can that have to do with the three young women that were strangled and dumped recently?"

"I don't know," said Evan, writing a note on his pad. "But I'm sure as hell going to dig for a connection. If I find a suspect in one murder, I'll take a hard look at him for the others, including Ken's."

"I miss this sometimes," said Sam with a wry grin. "I loved putting the puzzle pieces together. It was grueling and frustrating, but damn it felt good when I figured it out."

"I completely get that."

"So . . . where were we?" asked Sam. "Rowan told me a smaller skull was found with the others yesterday?"

"Yes," said Evan. "But we don't know the sex yet. Why wouldn't Rowan say anything to me about those murders twenty-five years ago when she learned of the current ones? She has to see the similarities."

Sam took a deep breath as he pondered. "Well . . . the man who tortured her is in prison. In her mind, he is gone. Out of the picture. Locked away. She feels safe. Her brain might have a wall up that keeps her from looking beyond and questioning how this is happening again."

"She must suspect the skeletons we found yesterday could be from when he was killing back then. Especially since one could be her brother, but she didn't say anything about that possibility." Evan met the detective's gaze. "The new cases could be the work of an accomplice. Maybe a copycat. Was another man under investigation back then? A friend or a relative of Jerry Chiavo?"

"No," Sam said firmly. "We had no suspects until—" He stopped and stared out the window. "Until his neighbor reported finding the babysitter's car on his property five years later." His gaze swung back to Evan's. "You'd think Chiavo would turn the tables on his neighbor or anyone else who was an accomplice. Chiavo never made that assertion."

"I need to look at his associates from back then."

Sam shook his head. "I don't think you'll find anything. Jerry Chiavo was prosecuted for murdering three women. If I was in his shoes, I'd be spilling my guts if I knew who really did it. His defense never suggested anyone. I always felt deep inside that Chiavo was the killer."

Evan understood. He listened to his gut too. But always searched for the facts. He respected the logic of Sam's assertion about associates— but Evan still had to investigate.

And talk to Rowan.

He frowned, considering how to approach her with the delicate topic. "How is Rowan when it comes to discussing her kidnapping or the murders? Does she mind talking about it?"

Sam snorted. "She hates it, but she'll do it. She's a smart, rational woman. But remember she saw things through the eyes of a five-year-old. Those aren't the most accurate memories. If I were you, I'd read everything you can find about the case before approaching her. Have your facts in line first."

Evan nodded. The detective was right. He had work to do first.

Confident clicks sounded down the hall, and Noelle Marshall appeared in his doorway, balancing two cups of coffee in a cardboard holder and a white paper bag with faint grease marks near the bottom.

Evan's stomach growled.

"You beat me in again," Noelle said with a grin. "One of these days I'll be here before you." She smiled at Sam, no recognition in her gaze. "Looks like I should have grabbed another coffee."

Sam stood. "Thank you, but I've got a cup of department brew."

"It's garbage," stated Noelle, raising a brow. "You'll need an antacid."

"True," agreed Sam.

Evan made quick introductions, and Noelle set her load on his desk to shake Sam's hand.

She looked from one man to the other, curiosity in her face. "Looks like you two have something to share."

"Pull up a seat," said Evan. "Sam has an interesting angle."

Eagerness replaced her curiosity, and she grabbed a chair.

While Sam told Noelle his story, Evan's mind strayed to Rowan.

Has she realized the recent women's murders are similar to the old murders yet?

19

Thor paced back and forth in front of the slider to the backyard and growled. Rowan rinsed her hands at the kitchen sink and looked out the window, checking for something in the yard that would have upset Thor. He rarely growled.

If a rabbit or chipmunk caught his attention through the slider, he would whine, frozen in place with his gaze locked on the animal. Rowan would never open the door. She liked all fuzzy critters and didn't want to learn what Thor would do if he caught one.

She couldn't see anything in the yard but suspected a coyote or bobcat had wandered through. It happened occasionally.

"Thor. Come here." She dried her hands, waiting for him to obey.

He gave her a reproachful look and took one more long gaze out the window before reluctantly coming her way, his head down.

"Can you walk any slower?" she asked with a grin.

He looked over his shoulder at the door and then at her.

/out/

"You already went out this morning, so I know you don't need to go already. And there's no way I'll let you confront a wild animal."

/out/

"Not happening." She bent down to give the dog a kiss on the top of his head and a hug. He squirmed out of her hold. "I'll be back soon. Don't stare out the back door the whole time I'm gone."

She grabbed her bag and turned on soft classical music that played throughout her home. Rowan always left music on when Thor was home alone. She didn't know if he cared, but it made her feel better.

Take him.

She'd struggled with the decision to leave Thor home. Ken's funeral was in half an hour. She knew there'd be other dogs, but she didn't want to upset him by crying through the service. He was sensitive to her moods. Tears stung her eyes. Today would be emotional. She'd need every bit of her energy to hold it together.

Rowan gave Thor another kiss. "Be good," she instructed firmly.

His head drooped the tiniest bit. Thor knew those words meant she was leaving. Rowan turned and headed to her garage before she could change her mind.

The little outdoor amphitheater was packed. Rowan stood at the top and scanned the crowd. She wasn't surprised at the numbers. Everyone had loved Ken. A dozen dogs were interspersed throughout the huge group, and for a second she regretted not bringing Thor. She spotted familiar faces and nodded at several who lifted a hand in greeting. Rowan wasn't ready to talk and be social; her grief was still raw. She looked for a seat where she could be alone for a bit and found Evan Bolton.

He stood about ten yards away, also keeping apart from the crowd, looking directly at her. Even through his sunglasses, Rowan felt his gaze, and roots of attraction stirred deep inside her. She liked him and wanted to know more about him. There was no denying it. But a funeral wasn't the place for those feelings. He moved her way, and she took a deep breath, pulling herself together.

I'm glad he's here.

But Evan wasn't here because he had loved Ken. He was simply on the job. She shouldn't read any more into it than that. He stopped in front of her and removed his sunglasses.

Rowan nearly broke down at the sympathy in his eyes.

"Are you here on a professional level?" For a greeting, she knew it was rather rude, but her emotions were all over the map.

His gaze softened. "No, I'm here because he was important to . . . a lot of people."

"I'm sorry. I was rude," she blurted, feeling even worse about her greeting. "I'm a mess."

"Completely understandable." He eyed the amphitheater. "Would you like to sit down?"

Rowan nodded, not trusting her voice. Evan lightly touched the small of her back and guided her down a few steps to a bench that wasn't packed with people. She concentrated on stepping firmly with her bad leg, not wanting to lose her balance.

"Or would you rather sit with some friends?" he asked.

"This is perfect." Rowan sat and inhaled deeply.

He took the spot next to her. "No Thor today?"

"He gets stressed when he knows I'm upset." She gave a shaky smile. "And I knew I'd be emotional today."

"I see Shannon Steward. Is that Ken's dog beside her?" Evan pointed at a black Lab sitting next to a golden.

"Yes."

"Who's sitting next to her?"

"That's Ken's cousin Eric, and on her other side is Ken's ex-wife Lisa. His first wife, Carolyn, is sitting directly behind Shannon with her husband, Steve."

"I'm still stunned that all the exes get along," Evan said. "What about the rest of Ken's family?"

"That's it," said Rowan. "He was a single child, and his parents passed away a long time ago. Eric is the only cousin that he keeps in touch with. I think he told me one time he didn't bother with extended family, nor they with him. His friends were always his family."

"Who does the German shepherd belong to?" he asked, eyeing another dog behind Shannon Steward.

Rowan knew he was trying to distract her, and she appreciated it. "That's Rees Womack's dog. I'd say he was as close to Ken as Shannon. His dog is Gunnar." She continued to share the names of other dogs and owners she knew—which was nearly every pair. She recounted amusing anecdotes about several dogs and the missions she'd worked with them. The tightness in her chest eased, and she no longer felt as if she were about to melt into a sea of tears.

The service started and she focused on the speakers. Thirty minutes later, her cheeks were wet from her laughing so hard. Ken's three ex-wives had organized the service and had clearly instructed the speakers to recount their funniest experiences with Ken.

There were a lot of stories. For someone who had dedicated his life to SAR, Ken was known for his poor sense of direction and being rather clumsy. Failings he was well aware of and joked about often. Many of the speakers shared their adventures with Ken that had resulted in sprained ankles, broken bones, or getting lost.

Afterward Rowan rose to her feet, her heart light for the first time that day. The service had been cathartic. Shannon Steward made eye contact with her and grabbed Lisa's and Carolyn's hands, pulling them in Rowan's direction. The three men who'd been sitting with the exes trailed behind.

Rowan was finally ready for a bit of social chat. She exchanged hugs with the women and introduced everyone to Evan.

"You're the detective," said Eric Steward as he shook Evan's hand. Ken's cousin was grim, dozens of questions in his eyes. Steve and Rees silently shook Evan's hand. Their gazes were also suspicious and unhappy. Rowan suspected they viewed Evan as someone who hadn't done his best because Ken's killer was still on the loose. Until Evan found him, the men wouldn't put their trust in him.

"Yes. I'm sorry for your loss," said Evan.

"Ken's case is in good hands," Shannon said quickly with a glance at Eric. "Detective Bolton is known for getting things done. I've been reading up on him."

"Me too," added Carolyn.

The women see the men's distrust too.

Evan raised his brows but said nothing. Eric looked away, frustration on his face. Rowan suspected he was biting his tongue, holding back dozens of questions because he knew this was not the place or time for them.

Today was for remembering the good times.

Rowan praised the women for the memorial service, and after a round of goodbye hugs, she was suddenly exhausted.

"I'll walk you to your car," Evan told Rowan, following her up the steps out of the amphitheater. His tone had changed. "I need to talk to you, but I hate to bring up business at a memorial," he said.

"It's not business; it's Ken's murder."

"My job isn't nine to five," Evan said. "I'm always working. My brain never stops." He paused for a long moment as they followed the path back to the parking lot. "Earlier today I spent several hours reading up on your kidnapping. After that woman's body was found yesterday, why didn't you mention the murders of other young women that happened at the same time as your babysitter's?"

Rowan's steps slowed as her brain tried to process what he'd said.

"You had to see they were similar to my two current cases and the woman you discovered."

Ice traveled up her spine. It'd never crossed her mind. "What does it matter? It can't be related. He's in prison." She refused to say his name. "He'll never be out. He'll die in prison."

Why am I so unsettled?

Evan touched her arm and she stopped, turning to stare at him. His eyes were patient. "The victim you found was close to the location where your babysitter was found. The other two women he killed back then were also strangled and found in similar situations. This can't be a coincidence."

Rowan's mind raced. "He's in prison," she repeated.

"Who else knew about the location where your babysitter was found?"

"I was *five*," she snapped. "You're asking *me* details of a case more than two decades old? You're the detective with access to all the old records. You figure it out." Her heart felt as if it'd pound its way out of her chest.

"I'm working on it. Sam Durette came to me with the connection this morning, which led me to dig into the past."

Rowan was quiet as a sense of betrayal swamped her. Sam must have made the connection during their birthday phone call. "He didn't say anything to me about those deaths."

Why would he keep that to himself?

"Sam cares about you," said Evan. "I think he didn't want to drag you into the past. He worries because you still search for your brother." His voice was soft.

Her face flushed. She didn't discuss her brother with anyone outside her family except Sam. And Ken. But it was clear now that Evan knew everything. Standing before him, she felt raw and exposed, all her secrets on display.

Defensiveness welled up in her. Rowan had researched Evan Bolton's past too. His sister had gone missing nearly fifteen years before as a teenager—but had turned up recently.

"Did you ever stop searching for her?" she asked quietly, holding his gaze, deliberately not saying his sister's name.

He looked away. "No."

"Could you have lived with yourself if you had stopped looking?"

"No."

"Did you think you were crazy because you hunted for someone you loved?"

His gaze returned to hers; his eyes were haunted. "Sometimes."

That's how his eyes looked when I first met him.

The weight of his sister's disappearance had dogged him, and Rowan understood that burden; she'd felt the same one for decades. A bond suddenly simmered between them, crafted by their similar, devastating experiences. The swift connection was surprising and strong, making her light-headed.

There is definitely something between us.

She wanted to explore it. But not right now.

"I didn't think about the other women who'd been murdered back then," Rowan confessed. "I've put them out of my mind because to me, their tragedy was solved. I think of our sitter Carissa's murder as being closed. Finished. No more questions. Malcolm fills my thoughts. Finding where *that man* buried him is the only thing from the past I think about." Her throat suddenly tightened. "It's too painful to think about what he did to us—or anyone else."

"There's a good chance those bones are more of his victims from back then," Evan said. "The location makes me consider that."

"And one of them could be Malcolm." Rowan could barely speak.

Is my search almost over?

"I'm going to see Dr. Peres tomorrow afternoon," said Evan. "She should have some preliminary results on the remains."

Rowan searched his face. It gave no clue to his thoughts, but she could feel his concern for her. "You'll let me know what she says?"

Evan took her hand and squeezed it. "Of course."

"Thank you." It'd been a long time since she felt that someone actively had her back in her search for Malcolm. Sam and Ken had always been supportive, but this felt different.

Why?

Evan felt like a partner. More than a friend. More than someone with a file on his desk.

He continued to hold her hand and her gaze.

An unfamiliar type of hope filled her heart.

20

Guilt overwhelmed Rowan and she cried.

She'd tried to be strong. But the man hurt them and made Rowan and Malcolm hurt each other every single day.

She hated him.

They were outside and blindfolded. And the man was making them punch one another. Over and over. Rowan swung her arms wildly, not caring anymore how much she hit Malcolm. As long as she was hitting Malcolm, then the man wasn't hitting her. She hated herself for hurting her brother, but her sense of self-protection was stronger.

"Harder! You're barely touching her!" the man hollered.

It was true. Most of Malcolm's hits hadn't hurt at all.

Below her blindfold, Rowan caught a glimpse of the man's boots. He wore hiking boots with red laces. She flailed her arms around again, spinning them in huge circles, landing a few punches. Not being able to see made it almost impossible to fight her brother. She tripped in the dirt but stayed upright. She wanted to win the fight. The man always picked a winner. The prize was not getting kicked in the stomach by him.

The loser got the kick.

After the man kicked her yesterday, she'd thrown up the watery soup he'd fed them.

Right now she hated Malcolm. Her big brother was supposed to protect her from people like this man. Instead, he was hitting her. She knew Malcolm had no choice, but her hate and fear bubbled in her chest.

The only thing to do was to fight back as hard as possible.

The man was in control. She and Malcolm were like puppets to him. They did everything he ordered and tried their best to make him happy. *Happy* wasn't the right word; they tried to keep him from getting mad. When he got mad, things got worse. More pain. Less food. More yelling.

"This is ridiculous! You *both* fight like girls."

Rowan put all her strength into hitting her brother. Her nose was running, and she could taste it in her mouth, but she didn't care. She wanted to win.

"Stop."

She halted midswing and stood frozen, panting. Malcolm made heavy breathing noises a few feet away.

Who won?

She knew better than to ask. One time she'd asked, and he'd said she had won but since she'd dared to ask him a question, she was now the loser.

He didn't like questions.

Her shin had hurt for days after he kicked her with his hard boots.

Rowan brushed away the hair sticking to her cheek, hating how short it was. When she'd lost a fight two days before, the man had handed Malcolm a pair of blunt kids' scissors and told him to cut her hair. He'd locked them back in the shed and told them they had five minutes.

Rowan had cried. She loved her long hair. Her mother would braid it or curl it on special occasions, making her feel like a princess.

Cutting it had taken longer than five minutes. The scissors were dull, and Malcolm could only cut small bunches of hair at a time. Tears had run down his face as he did it. "It'll grow back," he repeated over and over. "We have to do what he says."

Now she had boy hair.

But at least she hadn't been kicked for being the loser that day.

Now, still panting, she waited for the man's announcement of the blindfolded fight's winner.

"You both did horrible. You're stupid kids!"

He's going to kick both of us.

I tried so hard.

Tears soaked the edge of her blindfold, and Malcolm sniffled.

He's scared too.

"New game," announced the man. "Boy, come over here."

Relief swamped her that he'd called Malcolm instead of her, but guilt immediately followed. She didn't want the man to hurt her brother. But when he was hurting her brother, it meant he wasn't hurting her.

"Throw these at her," the man ordered.

Rowan tensed. A second later, something hit the dirt off to her right. And again.

Rocks?

"Aim better!"

"I can't see her," Malcolm said in a tiny voice.

Rowan sucked in her breath, terrified for the sound of the slap she knew Malcolm was about to receive.

It didn't come.

"Bark. Bark like a dog, girl."

He never used their names. She didn't think he knew them.

"Bark!"

"Arf, arf," Rowan barked, cringing as the man laughed.

At least he's not mad.

She continued to bark.

Something bounced off her thigh. It stung a little but wasn't too bad. More rocks hit the ground than hit her.

"You have crappy aim for a boy. I expect that from little girls like your sister. Are you a girl?" he taunted.

Malcolm said nothing, but a rock hit her stomach. Again, it wasn't horrible.

"This is stupid. Use these bigger rocks," the man said to her brother.

"This one will hurt her," said Malcolm.

Don't talk back, Malcolm!

Rowan covered her face with her hands. The next rock hit her elbow, and pain spiked up her arm. "Owww!"

The exclamation slipped out, and she knew the man would enjoy that she'd been hurt. Another big rock hit her in the stomach, knocking her off balance, and she fell to the ground. She cried and stayed down, pulling her knees up to her stomach, trying to catch her breath.

"Throw this one."

"It's way too big."

"Use it!"

"I can't lift it," said Malcolm. Fear filled his tone.

How big is the rock?

"You must want me to throw it," said the man. "I'm bigger, so I can hurt her much worse. That's what you want, isn't it, boy? You want her hurt really bad because you hate her, right?"

"Yes," Malcolm said quietly. "I hate her."

"Pick it up!"

It was silent for a moment, and then Malcolm gave a small grunt. "I can't throw it. It's too heavy."

"Just drop it on her."

Still on the ground, Rowan covered her head again.

"Bark, girl!"

Rowan barked.

One of Malcolm's shoes touched her leg. A thud shook the ground near her stomach.

He'd missed. Rowan tipped her head back, peeking below the blindfold, and wondered how her brother had picked up the huge rock that lay next to her.

"You worthless idiot! I'll do it."

The hiking boots came into view again, and Rowan cowered under her arms.

"This is from your brother, girl! Now you'll know how much he hates you!"

Malcolm doesn't hate me.

"No, please," said Malcolm. "Let me do it! I can do it better!"

Fire exploded in her leg and shot up to her brain.

Stars danced in her eyes, and then her world went black.

21

It was nearly 8:00 p.m. as Evan worked at his desk, crafting his interview questions for Jerry Chiavo. Noelle had run out to grab some Thai food. The two of them hadn't noticed they'd worked through dinner until Noelle's stomach grumbled loudly. Evan had an appointment to visit the Oregon State Penitentiary the next day and was reading everything he could find about the murderer.

He speed-read through decades-old murder binders, noting Sam Durette had made the majority of the entries as the lead investigator on the women's deaths.

I should talk to Sam again before the interview.

Reading about a case was one thing; talking to the investigator was another. Evan set the binders aside and picked up the kidnapping files on the Wolff children for the second time that day. They were thick. Evan shuffled through papers and stopped at Sam's notes from an interview with Rowan Wolff. Age five. He'd skimmed it that morning, but now Evan forced himself to slow down and read every word. Rowan's mother had been present as Sam questioned the child. This had taken place six months after Rowan had been found.

Sam had noted Rowan was alert, sharp, and not fearful of him. Which didn't surprise Evan since Sam had visited her frequently after she'd been found. The detective had worked hard to gain the little girl's trust.

Rage grew in Evan's chest as he read Rowan's description of her kidnapper's games. He'd made the children hurt each other. Punished Malcolm in front of her and then blamed Rowan, claiming it was her fault he had to beat her brother. There was little food. Little to drink. Isolation in a hot shed that often got very cold at night. Rocks. Sticks. Fights.

Jerry broke her leg by slamming it with a heavy rock.

Evan looked away from the page.

My God, what he did to those kids.

He was surprised Rowan had turned out normal. Someone else would be locked away in a mental hospital. Or in prison because they'd learned to hurt others.

His phone rang and he immediately grabbed it, desperate for a distraction from the horrors he was reading about.

"Bolton."

"This is Detective Jason Glass with the Shasta County sheriff's office. You're handling a Jane Doe found two days ago in Deschutes County, correct?"

Evan pushed Sam Durette's notes away. "I am. You're with Shasta County as in Northern California?"

"I am. I've been handling a case of a seventeen-year-old runaway who vanished five months ago. Jillian Francis. Her basic description matches your Jane Doe."

"Which parts of the description?"

"Five foot five, one-twenty-five, blonde hair, green eyes."

"That lines up."

"Hair might be dyed a hot pink in places."

"No, don't have that. But you said it'd been five months. Any distinguishing marks?" Evan held his breath.

"Two tattoos. A yin-yang on her neck and a daisy—"

"On her ankle."

The line went silent for a long moment. "Shit. This isn't how I wanted to find her."

"What's the story?"

"Fight with the parents. Took off. A witness claims they saw her get in an eighteen-wheeler at a rest stop. Said the pink hair caught their notice and that she seemed quite young."

"And somehow she ended up in Oregon. Do you have dental records?"

"I sent them to your email two seconds ago. Along with photos of Jillian and her tattoos."

Evan made a few clicks with his mouse and a moment later was studying a school photo of a blonde girl. "How old is this school photo?"

"A year ago. She was to start her senior year of high school this month."

Evan tried to see the girl's face in his memory of the Jane Doe. Maybe. "Gotta tell ya, she'd been dead about a week when we found her. Visually I can't make an ID."

"Understood. But the tattoos are clear?"

Evan opened the photos of the tattoos and immediately recognized the daisy, even though it had been distorted on the autopsy table. "I saw the daisy. It's a match. I didn't personally see the yin-yang because of her position during the autopsy, but I know it's in the photos from the report. I assume you want a dental comparison before notifying the family?"

"I want it, but this family wants to be told if the tattoos match up. That's proof enough for them. Frankly, for me too, but we'll move forward with the dental. Do you know what happened?"

Evan hesitated to tell the detective that Jillian might have been a victim of a serial killer. He had no proof. Just two other nearly identical dead women several weeks apart. "Not sure. She was found in a remote part of the Cascade Range by a hiker. Nude. Strangled. Half in a creek."

"Dammit."

"Detective." Evan paused. "There might be more to it. It's a theory I'm pursuing, but at the moment that's all it is: a theory. I hesitate to even share it with you."

"Understood. Go ahead. You have my discretion."

"Jillian is the third woman that's been dumped in the county in the last six weeks. All nude. Strangled. Blonde and young. One was a runaway living on the streets of Portland. The other took off after a fight with her boyfriend. The dumping locations are spread out, but I can't ignore the commonalities."

"You don't have a theory; you have a serial killer." The detective let out a string of curses. "Where is he collecting these girls?"

"I don't know yet." Evan grimaced, knowing the other detective was right. He didn't like to jump to conclusions, but after hearing Jillian's age and how she'd disappeared, these killings pointed at a possible single killer.

"Have you contacted the FBI?"

"I'll do it right after I finish talking to you. There is a definite pattern now. Even how the girls all had left their home base and possibly needed a place to stay."

"I need to contact the parents. Do you have images of the tattoos I can show them?"

"Yes." Evan tucked the phone between his cheek and shoulder to use his keyboard. "I'll get them right over to you."

"Appreciate it. It's not going to be an easy evening in the Francis home."

"It's not. Good luck."

The detective ended the call.

Evan leaned back in his chair. His victim was no longer the river woman; she was Jillian Francis.

And it appeared he had a serial killer in his county.

"Fuck!" He grabbed the phone again, pulling up Mercy Kilpatrick's cell number. Voice mail. "Mercy, it's Evan. I need you to call me back

ASAP." Mercy was a close friend in the FBI and the best person he could contact at this time of night to get things moving with the agency.

"Noelle to the rescue," announced Noelle as she entered his office, two big takeout bags in her hands. "Good to see you haven't fainted from hunger." She set the bags on his desk and started unloading. The scent of curry made Evan salivate.

"Things happened while you were gone." He quickly updated her on his call with the Shasta County detective.

"I'm glad we provided answers for her parents," said Noelle. "Too bad they weren't the answers they'd hoped for." She sat down, slid a chair up to Evan's desk, pulled out her phone, and scrolled as she took a bite of pad thai. She suddenly straightened and set down her fork, her eyes on her phone. "Check your email."

Evan pulled chicken off a skewer with his teeth. "I was just in my email," he said with his mouth full.

"This just landed. They've found Ken Steward's Explorer."

"Where?"

"Eagle's Nest. The police chief found it abandoned near the town, ran the plates, and it pulled up our BOLO."

"Chief Daly?"

"Yeah. I've heard of him but never met him. Know him?"

"Good friend. He's married to the FBI agent I just left a voice mail for."

"Small world on this side of the Cascades. I'll get a forensics team en route," said Noelle as she struggled to keep noodles on her plastic fork. "And then a tow."

Evan glanced outside. The barest hint of daylight lingered. If he wanted a look at Ken's vehicle tonight, he'd be doing it by flashlight.

"I know what you're thinking," said Noelle, eyeing him. "I don't want to wait until tomorrow either."

Evan shoveled food in his mouth. "Eat fast and let's go."

"You'll drive and I'll eat."

His grumbling answer was muffled by a mouthful of chicken.

22

Ahead, off the rural lane, Evan spotted the county forensics van with its bright lights shining toward a large mass of dense brush. An Eagle's Nest SUV was parked behind the van, and he recognized Police Chief Truman Daly standing with his arms folded across his chest while he watched the forensic tech. As he drew closer, Evan saw a Ford Explorer behind the brush twenty yards off the road.

Truman's face lit up as Evan stepped out of his vehicle. "Bolton!" He strode forward and shook his hand. Evan introduced him to Noelle.

He and Truman went back a couple of years. They'd worked on a number of cases together, and Evan found the chief of police to be honest and an overall good guy. Evan glanced at his phone. The chief's FBI agent wife still hadn't called him back.

"I left a voice mail for Mercy almost an hour ago," Evan told Truman. "Do you know what she's doing?"

"She's at her sister's house. She and Rose are working on some project for baby Henry's bedroom. And I know wine is involved." Truman glanced at his own phone. "She hasn't returned my text either."

"Shouldn't you be calling him 'toddler Henry' by now?"

Truman snorted. "Mercy and I had the same conversation. I'm worried the name 'baby Henry' will stick through high school."

Evan shook his head, his face dead serious. "You can't let that happen. He'll never have any friends."

Truman turned his attention back to the Explorer. "The closest home is a couple of miles away, and this road isn't used much except by locals. One of them called me. He was positive the vehicle wasn't here when he drove by this morning. I saw the gas tank wasn't empty. So unless there was an engine issue, someone deliberately dumped it today."

"We're in the middle of nowhere," said Noelle. "Someone must have picked up the driver."

"He could have hitchhiked," said Evan. "But that's awfully risky when you're abandoning the vehicle of a murder victim. Most likely he had an accomplice of some sort."

"I read about the owner's shooting," said Truman. "Frankly, it sounded like an assassination. How many days ago was that?"

"Three," said Evan. "And it looked like an assassination too. But I haven't found anyone who will say a bad word against the victim. He was liked by everyone."

"I never believe that when I hear it," said Noelle. "It just takes one angry person."

"Do you remember Rowan Wolff?" Evan asked the police chief. "The search—"

"And rescue canine handler. Hell yes, I remember her. She saved Mercy's life. I'll never forget."

"The victim was a good friend of hers. Almost like an uncle. They were very close."

"I'm sorry to hear that." Truman watched the forensic tech move to the other side of the vehicle. "I checked all the doors," he told Noelle and Evan. "Locked. Whoever stole it made a big mess inside." He moved to a window and shined his flashlight on the floor of the back seat. It was covered in fast-food wrappers and bags.

"The mess could have been left by the owner," said Evan. Beside him Noelle ran her flashlight over the back seat and then moved to look in the cargo area.

"Lotta crap back here too," she said. "I wish it wasn't locked. We'll have to wait until tomorrow to get in."

Evan was impatient too.

Truman gave him a side-eye. "How bad do you want in tonight?"

"You have no idea."

"Have you finished processing the outside?" Truman asked the tech.

"Yes," said the young woman. "I'll wait around until the tow truck gets here. We'll do the inside back at the department."

Truman strode to his vehicle and opened the back.

"Is he getting what I think he is?" Noelle murmured to Evan.

The police chief returned, a thin piece of metal in his hand.

"Yep," said Evan. He gestured at the tech. "Can you film this?"

The tech immediately understood the situation. "On it."

Without a key, the Explorer would eventually be opened by unconventional means. Evan had no problem with its being done in the field, but he wanted every second documented in case the procedure was challenged down the road.

The chief waited impatiently until the tech gave him the go-ahead, and then he slid the metal piece down into one of the doors before jerking it up and down.

"Photograph everything inside," Evan told the tech. "We can poke around, but try not to move much," he said to Noelle.

"I got it!" Truman said. He carefully opened the front passenger door with a gloved finger as the forensic tech filmed. She moved to the open door and started recording the interior.

"Thanks," Evan told Truman. "That never works for me."

Truman shrugged. "I lived in California," he said with a wink.

"So did I," said Noelle. "I can't do that."

"Then you didn't hang around the right people," said Truman. The tech unlocked the rest of the doors and continued to record. Truman waved an arm at the interior. "All yours," he told the detectives.

Evan covered every inch of the front passenger area with his flashlight. The seat was covered with black dog hair. He peered in the door pocket and then under the seat, occasionally turning over a crumpled receipt or food wrapper with his pen. There were scattered dog kibble, straw wrappers, and several pens. He opened the glove box. It was crammed with papers and manuals.

"We better wait on that stuff," Noelle said. "Have forensics go through it first."

Evan agreed. He popped open the storage between the seats. Apparently it'd been used as recycling storage for soda cans. Either Ken or his killer liked Mountain Dew. Most likely Ken. The murderer would have thrown the cans on the floor, not saved them to recycle.

Noelle was searching the driver's side. She pulled a folded newspaper out of the pocket in the door.

"What's the date?" asked Evan.

"Yesterday," she said, setting the paper on the seat. "So we know our guy definitely handled this. Fingerprints will be tough to lift but not totally impossible. I've seen it done." She shined her flashlight in the door pocket, then returned to the newspaper and flipped it over, and her gaze locked on a photo.

Evan leaned closer to look. The paper had been folded to show an article and photo on page five.

The headline was about Geoff Jensen's murder of his wife, Summer. Evan's murder case where Thor had found the five-year-old boy hiding in a bedroom nightstand. It'd been a week since the murder, and the article appeared to be a rehash of old news with a few bits thrown in about the family's history along with some new photos. The largest image was of Rowan and Thor in front of the Jensens' home. She was on one knee, speaking to Thor, whose ears indicated he was hanging on every word. The photo's caption identified the pair and stated their role in the discovery of Wyatt Jensen. Geoff Jensen was visible in the background, sitting in the back of a car with a cop speaking to him. Evan knew it had been taken before the boy was found.

"The paper is deliberately folded to see this photo," said Noelle. "The other accompanying photos are hidden by the fold. Same with two-thirds of the article. Look." She carefully opened the paper, demonstrating how someone had made awkward folds to center the photo.

Evan stared at the photo, his mind racing with possibilities. Most of them negative. "Why . . . ?" He met Noelle's gaze. Her expression told him she was struggling to understand too.

"It could be nothing," she said, but her eyes didn't agree with her words.

"Let's go through the rest." Evan moved to a rear door to examine the debris in the back seat. Crumpled receipts told them the fast-food bags were Ken's. In the cargo space, they found SAR equipment and dog supplies.

"This is expensive equipment," said Noelle. "Why didn't they . . . or he . . . take it?"

"Money wasn't the goal," said Evan.

"What was the goal?"

"Beats me."

"If the date on that paper was older, I wouldn't be surprised to find it folded that way, considering Ken's relationship with Rowan," said Noelle.

Evan had had the same thought. "Whoever was in here knows her. I can't believe someone would randomly highlight that photo without knowing her."

"Agreed." Noelle looked at him.

Frustration rolled through Evan as he remembered how Rowan was linked to several of his cases. Now she was tied to Ken's missing SUV.

Why are there so many connections to Rowan?

23

Rowan leaned back in her chair, sipping a cup of coffee, her other hand resting on Thor's head. They were on a restaurant's outdoor patio, waiting for Rees Womack, and she'd been lucky enough to get the last available table. In the ten minutes since she'd sat down, a large crowd had formed at the front of the converted old house. Locals were willing to wait long periods for brunch at the popular restaurant. The owners made the outdoor waits as pleasant as possible by providing a window to order coffee and other drinks, lots of room to sit, and even live music.

Rowan had ordered biscuits and gravy and a pitcher of white sangria. Rees was late, and she wanted to eat if he didn't show up. He'd texted her the night before, asking her to meet, but had been vague when she asked why, saying he wanted to talk about Ken. Thinking back, she realized she'd never met Rees one-on-one. Someone else had always been present. But he was a pillar of their close-knit group. Rees wasn't much of a talker, but people always listened when he did speak up. He thought things through and often presented avenues the group hadn't considered. He was a valuable SAR member.

Thor's head lifted a fraction, and his ears swiveled toward the crowd waiting at the front of the restaurant. Rowan spotted Rees and his German shepherd, Gunnar, working their way through the group. He was frequently stopped, usually by women asking to pet his dog. Rowan often had the same problem. At least people were better about asking to pet Thor these days. In the past they'd touch without permission. Thor loved attention from everyone, but some dogs did not.

Rees finally made it to the table and sat heavily in a chair. "Sorry I'm late." The dogs sniffed noses and then ignored each other. Rees was close to Ken's age, and Rowan had never seen him without a hat. Usually it was a baseball cap, but today it was a pale-blue bucket hat. His long beard was salt and pepper, and his brown eyes had deep lines from squinting in the sun.

They made small talk for a few minutes. When the waitress brought the pitcher of sangria, he ordered coffee and an everything omelet. When she left, he poured two glasses and held up his drink. "To Ken."

"To Ken," repeated Rowan, then took a sip, noticing Rees looked very tired and sadness lurked in his gaze.

I probably look the same way.

After some general talk about the funeral, Rowan got to the point. "What did you want to tell me about Ken?" Since he'd sat down, Rees had made poor eye contact and seemed distracted.

He leaned his forearms on the table, drained his glass, and then poured another. The waitress reappeared with his coffee and vanished again. He added three creamers and focused on stirring it in.

"Rees. What is it?"

He always likes to think before he speaks.

"It's Ken. Something was off before he died."

Rowan waited a long moment for him to collect his thoughts. "Like what?" she finally asked.

"He was stressed. Couldn't sit still. Always doing something. Seemed anxious." He met her gaze, concern and certainty in his eyes.

"The 'couldn't sit still' sounds like him," said Rowan. "The anxious part doesn't. Was he having money problems?" She knew from Shannon that Ken wasn't the best with money, which was why he drove for Uber. The flexibility worked for him. According to Shannon, he was always out of money but rarely let it bother him. When his account got low, he'd drive extra hours or take on a private client to train their dog. People all over the US asked to work with him.

"I don't think so," said Rees, finally looking right at her. "I think it had something to do with you."

"Me?"

"Yes. Your name constantly came up during the last two weeks before he died. I know he's always been protective of you, but this seemed unusual."

A chill went through her bones. "He thought I was in danger?" Her mind flashed to Thor's growls the day before.

Those mean nothing.

"He never said that. He did say that he couldn't talk to you about something and seemed very worried that you'd never forgive him."

Rowan was speechless.

"He brought up that day he'd snapped at you in training. He felt horrible about it and was going to apologize."

Tears threatened. "I've often thought about that day. I never got the chance to talk to him about it." Guilt racked her. "You think that incident upset him that much?"

Rees shifted in his chair and Gunnar suddenly stood, his full attention on his person. "I don't think that was the problem. The anxiety started before that. His behavior toward you may have been a by-product of what was bothering him."

"I don't know why you're telling me this. I know Shannon had said he was distracted in the weeks before his death . . . more forgetful than usual. Maybe something was going on with his health."

"Could be."

Judging by his expression, Rowan knew he didn't think much of her suggestion.

"He kept talking about you."

"What about me?"

"Everything . . . the training he knew you were working on. That case where the five-year-old was found in the bedroom. The hike you always do for your brother's birthday." Rees frowned. "You know he hated that you did that every year, right?"

"He was always very understanding about why I needed to do it. He used to go with me." Rowan was surprised. She thought Ken had been one of her biggest supporters of her search for her brother. "*Hate* is a strong word. I think you're wrong about that."

"I don't think so. He said harsh words about it to me. Several times. But always would end his rant with saying he had to support you because you were important to him."

That stung.

He lied to my face?

He was protecting my feelings.

Rees's eyes widened as he watched her think, and she softened her expression, suspecting he'd been surprised by the flare of anger. She blew out a breath and drank the last third of her sangria. "I still don't know why you asked to meet. You could have kept all this to yourself— although I appreciate knowing he felt bad about that day at training."

He looked away. "I was supposed to go camping with him."

"The night he was shot?"

"Yes."

"Why didn't you?" She wondered if this was the main reason he'd wanted to meet—that he felt guilty and needed to get it off his chest.

"Gunnar was sick." He touched his dog's head.

Rowan didn't believe him. She used her dog as an excuse to get out of things she didn't want to do. And she suspected that Rees had done the same.

There's something he's not telling me.

"Why didn't you want to go?" She infused understanding into her eyes and tone, trying to convince him to be open and honest.

He leaned forward. "Do you know where he was found?"

141

"Yes."

"Doesn't that seem like an odd place for him to camp? He always goes way the fuck out into nowhere, and there has to be a creek or lake nearby. Why would he decide to essentially camp in a spot miles away from water where lazy-ass rookies go to camp? I had no interest in that."

"Did he tell you that's where he wanted to go?" Rowan agreed with his assertion. Ken liked to go off the map when he camped.

"Yes. I tried to get him to pick a different location, but he was adamant."

She thought for a long moment. "Do you think he was meeting someone? I can't think of why else he would pick that spot."

"I've come to the same conclusion."

"You need to tell Detective Bolton," she said.

"Tell him what? That Ken had been stressed and that's an unusual place for him to camp? How does that help the police? I'd be wasting his time."

Rowan considered. Rees had a point. "But you wanted me to know. I doubt you could have changed things," she said quietly. "You might have ended up being shot too."

"I've wrestled back and forth with that."

The waitress set down two steaming plates of food. Rowan was no longer hungry, but she picked at her gravy. Rees faced his omelet with the same lack of enthusiasm.

One thought kept going through her head. "What could he have done that I never would forgive him for?" she asked softly. "I loved him. He was a good person."

Rees shook his head. "I've asked myself the same question, and I'm stumped."

"If he kicked Thor, I wouldn't let that go," she said with a sad smile, knowing Ken would kick her before he ever did such a thing to her dog.

"He wouldn't dare."

"He was the best," said Rowan.

Rees poured them two more drinks. He held his up. "To Ken."

"Do you think he'd be offended we're toasting him with wine instead of an IPA?" Rowan lifted her glass.

"Not at all."

Rowan agreed. "To Ken." She clinked Rees's glass and drank.

I miss him.

24

Malcolm, twenty-five years ago

The man was going to kill Rowan. Malcolm knew it.

He'd broken her leg.

Who does that to a little girl?

He does.

Malcolm shouldn't have felt surprised. Everything the man had put them through was evil.

She's going to die, and I'll have to watch.

He pulled her closer as she slept, trying not to bump her leg. He'd hit it accidentally a few times, and it'd made her cry out in her sleep. It had been three days since he broke her leg. She couldn't walk. Malcolm had helped her pee in the bucket, and it'd embarrassed her and she'd hated it. She'd tried to stop drinking, so she'd pee less, but he knew that wasn't healthy.

He made her drink.

At least the man had fed them that night. And he'd left more food than usual. Maybe he felt guilty for what he'd done. Rowan hadn't wanted to eat. Malcolm had had to beg her to do it. She'd said she wasn't hungry anymore.

How can that be? She has to be starving.

Malcolm wiped his nose with the back of his hand. It kept running because he couldn't stop crying. Everything was such a mess, and he didn't know how to fix it.

I don't know what to do.

He hated him. Malcolm didn't understand why the man had thought it would be funny to tell him he would send Rowan home and then take it back. He thought the man had lied about his parents moving away, but then why hadn't anyone found them?

What if he's right? What if we're here forever?

Rowan needed to see a doctor. She needed a cast on her leg. Malcolm didn't know how she would ever walk again if no one fixed it.

I can't carry her around forever.

He suddenly wished his sister would die, and his tears flowed faster. "I'm sorry, God, I didn't mean it," he whispered. "I really, really didn't mean it."

He was a horrible person. Malcolm should be the one with the broken leg. Rowan would never think bad things about him as he just had about her.

The locks on the door clanked. Malcolm panicked and scrambled for their blindfolds.

He didn't warn us!

At least the man didn't make Rowan get in her corner anymore since she couldn't get around very well. Rowan didn't wake at the noise of the locks or when he lifted her head to place her blindfold. It was dark, and his fingers were clumsy as he fumbled with the ties.

Hurry, hurry, hurry.

He was still tying her blindfold when the door creaked open. He hunched over her, hiding his face, petrified to look toward the door, waiting for him to yell.

Silence.

After a few seconds he risked a look and squinted in the dark.

The silhouette was wrong.

The man was thin. Not big and bulky.

Someone is here to save us!

Malcolm lunged to his feet and then froze as he realized it was the other man. The silent friend.

He'll tell him we weren't blindfolded. We'll be punished.

But the man just stood there.

"What do you want?" Malcolm whispered.

The man stepped back, motioned them out of the shed, and then pointed at the woods. "Go."

His brain didn't understand. "Go where?"

"Just go. Get out of here. Take her."

Is he setting us free?

"Is this another trick?" Malcolm whispered. His heart was pounding, and he wondered if the man could hear it.

"No trick. Get the fuck out of here."

Malcolm stared at him for another moment and then bent over and shook Rowan's shoulder, pulling away her blindfold. "Rowan. Wake up. Wake up." His voice quivered.

She swung a hand to bat him away and nestled her face into the blanket.

He leaned close to her ear. "We can leave now." He spoke softly, but deep inside he wanted to yell. This was it. This was the moment they'd been hoping for.

"What?" She lifted her head.

"He's letting us go. But we've got to go now."

"What?" Rowan repeated. She spotted the man at the door and froze. "He's rescuing us?"

"No. He's letting us go. We need to go as fast as possible, but I'll carry you."

"You can't—"

He put his arms under her shoulders and knees and lifted.

She's so light.

Rowan whimpered as he jostled her leg, but she wrapped her arms around his neck.

"Sorry about that." Malcolm turned to the door. The man took another step back, leaving them plenty of room to get by. Malcolm moved out of the shed, Rowan in his arms.

"Get moving," the man told them.

"Thank you for doing this," he said.

"Don't thank me yet," the man said gruffly.

Malcolm looked around in the faint moonlight. There were tall, dark trees in every direction. He didn't see a road or path. They were in a forest. "Which way do I go?" He had no idea where they were.

"Doesn't matter. Go that way. Don't stop." He pointed toward a clump of trees.

Malcolm took a breath and started walking. Then he moved faster, feeling as if he were being watched.

Is he close by?

He broke into a jog, and Rowan cried out as her leg bounced.

"Shhhhh." Malcolm went back to a quick walk, trying his best not to jolt her. They entered the tall trees and the moon vanished. He plunged forward into the dark.

His arms ached. She was light, but he couldn't do this for very long.

I'll carry her for as long as it takes.

I can't stop. Must keep going.

Malcolm halted, panting hard, and leaned one hand against a tree, staring up at the hints of blue sky between the pine trees. It was the afternoon of the second day since he and Rowan had escaped. Yesterday he'd carried her all day but taken frequent breaks. They'd figured out a way for her to ride on his back that made it easier for him, but he still couldn't go that far without stopping. It was hard to carry her without bumping her leg.

This morning he had left her where they'd slept overnight, telling her he could move faster to find help and that he would mark the way so he could lead someone to her. He'd been dragging his heel, making gouges in the dirt and breaking branches, so he could trace his path back.

Was I right to leave her behind?

They'd drunk at a creek the evening before, but there was no food. He hadn't even seen berries on their trek. Although if he had, he wouldn't have known if they were poisonous and so wouldn't have tried them anyway. Desperate, Rowan had chewed a couple of leaves and spit them out, saying they were bitter.

Malcolm hadn't seen any trace of people. No roads. No paths. No tents. He kept thinking he heard cars or voices, but he couldn't find them.

Even if she was with me, we still wouldn't have found people to help us.

There had to be a town somewhere. The forest couldn't go on forever.

His feet hurt. He was thirsty. He was hungry. He was tired of crying.

But he started walking again.

"Where you going, boy?"

Malcolm froze.

Is his voice in my head?

"Answer me, boy!"

He slowly turned. The bearded man was twenty feet away, and he had a rifle slung over one shoulder. Waves of anger rolled off him. A few feet behind him was the man who had freed them.

Was this a game?

"You thought your sister and you could escape?" The big man shook his head in disgust. "Stupid kids. You'll be punished for this."

Malcolm wanted to run, but his feet hurt so bad. And the man had a gun. He had no doubt he'd shoot him if he ran.

Maybe being dead is better than going back with him.

But he needed to stay alive for Rowan.

The men moved closer. The smaller man took Malcolm's upper arm, and they followed the armed man. Malcolm stared at his feet for a long time as they walked but occasionally glanced at the man who had freed them. He wanted to read his face, see a sign of hope, but the man wouldn't look at him.

He wondered again if it had been entertainment for them.

Another cruel game to get their hopes up and then destroy them.

Malcolm halted as he realized they weren't on the path he'd made to Rowan. His throat started to close as he panicked.

How will I find her?

They hadn't asked where she was, so they must have found her first. The second man yanked his arm, and Malcolm stumbled along. He looked at the man again, hoping to see a hint that they'd already taken Rowan back to the shed. The man's face was stony and closed off, and Malcolm wondered if he'd gotten in trouble too.

No one spoke the entire walk. The big man didn't look back at Malcolm, who could tell he was still angry by his shoulders and stride. Malcolm didn't dare say a word.

It was nearly dark by the time they got back, but they didn't go to the shed. Instead, they headed toward a building, and Malcolm thought it was where he had been taken twice before. He'd never seen it from the outside, but it was rectangular and small.

Is Rowan back in the shed or in this building?

The bearded man led them around to the back. Behind the small building was a large wooden box. The man lifted the lid.

"The shed you were in is bigger than you deserve. This is more appropriate for boys who run away."

Tears burned down Malcolm's face. He tried to step back, but the silent man had a hold on his arm. The box was about the size of his mother's Jacuzzi bathtub. He wouldn't be able to stand.

"Get in."

Shaking, he peered inside, hoping to see Rowan. Instead, he saw broken chunks of wood and cobwebs in the corners. He wondered if it had been used to hold chopped wood.

The second man shoved Malcolm's arm forward, and he awkwardly climbed into the box. It smelled like dirt, dusty and old. He sat cross-legged, hoping the lid won't make him bend his head when he closed it. The two men stared down at him.

"You shouldn't have been bad and run away," said the big man as he frowned. "See what you've made me do because you need to be punished? I have no choice." His voice was sad.

"I'm sorry, sir." It was the first time Malcolm had spoken since they'd found him, and his voice was hoarse.

"Get him some water," the big man said, and the second one left.

Malcolm closed his eyes as thirst and hunger swamped him, and he swayed in the box. He dreaded the man closing the lid. It would be dark, and he wondered if there were spiders.

"Aren't you going to ask about your sister?"

Malcolm's eyes flew open. The bearded man looked very sorry, and Malcolm's stomach heaved. His mouth went completely dry, and he couldn't speak.

Something happened.

"We couldn't tell if it was a bear or cougar that got her, but—"

Malcolm leaned to one side and retched. Nothing came up. His stomach heaved over and over, and finally a tiny bit of bitter fluid came up his throat. He spit it out.

He could see Rowan in his mind, terrified and screaming as she was attacked.

Malcolm heaved several more times, but his gut was empty. He covered his face with his hands and bawled.

I left her and she died.

"You shouldn't have run away," he said. "It's all your fault she's dead. She was safe in that shed, but you made her leave, didn't you? She couldn't have done it on her own with that leg."

Malcolm fought for breath between sobs and felt as if his tears were drowning him.

"Good thing your parents won't ever know. They'd hate you forever for leaving their daughter to die. The police would arrest you for taking a little girl into the woods and abandoning her. This is all on you."

He's right. I did it.

Malcolm coughed and choked, and the tears kept coming. Something made a wailing sound, and he realized it was him.

"You're lucky we saved your life today. The animals could have killed you next. We didn't have to go looking for you. I could have spent my day barbecuing or shooting on my gun range. You should show some gratitude."

"Thank you. Thank you for saving me." He wailed and immediately vomited again as the man closed the lid.

I'm going to hell. I got my sister killed.

"Don't get too comfortable yet," said the bearded man through the lid. "We got another boy yesterday, and we don't need two. We'll have to decide which of you to keep. Maybe have you compete for the honor of being part of our family."

Visions of Rowan and himself competing assaulted Malcolm's brain. The fights. The pinching. The rocks.

Her broken leg.

I can't do it again.

25

It took Evan a few hours to drive from Bend to the Oregon State Penitentiary. He always enjoyed crossing over the Cascade Range from Oregon's high desert into the greener Willamette Valley. The scenery changed from highways edged with sparse ponderosa pine trees and sagebrush to dense, dark forests of firs.

FBI special agent Mercy Kilpatrick called him during the drive, and he shared his suspicions about a serial killer in his county. She agreed and promised him FBI resources. He asked her to contact Noelle to get plans rolling since he was on his way to the prison. The FBI could speed up the processing of the evidence recovered at each murdered woman's crime scene and hopefully pinpoint a lead to direct them to the killer.

Before he murdered again.

The number of cases on Evan's plate had been wearing on him. Noelle had brought some relief, and the FBI would bring more.

But first he needed to do this interview.

Jerry Chiavo was waiting for him. Instead of using the usual visitors' area, Evan had asked for a small interview room. Jerry sat, the chain from his cuffs looped around the bar on his side of the bolted-down table. Evan had handed over his weapon, passed through two metal detectors and several controlled doors, and listened as a guard told him not to give the prisoner anything or move to the opposite side of the table.

The guard left, closing the door behind him, and then stood watching through its large glass window.

Evan was keenly aware of the absence of his gun as he eyed Jerry across the table, even though the seventy-five-year-old man didn't look like a killer. He looked like an off-season Santa in prison garb instead of a red velvet suit. His hair was white and his nose and cheeks red. But not red in a jolly way—they were red in a poor-health way.

"What can I do for you, Detective?" Jerry's eyes were sharp, probing.

Evan was surprised the man had spoken first.

He's immediately taking charge of the interview.

Evan would let him think he had done so—if it meant Jerry opened up more. He set a thick folder on the table and added a yellow pad he liked to use for notes. "It's been a busy few weeks in Deschutes County. Maybe you've heard some of what's happened?" He raised a brow at Jerry and picked up his pen, ready to write.

"I don't follow news from over there."

"Okay." Evan rubbed his chin, trying to look thoughtful. "Let me back up a bit, then. You were convicted of three young women's deaths twenty-five years ago. I assume you remember where each body was found?"

"I was told their locations."

Still won't admit to their murders.

"You had to be told the locations they were dumped because you weren't the one who put them there, correct?"

"Correct." Jerry shifted in his seat, his brows coming together in annoyance. "I didn't kill those women. All the evidence against me was circumstantial, and their primary evidence was planted."

"Planted? Who would want to set you up?"

"I suspect the police did it." Annoyance filled his tone. "This can't be new information to you, Detective."

"I was aware your attorney tried to point some blame at the police. It didn't convince a jury."

"No shit. But it doesn't mean it didn't happen." He leaned over, his chains clinking. "The most likely dirty cop is Sam Durette. He was determined to see me go to prison."

"Why? What was his motivation?"

"Who knows with cops?" Jerry shrugged.

"You've had twenty-five years to think about it. Surely you have a better reason than 'Who knows.'"

Jerry looked away. "I think he wanted me in prison for what happened to that boy."

"Malcolm Wolff."

"Yeah."

"You admitted he died in an accident, and that you buried him in a panic."

"Yeah."

"And you tortured him and his sister after kidnapping them. Broke her leg."

Jerry met his eyes. "You trust the word of a five-year-old? I didn't hurt them. Durette planted all that shit in her head. I don't know how she broke her leg. She'd run off."

Evan sat back and flipped through the file, pretending to look for something as he dissected what Jerry had said.

Would Detective Durette have planted evidence of the three dead women to make sure this guy ended up in prison?

He remembered Durette's tone as he talked about Jerry torturing the children. Anger. Rage. Disgust.

Would he have done it to make this guy pay?

"I was convicted on planted evidence," Jerry said. "If our justice system wasn't corrupt, I'd be free like I should be. I didn't kill those women."

Evan changed topics. "Why not tell them where Malcolm Wolff was buried?"

"Can't remember," he said shortly.

"Or maybe he was buried with other victims you didn't want found?"

Jerry's face was blank, but confusion flickered in his eyes for the briefest second.

"Are you saying you have more deaths you want to pin on me?" His tone was incredulous.

"Yes." Evan wouldn't bring up details of the current deaths. He didn't trust that Jerry hadn't heard about them—he could have lied about not following news in Bend—and Evan didn't want to tackle it yet with the wily murderer. "Since you're already in prison, maybe you should just tell me about them. Or tell me who helped you back then."

"Helped me what?"

"Capture and kill young women." Evan paused. "How long would you keep them alive before killing them?"

"*I didn't kill anyone!*"

"Except Malcolm Wolff. You couldn't lead investigators to his grave . . . maybe you could describe the location?"

"There were trees."

"Anything else?"

"Rocks."

"Was it flat or hilly?"

"Flat. Why would I dig a grave on a slope?"

"Do you remember anything else nearby? Water? Clearings?"

"No water, no clearings."

"Remind me how you killed him again?"

"It was an accident. He hit his head." Jerry leaned to one side, trying to catch the eye of the guard. "We're done."

By the frustration on Jerry's face and the silence at the door, Evan gathered the guard was ignoring him.

"Then who set you up, Jerry? The police don't have a strong motivation to do that. It must have been someone else. Who hated you enough to do it?"

"You're talking in fucking circles." He banged his chains on the table. "Guard!"

"Is it Malcolm Wolff we found buried next to two other young women?"

Confusion flickered again. "You can't tell if it's him?"

"Not yet. What are the names of the young women?"

Jerry just stared at him.

"These two women were buried close to where Carissa Trotter's body was found twenty-five years ago," Evan continued. "I find it hard to believe that two separate killers would leave bodies in the same area. It's only logical that they were killed by the same person."

Jerry pressed his lips together, making them vanish behind his white beard and mustache. "Then you better figure out who their killer was. Because it wasn't me."

I could have handled that better.

Evan sat in his vehicle in the penitentiary parking lot. He'd thrown heavy questions at Jerry, and the killer had shut down a little more with each one. Too much too fast.

He is a convincing liar.

His answers about Malcolm's grave weren't helpful.

Was it possible Jerry *hadn't* killed the three women twenty-five years ago?

But he had kidnapped Rowan and Malcolm. And their babysitter, who'd been with them, had turned up dead. It only made sense that Jerry had killed her.

If Evan had been in Jerry's shoes, trying to avoid three false murder charges, he'd point fingers at everyone. Make his attorney dig to figure out who had set him up. He'd do a lot more than push a weak claim that it had been the police.

He didn't fight hard because he knew he did it.

He assumed Jerry must have killed the two women whose skeletal remains had been found next to the child's bones. It only made sense considering the location of Carissa Trotter.

Don't assume. Ass. U. Me.

But Jerry had seemed legitimately surprised when Evan brought them up. In his gut, Evan felt the guy hadn't been faking it.

I'm missing something.

Evan wished Noelle had come to the interview. She'd pull his brain out of this rut. But today she was working on Ken's SUV and interviewing more of his personal circle.

If Jerry wasn't the killer, then did he have motivation to stay silent about who might have killed the women twenty-five years before?

Is he protecting someone?

His wife?

Everything Evan had read indicated Jerry and Suzanne had had a perfect marriage. But his wife was dead. The only reason to continue to stay silent if his wife had done the murders would be to honor his marriage vows or the memory of his wife. Evan believed some men would stay quiet until their deaths, but he doubted child kidnapper Jerry Chiavo was one of those.

Who else was he close to?

Sam Durette had dug deep into Jerry's family and friends. And come up empty. For as kind as Jerry and his wife, Suzanne, had been purported to be, they'd had no family on this side of the US and no close friends. Just tons of casual acquaintances and foster kids. Sam had conducted more than forty interviews and hadn't heard a negative word about Jerry.

In frustration and needing distraction, Evan pulled out his phone and checked his messages. Noelle had texted that she'd interviewed Ken Steward's cousin Eric and his close SAR friend Rees, and she'd emailed

Evan her reports. She'd texted that they'd both been annoyed that it'd taken four days for law enforcement to interview them.

"We were working our way to them," Evan muttered. Noelle's texts didn't say that she'd found any smoking guns, so he would read her reports when he got back to Bend. He opened his inbox and scrolled past her emails.

He glared at an email from the prison. "Well, that would have been nice to have before my interview today." It was Jerry Chiavo's visitor list. Considering Evan had only filed a request the day before, it was actually quite prompt. He opened the email and halted at the name of the most recent visitor.

Ken Steward had visited Jerry two weeks ago.

"What the hell?"

Evan did a quick scan of the list. It wasn't long. One more name popped out at him: Rowan Wolff. She'd visited Jerry Chiavo one time five years ago.

He stared at her name for a long moment, his mind spinning.

As an adult, she'd probably had questions for the man who'd kidnapped her and killed her brother, so he really shouldn't be too surprised. It made sense.

But he was dying to discuss it with her.

Evan wondered if Sam Durette knew she'd visited, but he tucked his curiosity aside. Right now he was more concerned about Ken Steward's recent visit.

Ken's name did not reappear on the list. Evan put his hand on the car door handle, ready to head back into the prison and demand Jerry tell him what he'd discussed with Ken Steward.

But he knew he wouldn't be let back in without a new appointment.

"Shit." Prison interviews had to be requested via email. He took a few deep breaths and tried to concentrate.

What is the connection between Jerry and Ken?

The day before, he and Sam Durette had unsuccessfully struggled to figure out a connection between Ken's murder and those of the three young women who'd been killed recently.

Now he was trying to connect Ken with someone who'd murdered women twenty-five years ago. Evan opened his bag on the seat next to him and pulled out the yellow pad. He'd taken no notes while talking with Jerry.

He wrote Ken's name in the center of the page and circled it. Then he drew a line from there and wrote Jerry Chiavo's name at the end, making a note that the connection was that Ken had visited Jerry in prison. Then he drew a line from Ken to a circle containing the names of the three recently murdered women. He thought hard, trying to remember the elements of that connection. Sam Durette had come to Evan about the current murders and had been the investigator on the old murders and Rowan's kidnapping . . . and so Sam knew Ken. It wasn't a straight line from Ken to the women. It was choppy, with small offshoots, including Sam's name.

He hesitated and then added Rowan's name, connecting her to Ken. And to Jerry . . . and to Sam. And she'd found one of the recent victims . . . and one of the old murder cases had been her babysitter.

"Shit."

On paper it was uglier and more stark than his earlier thoughts about how she was connected with several of his cases.

She grew up here. It's not a huge community. It makes sense that her path would cross many people's . . .

He was making excuses. Rowan was in the thick of everything for some reason. The folded newspaper from Ken's SUV popped into his memory—also Rowan. And it couldn't have been put there by Ken. Most likely it had been placed by his killer or their accomplice.

Evan closed his eyes and leaned his head back against his seat. His brain hurt. It resisted seeing Rowan's involvement. He liked the woman. A lot. And it was messing with his analytical skills.

She hasn't done anything. None of her connections are suspicious.

But they were numerous.

He worried he had a blind spot where Rowan was concerned.

She's just a friend that I find attractive.

Then why was she constantly on his mind?

Should I be removed from these investigations?

His supervisor would never agree. They didn't have the extra manpower, and he and Rowan didn't have a relationship. His reasons were weak, and he was invested in the cases. He didn't want to give them up; he wanted to solve them.

Evan opened his eyes as he sat up straight and turned on his vehicle. He needed Noelle's point of view. She'd help him look at things differently.

But what will she say when she sees Rowan's connection to everything?

"And finds out that I *want* a relationship with Rowan?" Saying it out loud brought a wave of relief. He'd been pushing the feelings aside, trying to concentrate on work. "Still not appropriate."

As he pulled away from the prison, he wondered if he'd be arguing with himself for hours during the drive to Bend.

Probably.

26

Malcolm, twenty-two years ago

Three winters had passed since Rowan died in the woods, and Malcolm's days, months, and years had blended together. Sometimes he spent time in the box. Sometimes in the shed. He dug holes. He moved rocks. He stacked wood. He did what he was told. Occasionally one of them woke him in the middle of the night and made him run laps, or one took away his clothes for a week, or they sprayed him with a hose, saying he needed a shower. The men usually took turns telling him what to do, but sometimes they did it together.

Malcolm didn't care what they did to him anymore.

He was long past caring.

He wanted to die.

The bearded man had lied about a second boy the day Rowan died and they'd brought Malcolm back from the woods. He had simply wanted Malcolm to stress about having to fight. He'd been in the box for three days before they'd told him it was a joke. They'd thought it was hilarious.

But now another boy had been there for four days.

And they'd told Malcolm they'd only keep the best boy.

They made Malcolm and the boy fight and run races in competitions. The new boy was taller and stronger than Malcolm, so he often won. The boys were kept apart. If one was in the box, the other was in the shed.

Malcolm no longer wore a blindfold. And the men hadn't worn masks since the day they first brought Malcolm into their home. But the new boy was blindfolded, and Malcolm studied him closely, soaking in the sight of the first new person he'd seen in years. The boy had blond, curly hair and long legs.

The boys weren't allowed to talk, but they had a few brief moments when they exchanged whispered words when the two men were caught up in discussions.

The boy was ten like Malcolm, and his name was Elijah.

Malcolm ached to talk with him more, he craved conversation, but had been told he didn't deserve friends because Malcolm never moved fast enough or acted grateful enough.

He'd been told many times he was a bad boy.

Malcolm missed Rowan and dreamed of her often. Sometimes the dreams were of happy times in the past, but other times he saw her killed by animals. He'd wake shuddering and sweating, terrified.

One time several days went by with no competitions while Malcolm slept in the box, and the two men were bad tempered each time they brought him food. Malcolm had been jealous that Elijah had been in the shed for so long and had many bitter thoughts about the other boy. Clearly Elijah was ahead in the competition to be the best boy and was being favored.

After four days in the box, the thinner man hauled him out. "We've got some work to do."

Malcolm nodded. There was always work to do. He looked around for Elijah, but apparently only Malcolm was on duty today.

Maybe he doesn't have to work anymore.

Maybe he won.

What will they do with me?

The man took him deep into the woods and then ordered Malcolm to dig a hole. He heard water, so he knew they were near a river or creek. But the ground was too hard, so the man had to help Malcolm dig, and it made him angry. He wanted six feet deep, but they barely managed two. It was exhausting, slow work. The man wouldn't tell Malcolm what it was for, but Malcolm saw it was long enough for a body.

It's for me.

Elijah was the best boy.

I'm digging my own grave.

27

Noelle had agreed to join Evan when he met with Dr. Peres to review her findings on the skeletal remains near the river.

The two detectives stopped at the open lab door in the medical examiner's building where Dr. Peres had set up her investigation.

Investigations. Plural.

No other remains had been found in the area after the third skull, but Evan had requested that ground-penetrating radar be used in the area. He pitied the techs who had to get the machinery to the remote location.

"Come in," Dr. Peres said from the far end of the large room. "I don't bite."

Her assistant snorted and shot a grin at her boss. "You like it when people think you do."

"Only the idiots. I have no patience for stupid people."

The detectives entered. The doctor had set up three tables, each with a partial skeleton laid out along with several clear bins holding more bones. Bones had been labeled in pencil with codes assigned by the forensic anthropologist. Evan immediately zeroed in on the table with the smallest remains, where Dr. Peres stood.

"What can you tell us, Doctor?" he asked.

"First I can admit I was wrong out in the field. This is a male."

Evan caught his breath as he stared at the empty dark hollows where a little boy's eyes should be.

Rowan's brother?

"You didn't say for certain it was female," said Noelle. "You made it clear to us that you weren't sure."

"Thank you for that," said Dr. Peres. "Frankly, I shouldn't have speculated out loud."

"We pressured you," said Evan. He could tell the incorrect guess was bothering the doctor. She was a perfectionist. "But go on."

"Male," she repeated. "Age eight to twelve. We also found short, dark hair where the skull should have been in relation to the rest of his remains. Like I had said, somehow the skull was moved a short way. Most likely an animal."

Evan didn't rule out Malcolm because the age range skewed high. Malcolm was seven when kidnapped, but he could have died later.

"Any indication of cause of death?" asked Noelle.

"I can tell you what isn't the cause of death," said the doctor. "It wasn't a head injury, and there are no indications of damage to the bones from a bullet or knife—that doesn't eliminate those. They could have been in soft tissue. The hyoid is missing, so I can't evaluate if he was strangled. All three sets of remains have many missing small bones. Again, animals at work." She picked up the small skull and narrowed her brows as she studied it. "I know you want to determine if this is Malcolm Wolff, so I requested the dental films from his original file with the sheriff's department. My forensic odontologist picked them up and immediately began her examination." She looked from Evan to Noelle. "I haven't ruled out that this is Rowan's brother, but maybe Dr. Harper can. She's down the hall on your right."

Evan glanced at the other two sets of skeletal remains. They deserved equal attention. But if he could quickly eliminate the possibility that this was Rowan's brother, he could focus better.

He and Noelle headed down the hall, glancing into open offices until they found a petite woman frowning at a computer screen. There were dental X-rays on the screen, so Evan figured they were in the right place. "Are you Dr. Harper?"

The woman turned toward them and stood, her hand outstretched. "Yes, I am. You must be the detectives on this case? Victoria said you'd stop by today."

She had a wide smile and warm brown eyes. She seemed too young to be a forensic odontologist, but Evan wisely kept his mouth shut. He made introductions. "You're working on the dental comparison for the young male that was found the other day?"

"Yes. Please call me Lacey." Dr. Harper cast a longing glance at Noelle's shoes. "I love your shoes."

Evan studied the burgundy heels. They looked like torture to him.

"Thank you," said Noelle.

After a last look at the shoes, Dr. Harper picked up two tiny pieces of plastic off her desk. "These are the X-rays that Malcolm Wolff's dentist sent twenty-five years ago, when Deschutes County was investigating his disappearance." She glared at the films. "They're shitty copies. They're too dark."

"Why would they send poor films?" asked Noelle.

"I suspect an office staff member made the copies. Many don't know how to recognize a quality film. Anyway, I scanned them and did my best to lighten them."

"They seem too small," said Evan, thinking of dental films he'd seen in the past.

The forensic odontologist nodded. "They are standard child-size bitewing films. Smaller than used for adults."

"I thought everyone used digital films," said Noelle.

"Definitely not every office twenty-five years ago," said Dr. Harper. "And some dental offices still don't today."

"So what did you find?" asked Evan, impatient for answers.

The dentist sighed. "I can't confirm it's Malcolm Wolff. There isn't enough here to make a positive identification. These films were taken when he was five—two years before he was kidnapped—and show nothing out of the ordinary I can use as a marker for a comparison. I can see baby molars and part of his first adult molars. No fillings. No cavities. No distinctly shaped teeth." She returned to the computer and clicked her mouse. "On the screen are the digital films I took today of the skull."

"You took a lot," said Evan.

"I wanted to be thorough. This many are not taken on a regular basis in a private practice. Especially on a child."

There were at least a dozen films on the screen.

"The films I took today show a child with a mixed dentition," said Dr. Harper. "He's lost many of the baby teeth, and several of the adult ones are erupting into his mouth."

"So you can't compare the films, because the old ones show mostly baby teeth," said Evan.

"Correct. Granted, I can see part of the first adult molars in the original films, but I can't say without a doubt that they are the same first molars in the films I took today."

Dr. Harper touched her mouse, and a wide film of the skull's entire jaw appeared. "If I had been given the films I took today, I'd estimate this child to be closer to age twelve because of the eruption schedule. I know Victoria has said between eight and twelve, and I'll defer to her experience. She has a lot more information to work with from the child's skeleton."

"Is she wrong to include the younger ages in her estimate?" asked Noelle.

"No. I've seen early dental eruptions happen in young kids." She shrugged. "It happens. I'm never surprised when I see it, but I will acknowledge that it's much less common. The reverse is true too."

I can't confirm to Rowan that this is her brother.

Disappointment rocked Evan.

Dr. Harper looked from one detective to the other and slightly tilted her head. "Victoria made my examination a priority. She called me in Portland and told me to come ASAP. She's spent more time with that small skeleton than the other two. I don't know what's going on, but she's put everything she has into it."

"There is a chance that this is a friend's younger brother who has been missing for over two decades," Evan said quietly. "Now we still don't know."

The dentist nodded in sympathy. "That's the worst. Not knowing. I guarantee Victoria has left no stone unturned in her examination of those bones. If something there could physically connect to that missing child, she would have found it."

"Thank you for your report, Doctor." Evan shook her hand, appreciating the sympathy in her gaze. The detectives left the office and headed back to where Dr. Peres was examining the skeletons.

"I'm sorry, Evan," said Noelle.

"Why are you apologizing?"

"Because I know how important this identification was to you."

"They're all important."

"But this could be Rowan's brother. You're close to her."

I am?

Evan frowned as they walked down the hallway.

I am.

It'd crept up on him. He'd sought her out, wanting to know her thoughts and see how she was coping. He was drawn to her. Yesterday he'd taken her hand in sympathy, feeling her waves of sorrow, wanting to offer her comfort and hope.

Then he hadn't wanted to let go.

He'd wanted to find Malcolm for her today and end her years of wondering and questions. But he'd failed. And he felt that keenly in his gut. He acknowledged that he desired to give her what she wanted most in the world. Today would not be the day he did it.

Someday. Soon.

He knew the healing power of finding a lost loved one. His sister's return to his life had restored pieces of his soul he hadn't realized were missing. But he'd been lucky. His sister was alive. Malcolm wasn't. When Evan found the boy, Rowan would grieve. But then she would heal.

He wanted to be there for both stages.

She feels it too.

The previous morning there'd been a look of awareness in her eyes that he hadn't understood until this very second. A connection. An attraction. It wasn't one-sided.

Not now. It's inappropriate.

But why not be there to support her through a difficult time? If something grew between them during this hard experience, it could indicate a durability that was rare in relationships.

"You're not denying it."

Evan pulled out of his thoughts and glanced at Noelle. Her lips lifted on one side in a half smile, her eyes glittering with confidence.

"Everyone can see the subtle sparks that fly between you two."

"Everyone?" he blurted. "There's nothing . . . I mean . . . there wasn't, well, I didn't know . . . it's new," he finished lamely. "Doesn't feel appropriate," he muttered.

"I get that. You're the investigator and it's her family member. But she's no frail woman falling for the alpha law enforcement detective. And you're not reacting to some inner caveman wanting to save a damsel in distress. You're both competent, independent adults. There's nothing improper with how you feel."

"It's not professional."

"Fuck that. You're not taking advantage of her. People meet in unusual situations all the time. Paths cross for a reason. You've stumbled across something of quality. Don't let it go just because of a profession-al-conduct tenet. It's not a firm rule and it doesn't apply here. You're not some horndog cop looking to get laid."

True.

"You've seen us interact once. You learned all this from watching us at a crime scene in the woods."

Noelle lifted her chin and grinned. "Yep. And I've been watching you for days. I see your reactions when her name is mentioned. You've got it bad, and I think you're just now realizing that."

Noelle was right. "Maybe," he said. "Shit."

She elbowed him in the ribs. "It's all good. Trust me."

They stepped back into Dr. Peres's lab. The doctor's gaze imme-diately met Evan's, and disappointment flashed across her face. "Dr. Harper couldn't make an identification?"

"No," said Evan. "The films she received are too old."

"Damn. I was afraid of that." She took a deep breath and moved to one of the tables holding an adult skeleton. "We'll move on for now."

Evan mentally shifted gears. Somewhere there were families of these two unidentified sets of remains waiting for news of their missing loved ones. He could do this. "What do you have, Doctor?"

I won't give up on finding Malcolm.

But the boy had to take a back seat to the other mysteries in the room.

"Both female," said Dr. Peres. "Caucasian. Both between eighteen and thirty. Both blonde."

"You found long, dark hair at the site," said Noelle. "We saw it."

"It had picked up color from the dirt. We determined that it was actually blonde." The doctor pointed at a group of mottled, brownish ribs. "It's normal for bones that have been buried for a long time to absorb some staining. The color and amount depends on what kind of soil they're in. Hair can do the same thing."

"Blonde," said Evan. "Like the three recent murders."

"And like Jerry Chiavo's three victims from decades ago," said Noelle. "Someone—or some people—has a type. Can you tell how long ago they died?"

"I can't. Could be as recent as a few years to as old as forty years ago—maybe longer. Taking into account how much color has leached into the bones, it's been more than a year or two. I don't have a lot to work with here as far as establishing a timeline. Dr. Harper found composite dental fillings in both of them and believes they both had braces. Both of these things weren't nearly as common forty years ago as they were in the last twenty. So I have more a likely date range than an absolute." She narrowed her brows in frustration. "Usually I find stuff with a body. Nothing was found with all three of them."

"You mean like buttons and zippers," said Noelle. "You were looking for those the other day."

"Correct. I especially like it when we find shoes. Shoes can last a long time and aren't too difficult to research when they were first made. Glasses are good for that too. If there is clothing, we can study the style, and if there are tags, we can contact the manufacturer."

"Anything useful for identification from the skeletons themselves?" asked Evan.

"The teeth, of course," said Dr. Peres. "But we need previous dental films to make a match. This set of remains shows an old, healed break at the medial end of the left radius. Right at its neck." She picked up a bone and showed them. "It will be useful for whittling down the match possibilities."

"What is this? It looks odd." Noelle indicated several small crisscrossing grooves in the bone below the skull's eye orbit.

"Teeth marks," said Dr. Peres. "A rat or something similar."

Noelle blanched and jerked her hand away.

Not liking the mental picture either, Evan glanced at the table with the other set of female remains. "One was buried on top of the other. How did you keep them from mixing together as you uncovered them?"

"By being extremely careful. Slow removal. Lots of record keeping as we went along."

"Can you tell if they were buried at the same time?" asked Noelle.

"I believe they were not. There was a layer of soil between them. If they were buried at the same time, usually there is no dirt between them."

"You've seen that?" asked Evan.

The doctor's face lost all expression. "Yes," she said shortly. "I've worked pits where a dozen bodies were thrown on top of each other before being buried." She laid the radius back in its position on the table and gently straightened a few other bones, keeping her eyes averted.

Evan faintly recalled an article that mentioned the doctor had worked in war-ravaged foreign countries, helping identify the remains from mass murders.

Humans did horrible things to one another. Evan had seen more than enough.

The doctor had seen worse.

"Does anything indicate the cause of death?" asked Noelle, filling the awkward silence.

Dr. Peres shook her head. "Same as the child. No marks on the bones from stabbing or gunshot. No head trauma. This one's hyoid is missing, along with several small bones from her hands and feet." She looked at the other table. "That victim was on the bottom. Her hyoid is intact, but that doesn't rule out strangulation. People can be strangled and the bone not broken. By itself, a broken one only indicates the possibility of strangulation, not a definite."

"Thank you, Doctor," said Evan. He'd known once the remains were found that it was possible they were related to either the old Jerry Chiavo murder cases or the three women who'd been murdered in the past few weeks. Or both.

In his gut he felt Chiavo was at the center of all the deaths somehow. He and Noelle silently left the building.

"I need to call Rowan," Evan said. "I wish I could confirm that this was Malcolm."

"Her family has been suffering for twenty-five years," said Noelle. "We all want to change that. Are you going to call her now?"

"Yes. From my car."

I wish I had better news.

28

The homeowner watches me as she stands in the bathroom doorway, suspicion in her eyes. I get it. I need a haircut and my beard is rather scraggly. But my red shirt with its cheerful Sam's Electric logo is clean, and so are my jeans.

I step back while the other electrician balances on the stepladder and lifts the light fixture to the ceiling. Liam has got this part under control and doesn't need my help. We've done this dozens of times and have a routine. He's been a competent trainer over the years.

I duck my head and look away, self-conscious because I made eye contact with her. I'm not here to interact with people. I'm here to do my job, and I'm good at it. I've learned a lot as an apprentice. Electricity makes sense to me. It's logical. It acts like I expect it to. Not like people, who are completely unpredictable.

He's got the fixture all wired and has moved the canopy into place against the ceiling. I hand up the bulbs, and he screws them in one by one. He nods to me, and I head to the garage to turn the breaker back on. I hit the switch and a moment later hear a happy "Oh, that looks great!" from the homeowner.

Another job well done.

I go back to the bathroom and start picking up. Then I sweep, vacuum, and wipe everything down, wanting it perfect for the customer. I take pride in not leaving any sign that work has been done. I never leave smudges or fingerprints or dust. I make it immaculate.

This was our last job for the day, and I have a strong need to be back home. I don't like being away for too long. My anxiety level goes up, and I can't relax. It feels like something is crawling under my skin even though I know it is just in my head. It feels dangerous to be out in public; home is safety.

"Ready to go?" Liam asks as he does a final inspection of the bathroom.

"Yes." I watch him, holding my breath. No matter how long we've worked together, this part makes me nervous.

I always want to do my best.

He claps me on the back. "Looks good. Let's get out of here, I'm starved."

Relief swamps me, and I realize how hungry I am.

Things are different. I've felt it change over the last several weeks.

He's distracted. Lost in thought. Stressed. Spends a lot of time on the computer. Like right now.

I sit in my corner and watch. The computer is off-limits for me. Password protected. But occasionally he leaves without closing the lid and my curiosity gets the better of me so I look. I never did figure out how to get past the password, but I'll watch him type and scroll for hours, jealous of all the information to read. I almost threw up the first time I touched the keyboard, terrified it was a trap.

He likes to set traps for me.

The cupboards with the food are locked, but he can't lock the refrigerator. Instead, he ordered me not to touch anything.

The first time I snuck some of the milk, he left me in the box for three days. I denied it, but he said he had been watching. I knew that wasn't possible. He'd been away from the property. The next time he left, I examined the refrigerator door and saw a half-inch-long hair stuck in the closed door.

It took me weeks to risk opening the door. During that time, I saw the hair was always replaced. But often in a different spot. So I opened the door, drank some milk, added water to the milk carton in case he'd marked the level, and replaced the tiny hair.

I was nauseated all night, expecting him to accuse me of opening the fridge. I never know what the punishments will entail. Sometimes he takes away all my clothes. Sometimes he ties me to a tree for a day or two without food. I always want more food than he gives me. He makes fun of my bony legs and ribs, then says my body doesn't require much food since I'm so thin. He says he can't give me more because I'll get fat.

No one wants to be fat.

I only got to wear shoes when I started accompanying him on the electrical jobs. At home he knows I can't escape into the woods very far without shoes. They are locked in the cupboards with the food. I always walk carefully outside. The area around the house is covered with small sharp rocks and tree roots.

Most of the time he just gives me chores for punishment. Cleaning. Weeding. Chopping wood. We don't have a fireplace; he sells the wood. He doesn't let me wear clothes for the chores. He says I'll get them dirty or make them stink. One time I hit my foot with the axe. I knew I should have stopped before that. I was tired and not seeing straight. I remember staring as blood gushed from my foot. The next thing I knew he was standing over me. I was flat on my back and soaking wet. He'd dumped a bucket of water on me to wake me up and to wash the foot. He yelled at me for being a stupid idiot, and that I deserved the injury for being careless. I couldn't walk for a few days, and he was angry, saying I made extra work for him. He ripped up one of my shirts to wrap the foot and pointed out that now I only had one shirt left, so I best take good care of it.

My work shirt doesn't count. I only get to wear it for jobs.

It's not really a house that we live in. He once said it had been a portable office at a jobsite. The one bedroom is his. I sleep under the table when he doesn't put me in the box. I feel very lucky on the nights I get to sleep inside. I don't worry about cold or bugs. Or that he might forget me.

I wonder what would happen if he dies while I'm in the box.

Once I beat my hands bloody inside the box when that thought occurred. I had to get out. I couldn't breathe. I shook and screamed to get out.

No one came.

Books are my rewards. Sometimes he visits the library and checks out books. The ones he gets for me are always kid books, but I read them over and over. Sometimes there are longer ones with actual chapters and the characters go on adventures. He likes super-thick books for himself. Books about the lives of people who lived long ago or mystery books with police and crimes.

I know this because I read all his books too. I have a spot under the table where I can hide one to read at night. He always borrows many books at a time, so he doesn't notice when I take one from the bottom of the stack. I know I'm risking a beating, but I can't stop.

Several months ago I stopped swallowing my pills. He's always told me I'd die without them. When I stopped them before, I got very sick. And as soon as I took them again, I got better. So I believed him. Every night he gives me the pill and then asks me to open my mouth and stick out my tongue, so he can see that I swallowed it.

He stopped looking that closely in my mouth a long time ago, which drove me to stop swallowing and tuck them high in my cheek. I'd become ill, but I noticed that I was less tired and my brain less fuzzy.

I wanted that back. That clarity of mind.

This time I stopped the pills differently. In one of his books, I read about a character who was trying to get off pills and cut the amount a little each week. I tried it and it worked. I didn't get sick, and I've been completely off the pills for several weeks. I feel as if I can think. I can read his books faster, and they make more sense.

They give me ideas.

People don't treat each other the way he treats me.

I don't belong to him.

But I'm scared to leave. He says I will go to prison, and I know he's right.

Because of the bodies.

29

Rowan pressed her cell phone against her ear, her heart breaking.

Why do I get my hopes up?

"I'm sorry I don't have better news," Evan said on the other end of the call.

"It's okay. We're used to it." Her voice was stiff, her tongue struggling to get the words out.

"I'm sorry," he repeated.

"I'm sure you'll figure out who it is."

"I suspect it's related to Jerry Chiavo too."

Rowan closed her eyes, and Jerry's despised face appeared. She let the hate flow over her and wallowed in the sensation. He was the only person who raised it in her. "My parents pleaded several times for him to tell them where Malcolm was buried. I—" She stopped and opened her eyes, surprised at what she'd almost admitted.

Evan was silent for a moment. "You talked to him too," he finally said. "I saw your name on his visitor list."

"Yes." Guilt and shame replaced the hate boiling inside her. "He told me nothing. I got nowhere with him. There was no point in trying again."

Evan sighed into the phone. "I'm sure that wasn't pleasant for you."

"It wasn't."

"But I fully understand why you did it."

"Thank you," she said sincerely. "Many times I've regretted going. That perhaps I made a big mistake." She'd never told her parents or sisters that she had gone.

"You had to try."

He understands.

"I did."

Evan ended the call a minute later, and Rowan set down her cell phone, suddenly realizing that Thor was pressing hard against her thigh, his head raised to meet her eyes.

"Hey, boy." She knelt to give the dog a quick hug. "You always know when I'm struggling, don't you?"

He wagged his tail faster, his eyes cheerful, believing she was no longer stressed.

If you only knew.

He darted away, snatched up a rubber ball, and moved to the door, looking at her expectantly.

/ball/

Rowan grabbed the long-handled ball thrower. It hurled the ball much farther than she ever could. Thor would wear himself out with the sprints. "I need a distraction," she told him as she opened the slider. He raced out the door and to the edge of the field, a black blur against her grass. She strode after him, trying to force down the memory that had been bubbling since Evan had brought up Jerry Chiavo.

It didn't work.

Five years ago

She'd only seen his face in past newspaper articles. It didn't match the face of the old man who had just walked into the visitors' room, a long chain leading from his cuffed hands to the shackles at his ankles. He was seventy now, and his hair had gone completely white. The large, soft build she'd seen on the news had turned into a very overweight body with stooped shoulders.

She immediately looked toward his feet, where she'd always kept her gaze. Even when she hadn't been blindfolded and he'd worn a mask, she'd kept her eyes on his feet. She half expected to see the hiking boots with red laces that he'd often worn. Instead, she saw prison slippers.

He sat heavily in the chair and looked her over.

His eyes were sharp as he assessed and judged her.

It made her skin crawl, and she was thankful for the perforated plexiglass barrier between them.

He was an old, broken man on the outside. But his eyes revealed that inside he was as cruel and manipulative as ever.

"The girl has grown up."

Rowan caught her breath but sat perfectly still, not allowing any expression to cross her face at his continued refusal to use her name. Like his body, his voice had aged. It was deeper and rougher. Perhaps he'd taken up smoking in prison.

She did the same slow perusal of him he had done to her, finally returning to hold eye contact.

Rowan said nothing.

She had two goals for this visit. The first was to sit in his presence without fear, facing the demon from her dreams, the twisted man who'd tortured her and killed her brother. She focused on her breathing as she stared at him, feeling her lungs expand and contract, counting to three with each inhalation and exhalation.

She searched for her fear; it wasn't present. She was calm and centered.

First goal scratched from her list.

Her second goal was to find out where he'd buried Malcolm. She ignored her impulse to immediately ask. The visit was an hour long. There was plenty of time to draw it out of him.

So she continued to steadily breathe and study him.

"Do you no longer speak, girl?"

"My name is Rowan."

His lips twitched. "I knew that."

"You never used my name." She continued to hold his gaze.

He shrugged.

"You broke my leg."

He briefly broke eye contact. "And? Looks like you get around just fine."

She needed to be less confrontational. If she pushed too much, he could end the visit before she asked about Malcolm. Jerry had been known to get up and leave when questioned by reporters, and he'd done it to her parents when they'd come to plead with him to share where he'd buried Malcolm.

But Rowan suspected he was curious about her and would try to emotionally manipulate her again.

He thrived on control and power.

It'd been the need behind every sick game he'd made her and Malcolm play.

No doubt most of his control had been stripped from his life when he went to prison. If she gave him a tiny taste, he might stick around long enough and say something to help her reach her second goal.

She licked her lips and looked down at her lap, letting him think she was affected.

"Why are you here, girl? Did you miss me?"

She tasted vomit in the back of her mouth and swallowed hard. Keeping her eyes averted, she decided to take a risk. "I'm looking for Malcolm."

Silence.

Rowan looked up, keeping her gaze meek.

"This again?" he asked. "I'm old. I don't remember where he's buried."

"Then tell me why you wouldn't tell anyone back then, when you could remember."

Jerry shifted in his seat, glancing to his right and then his left. "Don't need to tell you nothing."

"True."

His eyes narrowed. "Why all the concern for your brother? As I remember, you hated him. Told me that yourself. You hit him and threw things at him."

Now.

Rowan rose to her feet and made the angriest face she could. "You asshole! You know exactly how I truly felt about my brother. I loved him! Your wife is dead, and I hope it hurt that you were locked up in here when she died, her brain scrambled and confused with dementia, wondering why her husband had abandoned her. You're going to die alone, your legacy one of cruelty and murder!" She leaned toward the plexiglass, her hands balanced on the table, her legs shaking the tiniest bit.

That should feed his need for control.

Jerry stared at her for a long second, a new alertness in his gaze. "The girl has grown claws. I saw hints of them back then. But they were tiny newborn kitten claws. Soft and flexible." He smiled, a fake wide smile. "I won't die alone. I get visitors. I had two dozen kids, you know. And they all still love me."

Now he's talking.

That they all still loved him was a stretch of the truth. Rowan knew a few had purposefully distanced themselves, confused by the fact that the man who'd been so kind to them had turned out to be a murderer. Rowan slowly lowered herself back into her chair.

"Do your foster children know how you treated us?" she asked in a strained voice, shooting him a defiant but pained glance. She wanted him to feel he could still cause her pain.

"You mean did they hear the crazy stories from the mouth of a five-year-old who'd been lost in the woods? No one believed you." His chest seemed to puff out.

"They know you killed my brother. You said you did. That's impossible to forgive."

"An accident. I admitted he died in an accident and then I buried him because I didn't know what else to do."

"And conveniently forgot where that was."

"Yes." He gave another fake smile. "But he's in a lovely place. Lots of tall trees and fresh, clean air." A sly look entered his eyes. "But I guess the air isn't relevant to a dead person, is it?"

"And tall trees are?" she said, her voice cracking.

His eyes glittered at her comeback.

He's relishing this.

"So you do remember where he is."

Jerry leaned back and shrugged. "Give it up, girl." He looked over and jerked his head at the guard waiting in the back of the room. "I'm in a physical prison. The only payback I can give is to make sure you're in an emotional prison." He heaved himself out of the chair and shuffled to the door, his chains clanking.

Rowan frantically tried to think of something to say that would recapture his interest. Her mind was blank. She *was* in an emotional prison when it came to Malcolm.

She exhaled as the door closed behind him. "I got nothing," she said out loud.

No. I stared him in the eye, and I wasn't scared.

"That's a win."

30

"Those extensions are so obvious," said Iris, pointing at the TV screen. "Her hair is naturally wavy, and the extensions are straight. And don't get me started on how wrong the shade is."

"She should get her money back," agreed Ivy.

Rowan stared at the woman's hair. She couldn't see it.

On the reality show, the woman raised her champagne glass and pretended to be excited as she made a toast by the mansion's pool with a dozen other people. Then the show jumped forward to a slow-motion scene of the group dancing as they laughed and looked perfect, appearing to have the time of their lives.

"So fake," muttered Ivy. "Each one of them has been directed to act as happy and thrilled as possible. No one has that sort of amazing dance party with just a dozen people." She glared at the screen and took another handful of potato chips from the big bowl in front of the three sisters.

"It's all staged," agreed Iris.

No matter how much they complained, Rowan knew her sisters would watch every episode of the reality show, picking apart the outfits and makeup.

Rowan couldn't judge; she was just as guilty.

It'd become a weekly get-together. The three of them would gather and catch up on the multiple episodes that had come out that week, hopelessly addicted to the UK show about gorgeous twentysomethings living together in a mansion. It was packed with deception, romance, bare skin, and awkward conversations.

The sisters couldn't get enough.

Tonight they'd gathered at Ivy's little house. Her son, West, was spending the night with his grandparents, and Ivy had picked up six Italian meals from a restaurant downtown. She always bought more than was needed for the three of them, saying she and West were happy to eat Italian food for the rest of the week. It was a form of grocery shopping for her.

The delicious food had been attacked and the leftovers put away in the fridge two hours ago. The sisters had moved on to cookies, chips, and ice cream to watch the fourth episode of the evening.

Thor hopped off the couch from beside Rowan and paced through the kitchen. Rowan watched him out of the corner of her eye as she focused on the ridiculous kissing contest on TV. One woman was kissing every one of the blindfolded men as they tried to guess who she was.

"Gross. Bacteria. Spit. Now shared between all of them," stated Iris. Out of the sisters, she talked the most during the show, often stating the obvious.

Thor growled. He'd stopped at the door to Ivy's backyard and shoved his snout between the closed drapes and the glass.

"Does he need to go out?" Ivy paused the show.

"He just went," said Rowan, levering herself off the couch and feeling the pasta shift in her belly. "He did the same thing at my place yesterday. Do you have coyotes or anything?"

"Every house in this neighborhood has tall fences and little yards," said Ivy. "Coyotes would be trotting down the street out front—which I have seen. Would he growl if a cat was wandering around?"

"No, he loves cats for some weird reason."

Rowan pushed the curtain aside to see into the dark backyard. Something tall darted out of her vision, and she caught her breath.

"Ivy, there's someone in your backyard. He just ran to the far end of the house. Are your doors and windows locked?" She flipped the door's lock.

Her sisters simultaneously got to their feet, and Ivy went pale. Iris dashed to the front door. "This one's locked."

"Are your windows locked?" Rowan repeated, staring at Ivy. Her sister seemed unable to speak.

"I don't know," she finally said.

"Turn on all the outdoor lights," ordered Rowan, flicking the switch by the door. "Scare him off."

Breaking glass sounded from down the hall.

Rowan grabbed Thor's collar as he lunged in the direction of the noise. She pointed at Iris. "Call 911." She crossed the family room and took Ivy's arm. Her sister was frozen. "Where are your car keys?" Ivy silently pointed at her purse on the kitchen counter, and Rowan felt her shaking.

"Adam," Ivy whispered. "It's got to be Adam."

Adam was her loser ex-husband and West's father.

"We're taking your car and getting out of here." She pulled Ivy and Thor toward the garage door in the kitchen, pausing to let Ivy dig in the purse for the keys. Rowan had Ubered to her sister's home because sometimes TV night turned into margarita night or martini night. Iris spoke to the 911 operator, relaying what had happened.

"Why would it be Adam?" asked Rowan.

"Wait!" Ivy pulled out of her grasp and ran back to the sofa, dropping to her knees. Thor whined and pulled against his collar, wanting to follow. Ivy reached underneath and pulled out a wooden baseball bat.

"Jesus, Ivy." Surprise shot through Rowan's nerves. "What made you stash that there?"

"I've got two more. One by my bed and another near the front door." Her sister gripped the bat, seeming to draw strength from it.

"Why?" Rowan turned to Iris, studying her face to see if she'd known about Ivy's home protection system. Her eyes were wide, and she gave a small shake of her head, the phone still to her ear.

She doesn't know why.

Rowan spun back to Ivy. "What did Adam do?" She grabbed her sister's arm again and hauled her toward the garage door, Iris close behind. "Did he threaten you?"

The divorce seven years ago had been ugly. Especially considering the couple had only been married for two months. Adam had struggled to accept that Ivy no longer found him irresistible after he'd been charged with domestic assault. But when he'd discovered she was pregnant, he couldn't get away fast enough. He'd appeared a few times over the last seven years. Usually trying to coerce money from Ivy. Never interested in seeing West.

Rowan hated him.

"He wanted to meet with West," Ivy said as they dashed down the few steps into the garage. "I told him no, and he threatened to take him away."

"That makes no sense. He never cared before and gave up his rights." Rowan let Thor in the back seat as Ivy went around to the passenger side. Ivy clutched the bat with both hands, her knuckles white. Rowan let Iris, who was still on the phone, climb in after Thor. Then Rowan slammed the door and got in the driver's seat. "Tell them it's her ex-husband," Rowan said, buckling her seat belt and starting the car. "He's threatened to take her son."

"I have a restraining order," added Ivy as she sat, still gripping the bat. "Last time he came he said he had a gun."

Rowan's hand hovered over the garage door opener on the visor by her head as she tried to process Ivy's words. "He threatened you with a gun? And you bought *baseball bats*? Why didn't you tell me?"

"I wouldn't buy a gun with West in the house!" Ivy shouted at her. "I can barely shoot one even after the classes I took. Do you think

I could fire at a *person*? They'd take it away from me before I could squeeze the trigger!"

Rowan hit the garage door button, put the car in reverse, and held her breath, her eyes locked on the door that led to the kitchen. The opener's motor seemed deafening.

If he's in the house, he'll hear the garage door opener.

Does he have the gun?

The motor above their heads rattled and groaned, slowly sliding open the big door.

So. Slow.

Thor's panting filled the car, and Rowan flicked her gaze between the rising door in the rearview mirror and the door to the kitchen, praying for no one to open that door and shoot at the windshield.

"I don't understand why he suddenly wants West," Ivy whispered. "He's ignored his son all his life."

In the back seat, Iris told the dispatcher the man might have a gun and they were about to back out of the garage. She turned and looked over her shoulder. "Go, Rowan! It's high enough!"

Rowan agreed and stepped on the gas. The car shot out of the garage. A loud thump and crack sounded as something large hit the right rear fender. Ivy screamed, and Rowan hit the brakes.

I hit him.

"Don't stop!" Ivy shrieked.

Rowan twisted in her seat, trying to see out the windows into the dark, thinking she'd seen a flash of a male silhouette to the side.

Are there two men?

No one was visible in her mirrors or out the windows.

It had to be one man.

"Go! Go!" shouted Ivy. She slammed the bat on her lap.

"I don't want to back over him!"

"Fucking run him over!"

Sirens sounded and flashing lights filled the street.

"They're here!" Iris told the dispatcher. "Tell the police we're in the car in the driveway! And we might have hit the guy."

Two patrol units blocked the driveway. "Turn off the car!" one officer shouted.

Rowan turned it off and held her breath, watching the officers in her mirrors. Their weapons were drawn and pointed at the back of the car.

No. Pointed at the ground behind the car.

"Drop the weapon! Drop the weapon!"

Ivy shoved her bat to the floor.

"They're not yelling at us," Rowan said, trying to steady her voice. Ivy was panting, her face wet with tears. She covered her eyes and started to shake.

"Thank God West wasn't here." Her voice cracked on his name.

Rowan watched in the rearview mirror as one of the officers holstered his gun and bent over behind the car while two other officers covered him.

She let out a shuddering breath as Thor shoved himself between the front seats, trying to get to Rowan. She scratched his head. "Shhhh. Good boy."

It's over.

An hour later, Rowan was still on edge.

Ivy's ex was on his way to the hospital. The officers wanted him medically cleared before they took him to jail. He'd appeared to have a head injury and possibly a broken leg. Ivy had refused to get out of the car or look at the man. Rowan and Iris had identified Adam as he lay on the ground behind the car, moaning in pain and cursing Ivy. A small pistol had been found near one of the tires.

He was very, very drunk.

Rowan leaned against the counter in Ivy's kitchen, too worked up to sit down. The sound of breaking glass they had heard had come from West's bedroom. Adam hadn't entered the house through the broken window, possibly because it was so high. Instead, he'd come around the side of the house, probably when he'd heard the car or garage door. Rowan believed he'd lunged at the trunk area of the sedan, trying to stop them, and been knocked to the ground.

If she'd backed up any farther, she would have run him over.

At the moment part of her wished she had.

After the three sisters had given statements, Rowan had called her father and asked him to come get Ivy. He'd hugged his daughters and cursed Adam as he led Ivy out the door. Then Iris's boyfriend had shown up and taken her home.

Police and a forensics tech were still in the home, processing the broken window and the vehicles, including Adam's truck, which had been found two blocks away. Rowan paced in the kitchen, staying out of their way and waiting for them to leave. She had looked in the bedroom and shuddered at the glass scattered over a racetrack on West's floor.

What if West had been asleep in there?

Even if Adam hadn't been able to get to the boy, West would have been traumatized. It didn't make sense that Adam would be interested in his son. Rowan suspected it had more to do with Ivy. Either he wanted something from Ivy and would have used West to get it, or he simply wanted to hurt her through her son.

Outside there was blood on the driveway and a dent in the car.

I'm not going to sleep tonight.

She would lock up the home once the police were done and then call an Uber.

Opening the fridge, she eyed the containers of leftover Italian food. It seemed so long ago that the sisters had sat at the table, eating, laughing, and making fun of the reality show. Not a care in the world.

I should throw it out. Ivy won't want reminders of tonight.

Instead, she grabbed the half-empty bottle of red wine on the counter and poured a glass. She sat heavily on a stool at the kitchen bar, suddenly jealous of Iris, who had a boyfriend to comfort her. Thor lay on the kitchen floor, his head between his paws. His alert eyes had been following her every movement. Rowan made eye contact, and he lifted his head.

/food/

"Not now. We'll go home soon."

Disappointment flashed in his gaze, and he lowered his head. Rowan thought about how he'd growled, letting them know someone was in the backyard.

Just like he did yesterday morning at my house. Was that a reaction to Adam too?

But Adam had no motivation to be outside Rowan's home.

Or does he?

If his main motivation was to hurt Ivy, Adam could have hurt any member of their family to achieve that goal. But he knew Rowan had a large, protective dog. He'd be an idiot to choose her.

Maybe I'm giving him too much credit.

Rowan sipped her wine and stared moodily at the most important male in her life. She loved him beyond reason, but he didn't fill all the holes in her heart. A lot of them, but not all.

Voices sounded out front, and Thor got to his feet, his focus on the living room door. Rowan tensed and then remembered officers were still there. The door opened and Evan Bolton strode in, tension emanating from him. He locked gazes with Rowan and visibly relaxed.

"Thank God," he muttered, stopping to greet a tail- and hip-wagging Thor, who'd met him halfway.

Rowan watched him pet her dog, feeling something shift in her chest, a piece tipping into place.

I'm falling for him.

It wasn't just an attraction; it was more.

31

Evan had known the three sisters were unharmed, but his heart had been in his throat during the entire drive to Ivy's home. It wasn't until he'd stepped through the door and seen Rowan staring at him, a big glass of red wine in her hand, that his heart had returned to its proper place in his chest.

He stroked Thor's head and then crossed the room to his owner, the dog close at his heels. Rowan looked confused to see him and was silent, just staring, making Evan wonder how much wine she'd drunk. He pulled her into a hug without saying a word. She shuddered and then relaxed into him. He smoothed her hair down her back with one hand, realizing he'd never touched her in that way before.

It feels right.

"You're okay?" he finally asked.

"Yes. Just tired," she said into his shoulder. "I want to go home, but I'm waiting for them to finish so I can lock up the house."

He pulled back and searched her eyes, his hands on her shoulders. "You good to drive?"

She gave a half smile. "I've had three sips of wine in the last two hours. I'm taking an Uber anyway."

"I'll drive you."

"You don't—"

"I want to." He let go of her and looked around the room. "I want to walk the scene and talk to the officers. Then we'll go. They can lock up, and I'll get the key from them tomorrow. Now tell me what happened."

Rowan walked him down a hallway, explaining how Thor had acted strangely and she'd glimpsed someone in the backyard. Evan stepped into West's room, studying the broken glass.

Asshole.

"Did he know ahead of time that this was the boy's room?"

"I'm not sure. Ivy hasn't lived here that long, and I know Adam has never been in the house."

"I heard Adam might have a broken leg?"

Rowan snorted. "I wish it was more. He slammed into the car pretty hard at the same time I was backing up. I didn't see him until a split second before he hit." An odd look crossed her face, and she took a sip of wine.

"You describe it as him hitting the vehicle."

She thought. "He hit the corner of the car, and part of the dent is on the side. I was going straight back. And I saw him rushing toward the car. We collided . . . it wasn't just me backing into him." She started to say more and stopped, that odd look returning.

"What is it?"

Rowan looked at him, concern in her eyes. "For a split second I swear I saw two men before the collision."

"You think someone could have been with him?"

"I do. But it was so fast."

"You didn't tell anyone?"

"No." Her mouth twisted. "He'd be long gone by now. I should have said something, but it was all a shock and happened so fast."

"Do you want to come outside while I ask the officers some questions?"

Rowan tipped her head at her wine. "I'm good. Already been out there."

He'd already seen the dented car but wanted to ask what Adam had said during his arrest. And now take a look for signs of a second person. "I'll be back in a minute."

Evan left the house, wondering about what Rowan could have seen. The driveway had been lit up with bright portable lights that were almost better than daylight since they illuminated the scene from all angles. Evan noticed the closest streetlight was across the road and down several houses. The driveway would have been very dark when the accident happened. A forensic tech was packing up her equipment behind the car, and he showed her his badge and was joined by the sergeant he'd briefly talked with before entering the home.

"You were one of the first ones here, right?" he asked the sergeant. "I was."

"Any chance there was a second man involved?" Evan included the tech in his question.

The tech frowned and stood, pulling off her gloves.

"I only saw the guy on the ground," said the sergeant. "He was already down when we pulled up. I didn't see anyone else." He grimaced. "And we didn't look around for another person. The victims had seen the guy get hit and didn't suggest someone had been with him."

"There's a set of shoe prints in the dirt over there," said the tech, pointing at a bed of shrubs that divided Ivy's property from her neighbors'. A wide swath of grass separated the shrub bed from the driveway. "I could tell someone crossed the grass from the bed. And according to the officers who took the attacker to the hospital, he has on Nike tennis shoes. I called them to ask when I found the prints. Those are tennis shoes but not Nikes. The problem is I can't tell you how long ago the prints were made." She lifted her hands in a who-knows gesture. "Someone could have walked through there this afternoon. But I've photographed and recorded them."

"Good job." Evan could see the disturbance in the grass. A concrete walkway ran along the side of the house and then curved to join the driveway. Adam would have used it after breaking West's window in the back of the house.

Evan walked down the driveway and followed the sidewalk to the bed of shrubs. One of the portable lights shone on the shrub bed. The tech must have directed it that way to process the prints. He stood on the sidewalk, hesitant to step into the neighbors' grass or Ivy's, not wanting to ruin any evidence.

"You can walk on the grass, Detective," the tech told him. "I'm finished there."

He took a few steps in the grass and spotted prints near the biggest shrub. There were several, as if someone had stood there awhile, not simply walked straight through.

Rowan might have been right about seeing two men.

He scanned the slight depressions in the grass, seeing that they led straight to where Adam had been knocked down.

But where did the second man go after that?

Unless it had been a neighbor cutting through the yard earlier that day for some reason. Evan walked back around to the tech and sergeant. "What'd the attacker have to say?"

"Not much. Just cursing out his ex-wife even though he couldn't see her," said the sergeant. "He was drunk. I heard his blood alcohol at the hospital came back as a point-one-nine. He also hit his head pretty hard and was dazed while we cuffed him on the ground. Didn't seem aware of what had happened."

"Thanks." Evan headed back inside, ready to drive Rowan home.

Twenty minutes later they were almost to her house with Thor happily panting in the back seat. Evan had told her about the footprints, but she doubted they were relevant since the tech couldn't tell how old they were. Rowan had spent most of the time texting and having short calls with her sisters and parents, checking up on them.

She leaned back in her seat and sighed. "You now have another case on your plate. At least Adam was caught. That should make things easier."

"It's not my case."

Her head swiveled in his direction. "What? Then why did you come? How did you know?"

"Noelle is the detective on call tonight. It's her case. She's wrapping up another scene, and the sergeant will stick around until she arrives. She texted me when she learned it was your sister's home and that you were here."

There was a long pause. "You came just to check on me?" Rowan asked.

"Yes." He glanced her way, wondering what she would read into that.

"Thank you," she said after a moment. "But why would Detective Marshall think to text you?"

Tell her the truth.

He had nothing to lose.

"She's perceptive," he said.

"Women often are."

"I think she noticed that I care about you more than as a friend." He grinned at her. "What do you think of that?"

Even in the dark car, he saw her smile, and electricity flared between them. "I think she did us a favor." She reached over and touched his cheek, her fingertips gently dragging over his stubble.

Evan felt it all the way to his toes.

Then she slid her hand down his arm and took his hand in hers. He squeezed it.

"I've been interested in you since the first time we met," she said, squeezing his hand in return. "I think that was two years ago."

"At least," said Evan. "I noticed you too . . . but the timing was never right."

"Is it right now?"

The interview with Jerry Chiavo suddenly thrust to the front of his brain along with his earlier realization that Rowan was somehow intertwined with several of his cases. "I don't know," he blurted.

Her hand stilled in his.

"I mean . . . I'm ready. Definitely. And it appears you are too." He looked her way and she nodded. "But you're connected to several of the cases I'm working on. I don't know if I'm crossing a line somewhere. Honestly, I'm not sure where that line is."

"I understand." Her fingers tightened on his. "We'll figure it out. It's not like I'm a suspect." There was a smile in her tone.

"No, thank God." Evan turned into her driveway, and Thor stood on his seat, tail wagging, ready to be let out.

Rowan hesitated. "I told you that Thor growled before I saw Adam in the backyard. He did the same thing at my back door yesterday. He almost never growls."

"Shit. You think Adam was here?" Anger flooded him.

"I don't know what to think, and I can't come up with a good reason why Adam would come here. It really surprised me to hear a growl two days in a row."

"I'm going to check the house first," Evan said. "Give me your keys."

"Adam is in jail—well, he will be as soon as he leaves the hospital. I have nothing to worry about now. I'm sure it was a coyote or bobcat in the yard."

"Humor me." The image of those footprints in the shrub bed popped into his head.

Is there a second man?

He—or Noelle—needed to talk to Adam.

Rowan handed him her keys. She hadn't added any more protests, and that bothered him a little. Either she knew it could have been a person in her yard, or she was very tired.

He would put money on the latter.

Ten minutes later he'd cleared her home and brought her and Thor inside. It was nearly 1:00 a.m. He stood at her front door, his fingers on the handle, knowing he needed to leave but not wanting to. Rowan was tired, her usual energy dim. She looked at his hand on the door and then met his gaze.

"You should go," she said softly. Her eyes suggested something else.

Evan debated. He was highly tempted. But this wasn't how he wanted to start something. He wanted to take her to dinner or maybe a movie or perhaps on a hike, really get to know her. He was old fashioned that way, and he didn't want to mess this up. It was important.

He stepped away from the door and slid one hand around her waist and the other into her hair, pressing her mouth to his. She sighed into the kiss, and her hands were hot against his chest.

It felt right. More right than any other kiss he'd had.

After several moments he pulled back and touched his forehead to hers. "I'm going home. But you need to know that I don't want to . . . but I feel it's the correct thing to do tonight."

She nodded. "I know."

Minutes later Evan was driving home, his window all the way down and warm night air blowing over the giant grin on his face.

32

I never questioned Liam about the Ford that was parked outside for a few days.

It was none of my business, and I had a feeling I wouldn't like the answer.

Silence is always best.

A few days ago I dropped him off up in the mountains where he said he was meeting someone and wouldn't need a ride back. I don't have a license, but he'd taught me to drive. I always drive exactly the speed limit and never make an error. He'd told me if I was pulled over, I'd end up in prison once they knew that I'd helped with the bodies.

I don't want to go to prison.

The day I dropped Liam off was a good day. I rarely got to drive alone. I've been tempted to simply keep driving, but he said there is a tracker on the truck. I know these exist; I've read about them in books, so he'd always have a way to find me. And if he didn't find me, he knew where my previous family lived and would kill them.

I know he can kill.

But still I dream of leaving, having a real bed, shoes always to wear. But I have no money. No identification. He's been good to provide for me.

Family is forever. We never betray the family.

That is the worst sin of all.

So instead I rolled down the windows in the truck and carefully drove home. I turned on the radio but didn't dare adjust the volume or change the station. He would know.

It had been one of the best days ever.

A few days later my world changed.

Liam said it was time to return the Ford. I would drive it and he would follow in the truck. But when I got in the Ford, I noticed it was almost out of gas. He was angry about that, yelling that he didn't want to make an extra stop. I'm not sure how that was my fault. He told me to stop at a station and gave me ten dollars to pay for the gas, saying it would be enough for the distance I was driving.

We left, and I pulled into the station. He parked the truck at the edge of the station's lot, waiting and watching me. The attendant told me to pay inside since I had cash. I froze. I'd rarely been inside a store on my own. I got out of the Ford and caught Liam's gaze across the lot. I held up the ten-dollar bill, pointing at the store. I could tell he was annoyed, but he waved me on.

Inside I was accosted by bright colors and saw candy and chips I've never tried. I stared for a few moments, feeling overwhelmed, and then I moved to wait behind three other people to pay. I eyed the newspapers and magazines, reading every headline as quickly as possible. Stories were more appealing to me than any candy. A local newspaper headline about a bear attack caught my attention, and I took the paper out of the rack to read the article. I flipped the pages to continue the story and found a new article with a photo.

I read the caption and my world stopped.

I can't believe this.

"Hey! You paying or what?" The clerk behind the counter stared at me.

The waiting customers had gone. I was the only one left.

I couldn't make myself put the paper back in the rack, and my fingers crinkled its edges. I needed to keep it. I walked to the counter and gave him the ten. "Pump six, but I want this paper too, but all I've got is the ten."

"No problem." He punched some buttons, and the newspaper was mine. "Want a receipt?"

"No." I didn't want Liam to find evidence that I had used gas money for something else.

I was elated and terrified at the same time, my heart pounding out of my chest. I paused inside to read the article accompanying the photo. My vision tunneled as I read.

This can't be right.

I'd been inside the store too long. I tossed most of the newspaper, folded the rest as flat as possible, and tucked it in the waistband of my jeans, pulling my shirt over it. It wasn't perfect, but I couldn't leave it behind.

I walked back to the Ford, noting Liam still watched me from the truck. The attendant placed the gas handle back on the pump.

"Not gonna get far on that much gas," he said.

"It's okay."

Once inside the Ford, I laid the newspaper next to me and pulled out of the station. I followed the truck as he drove out of town, and I studied the picture at every traffic light.

How is this possible?

My mind spun with possibilities the entire drive. Ahead Liam suddenly pulled off the road onto a shoulder and waved me to drive up beside him. I rolled down my window, and Liam pointed at a big clump of brush. "Go park it behind that brush. Make it so it's hard to see from the road."

He wants the SUV hidden.

I knew better than to ask why.

It was so hard, but I left the newspaper in the door of the Ford. I had stared at it, committing the photo to memory, and then started to panic as I thought about what he'd do if he discovered I'd bought a newspaper. He'd put me in the box for days and days.

Liam was chipper as we drove back, whistling and in a good mood. But my mood was black.

He's a liar.

He and Jerry had lied to me for years. Sweat beaded on my temples and dripped down my neck. I bit my tongue to keep my accusations to myself, but inside I wanted to explode.

Don't ask questions. He'll get angry.

But I couldn't stop myself. "You said my family moved to Texas, right?"

"That doesn't matter. Let it go. I'm your family now. This is how it works. Jerry trained me and I helped train you. It's time for that to continue and expand."

"Expand?" Dread crawled up my spine.

"Yes." He chuckled, his gaze still forward. "Three is a good number. It was three of us for a long time and I think it should be again. I've got a good plan, and I'm pretty proud of it. Better than Jerry could ever do."

If I asked about the plan, he would say it was none of my business. Instead, I fed his ego. "You outsmarted Jerry?"

"Damn right."

I wanted to smack the smug grin off his face.

"Jerry wasn't as smart as he thought. The police found him." Liam grinned. "He thinks he got caught because our neighbor snooped, but that wasn't it."

I knew Jerry had gone to prison for killing three women.

"It was time for Jerry to move on." Liam scowled. "I'd had enough and told the neighbor his missing chain saw might be in Jerry's barn. I hinted that Jerry had stolen a few things. The neighbor went snooping and then decided to see if the nice car in the barn had been stolen too. It belonged to one of those women."

"Jerry didn't know you did it?"

"Nope." A frown crossed his face. "Although I felt a little bad when I saw how well he protected me from prison. He'll never speak about what we did all the way to his grave." He looked at me until I met his gaze. "That's how it works. You protect me, and I'll protect you."

He's talking about the bodies we buried.

"I won't tell anyone."

"Exactly. Jerry was very strict about that. Your family always comes first. No matter what."

Yet he betrayed Jerry.

He must have done something horrible together with Jerry.

Instantly I knew that Liam had helped kill the first three women.

At the very least, Jerry had made Liam an accessory as Liam had done to me.

I rubbed my face with one hand, overwhelmed. Each generation in this *family* was involved in murder. Jerry, Liam, and me.

And now he wanted to bring in another person.

"Anyway, it's important to leave a legacy behind."

A legacy of murder?

"And to have someone to pass on our values and knowledge."

Knowledge? Values?

I've gained most of my knowledge from sneaking his library books. And I don't think punishing someone by putting them in a box reflects good values.

"People who go against the family will pay."

I didn't like his voice's sudden change in tone, and I glanced at him as a shadow crossed his face. I suspected someone had paid with their life for their betrayal.

"A little insurance helps remind everyone that family comes first. I know you'll toe the line because if you don't, our new third might get hurt."

I stared at him, unable to speak, confused about who this new person was.

"This one will be the perfect age to train."

Looking back, I realized that was exactly what Liam and Jerry did to me. Trained me.

With years of emotional and physical abuse, they trained me to be so docile and frightened that I did everything they said. They needed full control. That power was what drove them.

How did I not question that before?

It had to be the pills. They'd kept me numb, emotionless. Helpless. I don't know what kind he fed me for years, but now that I no longer take them, my mind feels unnaturally clear and focused. Anger boils inside me. I was a zombie before. Very pliable. Obedient. Spineless.

How dare they do that to me?

But now I see it perfectly; I'm aware.

I won't let Liam hurt another child. Not like he did to me and the other boy.

The one we buried.

33

The next morning Evan leaned against the wall in the hospital room, listening to Noelle interview Adam Thornton. Noelle could be intimidating but would turn on the charm when needed. She didn't tolerate bullshit, and anyone who didn't take her seriously soon regretted it.

Ivy's ex-husband knew he'd screwed up and was currently putting an incredible amount of energy—and bullshit—into convincing Noelle that what he'd done was no big deal.

Breaking his son's bedroom window and terrorizing his ex-wife.

No big deal.

Adam's leg wasn't broken—just banged up—and the doctor had said his head should be okay in a few days. He had a concussion, a giant bruise on his forehead, and a broken nose. He'd been officially discharged but was still in the hospital, because Evan and Noelle had shown up at the same time as the deputy who was to transport Adam to the county jail. The deputy had agreed to wait until they had questioned Adam.

Evan was already annoyed and impatient with Adam's question dodging and obvious lies. The sound of his voice was grating, and Evan wondered how Ivy had ever fallen for him.

Evan squinted, studied the man, and acknowledged there was probably something attractive about Adam that would catch a young woman's attention. And maybe seven years ago it'd been even stronger. Ivy and Adam had only been married for two months, so she had quickly come to her senses. Evan observed something . . . slick about the man. He never quite told the truth and tried hard to convince them how wonderful he was.

Evan suspected Adam was like that in every conversation, not just when questioned by the police.

Adam said he had been at Ivy's home because he wanted to see West.

"Maybe ringing the doorbell would have been a better idea," Noelle said with a straight face.

"Yeah. Maybe." Adam glanced at Evan and then looked out the window.

"Were you planning to take West away?" asked Noelle.

"Nah. Just wanted to say hi. I'd never do that to Ivy."

"How much did you have to drink before stopping by?"

Adam screwed up his face in thought. "Not sure. I'd been at the brewpub with some friends. We went through a few pitchers."

"Did one of your friends go to Ivy's house with you?"

He looked surprised at the question. "No, just me."

"Did you see anyone else outside the house?" asked Noelle.

Adam sat up straighter in bed. "Why? Was someone else there? I don't know what they told you, but I didn't do anything."

"You broke the window," said Evan, unable to keep his mouth shut.

"Unless you think someone else did." Adam looked hopefully at Evan.

Noelle and Evan exchanged a pained glance.

"You hit the car awfully hard," Noelle said. "Did you think you could physically stop it?"

Adam gently touched his bandaged nose and winced. "Don't remember what I was thinking."

"You're lucky she braked. She could have run you over," added Evan.

The patient scowled. "I think I tripped and hit the car. Sort of remember falling hard into it." His eyes widened. "Someone pushed me! I remember feeling something hit my back."

Evan tensed but kept his face expressionless. "Who?"

"Was her twin outside? Iris woulda pushed me. She hates me. Rowan too." He looked from one detective to the other, an expectant gaze in his eyes.

"What made them hate you so much that they'd push you into a moving car?" asked Noelle.

Adam's mouth flattened into a tight line. "Not sure. Not my fault Ivy and I broke up."

"Do you remember anything else?" Evan asked, irked by the man's refusal to accept any blame.

"Cops yelling at me. Flashing lights. Pain in my head and leg."

"You just quietly laid there after hitting the car?" asked Noelle.

"Yep."

Evan recalled the sergeant's comment about Adam cursing out his ex as he rolled on the ground. "How often do you go to Rowan's home?"

Adam hesitated, flushed, and adopted a confused expression. "Why would I go there?"

"You tell me."

He looked away. "I've got no reason to go to Rowan's home. Haven't talked to her in years."

"Interesting. She had an outside prowler the other morning. Her dog let her know. Same way he did yesterday at Ivy's home." Evan studied the man. "Thor's a big dog, you know. She's trained him to protect her." The last was an exaggeration, but he wanted to plant a reason in Adam's head to stay away from Rowan.

Adam appeared very interested in what was happening outside his window.

Evan made eye contact with Noelle. She gave a tiny nod and stood. She was done too.

"Hey. When am I getting out of here?" Adam asked as they reached his door.

"There's a deputy in the hall, ready to transport you to the jail."

"My head was banged pretty bad. Probably shouldn't leave yet."

"The doctor already signed off, saying you'll be just fine," said Noelle. She opened the door and left with Evan on her heels, both of them ignoring Adam's protests.

In the hallway, she turned to Evan. "What do you think?"

"I think the only reason he was outside Ivy's home was to hurt her somehow. Either by taking West or causing damage. I guess his drunken brain decided it was time for payback and this was a good way to do it."

"I agree. Rowan had an intruder also?"

"No one was in the house. Thor acted out of character while looking outside the other day, and she said he did the exact same behavior last night."

"Adam seemed flustered when you asked."

"I noticed. I don't think he'll stop at Rowan's again, but I'll talk to both her and Ivy about security systems. I'll ask if Ivy has one at their hair salon too. Adam seems like the type to strike out at whatever he can. Especially if he's drunk."

"I know the type." Noelle squared her shoulders. "I need to get back to the cell phone records of Jillian Francis. I'm so glad we've pulled in the FBI on this—and I really like your friend Mercy. She's kicking things into overdrive to get more hands and eyes on these cases. I'm trying to find a connection between Jillian's and the other two girls' calls and texts. Somehow these three crossed paths with the same man. I'm determined to figure it out."

Resolve filled her features, and Evan believed she'd find it.

Evan checked the time. It was nearly noon. "I need to call Shannon Steward and ask if she knew that Ken visited Jerry Chiavo in prison."

"Did you ask Rowan?"

He grimaced. "I didn't. As far as I know, Jerry and Ken are connected through Rowan because of something that happened twenty-five years ago. It's logical to ask her, but something feels off."

"Feels off with Rowan?"

"Not exactly." He pulled out the notepad he'd written on after talking with Jerry. "Look. She's connected to all these cases in one way or another."

Noelle studied the page, running her finger from Rowan's name to each of the cases. "But her involvement isn't deliberate—it's just where life placed her. She was kidnapped and everything radiates from that . . . although I don't believe in coincidences, and this is a lot of them, so I see what feels off to you." She handed it back. "But if she's in the middle of everything, you *should* ask her the questions. What's holding you back?"

"I don't like so many connections either. I've never come across this in a case before, and it's making me hesitate. I feel like I'm missing something."

"Talk to her. Maybe she holds our missing piece. If you don't do it, I will." She raised a brow at him.

He knew she would. He was being ridiculous. "I'll call her after I talk to Shannon."

"Gotta go." Noelle lifted a hand at him and left, pausing ten steps later to greet a nurse she appeared to know.

Again Evan was glad Noelle was on his team. She sliced through things to see the heart of the matter. He took out his phone and snooped around for a quiet corner, ending up down the hall in a nook with three vending machines. He dialed Shannon Steward and eyed a bag of Lay's Classic Potato Chips in a machine. A weakness of his.

Shannon answered, and Evan identified himself.

"What can I do for you, Detective?"

"I have a quick question. Did you know Ken visited Jerry Chiavo in prison?"

There was a long silence. "What?" she finally asked. "Ken did that? When?"

"Two weeks ago. I saw his name on the visitor log. He only visited the one time."

"I don't know what to tell you. I'm a bit shocked because I know he hates—hated the guy. I can't think of why he'd go see him. Especially such a recent visit."

"Does it fall within the time frame of when you'd noticed Ken had been distant?"

"Well, yes, it does. I imagine the prison visit wasn't a pleasant one. It could have affected him, but he was almost impossible to reach for quite a while. I have a hard time believing one talk with the asshole would affect him for that length of time."

"You're insistent that he hated Jerry. Why do you say that?"

"From years of hearing Ken blame the asshole for what he did to Rowan. And her brother. You know how he felt about her. Very protective."

"Ken never spoke of a need to confront Jerry about what he did?"

"Not that I can think of."

"Would you say he discussed Jerry too much? Considering it was someone he'd never met?"

Shannon paused before answering. "Well . . . I don't know. Finding Rowan in the woods with a broken leg was a big event in Ken's life. Almost life changing, I'd say—although I didn't know him back then. Ken found a lot of missing people, but maybe because he was young when he found her, it may have left a bigger impression on him. His anger about that little girl's situation was all channeled at Jerry Chiavo after he was arrested. Rightfully so."

"From what I've read, the entire public was angry."

"It was a big deal around here. Did you ask Jerry why Ken was there?"

"Not yet. I found out after my visit. I'll line up a phone call and ask."

"Let me know if you get an honest answer."

"I doubt I'll get one. But I'd like to hear what he says about it."

Evan ended the call, made some quick notes, and sent an email to request a phone call with Jerry Chiavo.

Then he bought the potato chips.

34

The day after we hid the Ford, Liam took me to a house in town late in the evening.

That night didn't go as planned.

It was to be a reconnaissance mission, he said. Simply study the lay of the land around a certain home, but a drunken man showed up and broke a window. I heard the drunk call a woman a whore and yell that she would pay for how she'd ruined him. His words slurred as he stumbled around the outside of the house, shouting that she didn't deserve the boy.

I waited in the street near the truck but heard him clearly. The garage started to open, and I got in the truck and turned it on, ready to leave. Liam sprinted across the street a moment later, breathing heavily and saying we needed to leave *now*.

He said the drunk man put a wrench in things because the woman would now be on alert for anything strange near her home.

He said he might have to come up with a different plan.

Liam never tells me details, so I didn't care if he had to make a new plan. On the ride home he was angry the other man caused a problem, and he ranted about it for hours.

I didn't know why we were there. But now I think I know.

The boy.

The drunk man had shouted about a boy.

In the truck on the way home from hiding the Ford, Liam had said *we* needed someone young to train.

He had been outside that house to make a plan to take the boy. *Another boy.*

And he expected me to go along with it.

The same way *he* went along when Jerry took young children. *Victims for their extreme cruelty. To humiliate. To hurt.*

Maybe to kill.

And now Liam wants to start the cycle again.

I can't treat another person the way he treated me. I don't care if they put me in prison, I won't torture someone. I try not to think of his threats to kill my family.

I need to figure out how to get away from him, but it's not easy. He is always with me. If he's not with me, I'm usually in the box. I've thought about escaping at night. I know how to get to the main road from here, but he's said an alarm will go off if I open the door or windows at night.

He might have lied about that too.

I've considered leaving while we work at a residential job. That might be easiest. If he sends me to the truck to get a tool, I'll keep on going.

I know the computer could probably tell me where my family is, but I've never been allowed to touch it. He has a phone that could probably find them too, but it has a password. And I don't know how to use it. He never lets me look at it.

I've stayed for a long time because I had nowhere else to go. But now I do. My family won't turn me away, even though they haven't seen me in . . . I don't know how many years it's been. He says I'm in my thirties, but I don't trust him. I don't feel thirty.

I tried to leave once before. It didn't go well.

35

Rowan couldn't believe it, and she scanned Evan's eyes, hoping it was a joke. "Are you sure?" she asked. He had asked her to stop by his office.

Evan was grim. "Positive. Adam was processed and then released. The jail is already overcrowded, and all Adam did was break a window."

"You just interviewed him this morning at the hospital, and he's out *already*? He threatened Ivy!"

"I know. Believe me, I know what a shit he is. They know he violated the restraining order, but—"

"A piece of paper isn't going to stop bullets," snapped Rowan. "Last time he threatened her, he said he had a gun. And who knows what he wants with West. He'll take him away just to upset Ivy."

"I don't think he'll hurt his son."

Rage ran through Rowan. "Angry parents kill their children. We've both seen it happen. And someone always admits, 'I didn't think he'd really do it.' Has Ivy been notified?"

"Yes."

"I should call her."

"Tell her to check into a hotel for a while. At least until I get a security system installed on her home."

"She's a working mom," Rowan exclaimed. "It is not fair that she must spend money on a hotel to avoid the man who is making her life hell. She's done everything right—the restraining order and trying to live her own life. He's the one causing problems, and I know he'll continue. He tried to get into Ivy's house last night and do who knows what and walked away scot-free."

"He still has to appear before a judge."

Rowan didn't care. The man was free after the scare he'd given everyone. "He'll try again. Next time he'll kidnap West or hurt Ivy. I know this guy. Once he has an idea in his head, he'll stop at nothing—especially if it involves hurting Ivy somehow."

"You're preaching to the choir." His tone was calm, patience in his eyes as he let her vent.

Rowan spun around and paced, trying to calm her infuriated thoughts. She knew it wasn't Evan's fault. She had attacked the messenger. He appeared unruffled, but she knew he was angry about the situation too. He was the opposite of her ex, who would spout off and yell about anything that annoyed him.

Evan didn't yell. She liked that. She never feared what would come out of his mouth or wondered what she should have done differently to keep him calm.

How did I marry that guy?

Evan's eyes were nicer too. A dark brown that projected intelligence and kindness. When he was deep in an investigation, they would assess and analyze. Never accuse.

She felt safe with him. Not that she needed protection. But it meant she could be herself and relax.

Rowan took a couple of deep breaths. "I'm sorry."

"Don't apologize. You have every reason to be angry."

"I didn't need to attack you about it."

His brows rose. "You consider that an attack? People have lunged at me with knives and scissors and bats. Threatened to shoot me or break my legs because something I said pissed them off. This was nothing."

The corners of her mouth turned up; she couldn't help it. He was trying to distract her, and it was working. "That's horrible."

He shrugged. "Comes with the job. You can't be in law enforcement and let things push you over an edge into a reaction."

"You see horrible situations." Rowan had worked alongside law enforcement much of her life but had never witnessed a moment when one of their lives had been threatened. It took a special person to pursue the job. "How do you deal with it? I mean . . . when you were a deputy, you never knew what you would face that day. It could have been a traffic stop where you're fired at or an active shooter in a school."

Resolve entered his eyes. "You do what you're trained to do. I didn't get my deputy pay and excellent benefits to take reports about stolen lawn mowers or ticket speeders. I got it for the day I would have risk my life to save others without a second thought. You mentioned a school shooting. I'm trained to go in even if I am the only responder there. And if a shooter has locked themselves in a room with children, I go through that door. Hopefully with two other officers I trust. I go straight in, and the others follow behind me to the sides."

Rowan stared at him. She'd known they were trained to go after active shooters, but now she had a vivid image of Evan risking his life in that scenario to save others. And she was rattled to the core. "Thank you," she managed to say. "Few people would do that."

"There's little glamour in the job. We get spit on, called names, flipped off, and see some of the saddest or most disgusting sights you can imagine. Recruits know this, but until they experience it, they don't know if they have the heart and soul needed for public service. I joined because I want to help people, and that's what most officers will say is their reason. But there has to be a part of you that will sacrifice everything when called upon. Not everyone can stomach that." His eyes softened. "Sorry. I didn't need to go there."

"It's okay. It's the truth." Rowan blew out a breath. "We were talking about Adam. An actual coward."

"Ivy is at work today?" he asked.

Rowan checked the time. "Yes. She should be at the salon. I'll call her and then drive there."

"Before you go, I wanted to ask you a question about Ken Steward."

Her brain struggled to shift conversational gears, and she experienced a small wave of guilt because she hadn't thought about Ken in a while.

It doesn't mean I don't care about him.

"What is it?"

"Did he talk about Jerry Chiavo with you?"

Rowan stiffened. The man's name always did that to her. "Occasionally, I guess. We rarely said his name . . . just called him 'that guy' or 'he.' We both knew who we were referring to."

"Did Ken ever tell you he wanted to visit Jerry in prison?"

She blinked. "No. Why would he want to?"

"That's what I hoped you could tell me." He grimaced. "Ken visited him about two weeks before he was murdered."

Rowan was stunned. "I don't know why he would go."

"His only connection to Jerry Chiavo would be your case, correct? I talked to Shannon Steward about it, and she didn't understand why Ken would visit him either. She said Ken had a lot of anger directed at Jerry from what he did to you and Malcolm."

"Yes, Ken got angry when his name came up. I saw that several times. I don't find it odd, considering what Jerry did."

"I don't think the anger is unusual either . . . but a visit seems odd. Maybe he needed to have it out verbally with Jerry? But Jerry would have agreed to the visit, and he had to know Ken had nothing good to say to him. Jerry had very few visitors, especially since his wife died. Maybe he was bored and curious why Ken would set up a visit."

Rowan thought for a long moment, remembering how her visit had gone. "I can see him agreeing to see Ken for that reason. Wanting someone to toy with a bit."

"Shannon said Ken had been distant for a couple weeks before his death. Could his visit to Jerry have something to do with that?"

Rowan shook her head. "I honestly have no idea. Which reminds me, Rees Womack also told me that Ken was acting odd in the weeks before he died. Said he was anxious and acted distracted." She paused. "Rees thought it had something to do with me."

Even's gaze sharpened. "How so?"

"He didn't know. Ken told him there was something he couldn't tell me, and that he was worried I'd never forgive him for it. I've thought and thought, and I can't figure out what that could be. The man saved my life. What could I not forgive him for?"

"You might never find out."

"Rees also said he thinks Ken might have gone camping in that spot to meet someone. He'd wanted Rees to come along, but he backed out. He didn't care for the location and pointed out that it was an odd one for Ken to choose. Ken likes to be near a lake or creek and always goes far out in the boondocks. That site was rather close in for him. Rees said he refused to change the location."

"But he didn't say he was meeting someone?"

"No. It was speculation. But Rees and I couldn't come up with another reason for him to camp there. I hesitated to tell you because it didn't seem important."

"I never know if something is important until it suddenly is."

Evan was frustrated; Rowan saw it in the set of his jaw and the stiffness in his shoulders. He wanted to find Ken's killer, and she appreciated his determination. "You'll figure out who murdered Ken."

"I'll keep digging until I do," he promised, holding her gaze. "Go see your sister. Tell her I'm sorry about Adam getting out."

She stopped closer, slid a hand up his chest, and kissed him. She didn't know what they were to each other, and it didn't matter. She cared about Evan and knew he felt the same way about her. Labels could come later. Pulling back, she met his gaze and saw happiness with an undercurrent of desire.

"We're having burgers at my parents' this evening. Can you come?"

His face lit up. "Definitely."

A warm glow filled her chest at his reaction.

Yes. This is good for us.

36

After Rowan left, Evan opened Ken's murder binder.

Noelle had interviewed Rees, Ken's cousin Eric, and the other two ex-wives. Evan took a few minutes to read over her notes for the fifth time and still agreed no leads had been presented to follow up on. All the interviewees had stated that Ken was the best guy ever, with no enemies.

It's almost too consistent.

If Ken had been so wonderful, why had he been deliberately shot in the head? And according to what Evan had just learned from Rowan, Ken might have camped there to meet someone—and this person might not have agreed that Ken was the best guy ever. Noelle's report on Rees's interview did not mention that Ken had asked Rees to go camping with him or that he believed Ken was possibly meeting someone.

Witnesses often later remembered additional details. Evan always ended an interview with a request for the witness to contact him if they thought of more details, and he knew Noelle would have too. He was a little annoyed Rees had told Rowan instead of Noelle. He looked up the man's number and dialed.

"Hello?"

Evan identified himself. "We met at Ken's memorial, and I'm working with Detective Noelle Marshall on Ken's case."

"Yes. Of course," said Rees. "What can I do for you, Detective?"

"Rowan mentioned that you were invited to go camping with Ken that day."

"Oh. Yeah. Sorry I didn't mention that to the other detective. Honestly, I didn't remember it until later, and then I couldn't see how it was relevant to Ken's investigation. I've wondered a million times if it would have happened if I'd been there."

"You could've been shot too."

"Rowan pointed that out." His tone was glum. "Did she tell you we wondered if Ken was meeting someone there?"

"She did. That's the only reason you could come up with why Ken would camp there?"

"I really can't think of another. It's a shit location. It made no sense."

"You knew him well."

"I did. He was my closest friend."

"How far back do you two go?"

"Let's see . . . it's got to be close to twenty years."

"I was told he was an only child and his parents passed long ago," said Evan. "Obviously you know his cousin Eric. Did you ever meet more of his extended family?"

"Ken didn't really have family. His parents died when he was ten or so, and he bounced around in foster care until he was eighteen. If he had other relatives, none of them offered to take him in."

"I don't think anyone else mentioned Ken grew up in foster care," Evan said.

"Not surprised. He didn't like to talk about it. I don't think it was a good experience. His foster parents were real assholes, from what I understand. He had to figure out how to do everything on his own. I know he hated working for other people. Tried his hand at a few things. Restaurants. Lumber mill. Construction. Tried an apprentice-ship program for electricians. Complained about people looking over his shoulder all the time in every job. Got into dogs and SAR to be his own boss as soon as he could."

Evan's brain had stopped listening at the word *electricians*.

Jerry Chiavo had been an electrician.

Evan asked a few more random questions, thanked Rees, ended the call, and sat thinking for a moment.

Could Ken and Jerry have worked together?

He got up from his desk and walked over to where Noelle was working. She was on the phone but covered the receiver.

"What is it?" she whispered.

"Do you still have the old Jerry Chiavo files handy?"

She pointed at a storage box on a shelf by her desk.

"Thanks." Evan grabbed the box and took it back to his desk.

Evan dug through the box until he found the list of dozens of Jerry's work associates. He'd been an electrician and worked a long time for a big regional electrical company. According to the interviews Evan had skimmed through days before, everyone who'd encountered him had thought he was the best.

Evan ran a finger down the list of company associates, who were listed by last name.

"Steward, Steward, Steward," he muttered, making himself read every name.

There was no Ken Steward.

"Fuck."

I jumped to conclusions.

He scanned the names again and paused on Kenneth Riley and Kenneth Lynch.

Maybe a last name was changed. Hell. He could have changed his whole name.

The thought of researching every male name on the list for a name change made his head hurt.

He called Rees Womack again.

"Detective?"

"Yes, it's me again. Do you know if Ken changed his last name at some point?"

"Yeah. He did. I remember he told me that. Wanted to permanently separate himself from his family."

"Do you know what the name was before?"

There was a long pause before Rees spoke. "No. He told me a long time ago. Like before his first marriage."

"Could it have been Riley or Lynch?"

"Lynch!" said Rees confidently. "Now I remember thinking it was the same name as the movie director David Lynch."

Got him. He worked at the same company as Chiavo.

"Thanks, Rees."

"Anytime."

Evan hung up the phone and focused on the list in his hand, his mind going full speed. He flipped through the work associates' interviews, searching for Ken's, wanting to know what he'd said about Jerry Chiavo.

There was no interview for Ken Lynch. Sam Durette had marked him as "Unable to locate." Several of the company's employees hadn't been found for interviews.

Evan quickly did some county records research and determined Ken had changed his last name to Steward after leaving electrical work behind. His previous electrical employer had supplied the list of associate names, listing Ken by his old name.

No wonder Sam didn't interview him.

Evan would bet money that Ken had known Jerry Chiavo.

His brain started to spin as he thought about Ken finding Rowan and then five years later a man he'd worked with admitting he'd killed her brother after kidnapping the two of them.

Why didn't Ken make a statement?

"What the fuck?" It made no sense to Evan.

Ken had played both sides. Supporting Rowan and staying quiet about the man who'd done terrible crimes.

Unless . . .

Evan grabbed his files for the three recently murdered women, focusing on the estimated time of death of Jillian Francis, the river woman. Even Sam Durette had wondered if Jerry Chiavo had an accomplice for the old killings who could have committed the recent similar murders.

Could it have been Ken?

Ken Steward had been alive during all three women's deaths.

Had he learned to kill from Jerry Chiavo?

Evan leaned back in his chair, stunned. Was Ken Steward the killer he'd been searching for? The man everyone said was so wonderful? And now he was dead?

Evan didn't know who had killed Ken, but had he just found the answer to the recent murders of the three women?

He scrubbed his face with one hand. This wasn't the answer he wanted. It would hurt all of Ken's friends, especially Rowan. He had more digging to do. Just because Ken had worked with Jerry at one point didn't make him a murderer.

"Hey, Noelle?" he called to the other side of the big room.

"Yeah?"

"I need your help. We've got some research to do."

I can't tell Rowan until I'm positive.

37

As we park at the home of the first electrical job of the day, I immediately know it's in the perfect location.

It's in Bend and adjacent to a four-lane, busy street with lots of trees and shops. Plenty of places to dart between, take cover, and hide. It's exactly the setup I want.

I thought about my escape all night, mentally preparing in case the perfect opportunity presented itself. My best chance would be to leave from a work site near town, so I needed to be ready. Today I wore a T-shirt under my work shirt so I can remove that shirt and not stand out like a bright-red flag when I leave. I wish I had a hat, but only Liam has hats, and I didn't dare take one. I want to take the truck keys so he can't immediately come after me, but they're always in his pocket.

This homeowner hired us to install under-cabinet lighting in his kitchen. The owner is chatty, carrying on a conversation with Liam about baseball. I know little about baseball. I purposefully leave behind some tools in the truck, positive he will call me an idiot and send me back outside for them.

We start in the kitchen. I'm sweating, and I know it's not because I'm wearing two shirts on a summer day. My heart rate won't slow down, and I worry he'll ask why I'm nervous, so I prepare a lie.

My gut doesn't feel great.

He hates intestinal issues, and I know he won't ask more questions.

I'm terrified I won't go through with it, but I must. I try not to think about how angry he'll be if he catches me. He'll soak me with the hose and put me in the box for days with no food. He'll take away all my clothes for weeks. I'll have to move piles of rocks back and forth for no reason, naked in the freezing cold or hot sun. These punishments run on a loop in my thoughts.

I shove them out of my head.

My plan has to work. There isn't another option. I'd rather die than be brought back.

I have sixty-two dollars that I've saved over the years, finding a stray bill here and there. Sometimes at work, sometimes in our kitchen. Usually my money is hidden next to my borrowed book. This morning I tucked the stack of bills into my socks, knowing I need to be prepared to leave at a moment's notice. It's not much, but I don't need much. I've survived with very little for many years.

I'm confident my family will help me.

The problem is locating them. I'll need help. I can't go to the police and ask for assistance. They'll ask too many questions and might link me as an accessory to those murders. I have to find a stranger willing to help me.

This part of my plan frightens me. There are too many elements that can go wrong. I think I should ask a woman for help, but I worry I might scare her. I don't want to ask another man for help . . . What if he's no different than the man running my life now?

What if they call the police?

Twenty minutes into the job, Liam calls me an idiot and sends me out to the truck for the tools I left behind.

Time to go.

My heart tries to pound its way out of my chest.

At the truck I tear off my work shirt with shaking hands and shove it under the seat, so he won't know I changed. I pause, wanting to disable the truck somehow. I've read it's possible but don't know how to do it.

I quietly close the truck door and run.

I head toward the busy street, passing three other homes on this road. I feel as if eyes watch me from every window. I know people have cameras outside their homes, but I doubt he would knock on doors to ask to see footage. When I reach the main road, I turn and jog north, scanning the store signs ahead. I see a 7-Eleven, but it's too soon to stop.

I want to buy a hat and maybe shave my beard. But I need to put more distance between me and him. I keep running and my chest starts to hurt. I never run at home, and he keeps me very thin, so I know I'll need breaks. I pass two mothers with strollers. They are busy chatting and don't even look at me. A truck waits to turn out of a parking lot and waves me across in front of him.

I feel as if I'm under a spotlight, and being on my own seems foreign.

I've worked enough electrical jobs to know how to act in public, but I have the sensation of a big target on my back. As if something I'm doing is completely wrong and making me stand out to everyone. I know jogging in jeans isn't normal, but I don't think it's too bad.

Is it?

I cut through a parking lot and run behind a long line of stores. I feel a million times more comfortable in the shade and away from so many eyes. I pass two guys lounging behind a building, smoking cigarettes. They watch me run by.

"What'd you steal, man?" one of them yells.

"I'm late," I shout back.

"Yeah, right." They both laugh.

My anxiety doubles, and I struggle to breathe. What if he stops here and asks them if they've seen someone like me?

I should move to the other side of the busy street.

I run through a narrow alley and stop behind some bushes so I can study the road. There is a crosswalk at a light just ahead. I'll have to use it. The street is too busy for me to cross without stopping the traffic first.

But I can't stand at the crosswalk in view of every passing car while I wait for the light to change. One of those vehicles might be him. I crouch behind the bushes, panting hard, trying to catch my breath. I spot a woman in shorts jogging along the busy road and pray for her to hit the button to use the crosswalk.

She doesn't.

I can't wait much longer for someone to come along and do it. I eye a bush closer to the crosswalk. It's thin and not a great place to hide, but it's better than nothing. I jog several yards to the bush and then check the traffic, looking for his truck. An oncoming white truck makes my throat close, and I crouch lower. I clutch my head in my hands, panic speeding through my chest and head. But as it draws nearer, I see it's not his. The relief hits my gut like a punch, and I'm frozen in place.

I can't stop. I need to keep moving.

I scan the traffic and then dart to push the button and return to my hiding spot. A full minute passes before the traffic stops. Two more white trucks passed, neither of the right make, but they still sent jolts through my nerves. When the traffic is fully stopped, I check for white trucks and then start to jog across the road.

It's so wide, and I feel as if every waiting driver is studying me, wondering what is wrong with me.

I keep going so I can run behind the businesses on this side of the street. I pass dumpsters and more employees taking cigarette breaks behind their stores. This time I'm ignored. I continue for twenty minutes, alternating between walking and jogging. I have no stamina. I can't go much longer without a break. I spot a store that boasts of selling everything for a dollar and cautiously walk around to its front, looking for the white truck. Three cars are parked in front of it. The store looks quiet.

I wipe the sweat off my forehead and gather my strength.

I'm terrified to go inside.

But I do it.

Indoors there is one teenager at a check stand. I don't see any customers, and he's staring at his phone, swiping his thumb across the screen. He looks up. "Welcome in," he says in a monotone, and goes back to his phone, clearly not caring whether I'm there. I wonder if he can hear my heart pounding as I walk farther into the store, scanning the signs above the aisles.

I wander for a couple of minutes, avoiding the few customers in the store. I find a pack of three razors and a small pair of scissors, knowing I need to cut the beard before I can shave it. I also find a tan baseball cap. I'm annoyed that it's three dollars, not one dollar. I go to pay, and the teenager barely acknowledges me. I hate to part with a few dollars, but it has to be done.

"Can I use your bathroom?" I ask.

Without speaking or looking at me, he points at a back corner of the store.

In the restroom I quickly cut the bulk of my beard. I don't like my hair. It's long, past my shoulders. I always tie it back with a string to keep it out of my face when I'm working. I consider cutting it but decide to leave it as it is to save time. Using the perfumy soap from the restroom dispenser, I shave.

My hand shakes, but I get it all off and rinse the hair down the drain. I study my face. I can't remember the last time I didn't have a beard. Liam has cut it and then shaved it occasionally in the past, saying I scare the customers. My cheeks are smooth and the touch of my fingers on my skin feels odd. I pull the tag off the hat and try unsuccessfully to maneuver my hair up under it. I give up, then I use the toilet and double-check that I've left the sink clean.

As I head to the exit, I see the teenager on his phone again. There is one gray-haired woman near the kitchen supplies, but no one else is in the store now. I scan the parking lot. No white truck.

I stop at the check stand, and the teenager does a double take.

"You shaved."

I guess he did look at me after all. "Yeah, it was itchy. Can you look something up on your phone for me?" I'd pondered how to find my parents. I knew there was a world of information available through phones, but I'd never used one myself. I'd only watched.

The teenager frowned. "Where's yours?"

"Being repaired."

"What do you need?"

I give him a name.

"Like look up his phone number?"

A phone number won't help me; I don't have a phone. "How about an address?"

"In Bend?"

"Yes." I mentally cross my fingers.

He taps on his phone for a minute and then shows me the screen.

"That's current?" I ask.

He shrugs. "Hard to say." He scrolls the screen a bit. "No other addresses are listed, so most likely."

My family is still here.

"You did that so fast."

"You can easily find addresses if you know the name and city."

I'm swamped with a paralyzing need to see them. "Do you sell maps?"

The teenager scratches his head. "Like a paper map? One of those folded things? No one uses those."

I know the address but have no idea how to get there.

"Hang on." The teen taps on his phone a few times and then shows me the screen again.

It's a map with a red dot and the address. It means nothing to me. I have no idea where that is. I heavily exhale and run a hand across my mouth. I don't know what to do.

He sighs and then touches the screen again. A blue line suddenly marks the route. The same mapping tool Liam uses to locate the homes for our electrical work.

"Want me to print this for you?"

"Please."

"Hang on."

Two minutes later I walk out of the store and stand in the sun, still in shock, my mind racing, my new hat on my head, and the map clenched in my hand. It says I can walk there in two hours.

Today I will see them.

How many other lies was I told?

A white truck passes on the busy street, and I whip out of my shock. It's not Liam, but I've been distracted for several minutes. What if he'd walked in the store while I talked to the clerk? I'd completely forgotten that I need to hide. I shudder, imagining his anger if he finds me.

I need to stay alert.

I turn to continue my run behind the store, thinking about my parents. I have a new energy. A different energy than when I ran from the electrical job. I try to understand why it is different, and I realize I haven't felt it in decades.

It's hope.

38

It was burger Friday at Rowan's parents'. Even though they'd just gotten together not long ago for Malcolm's birthday, no one ever considered changing burger Friday. It was tradition. The family believed in keeping its traditions, so special attention was given to keeping the menu different from on Malcolm's day. Local microbrews were the drink of choice, and her mom always made a giant leafy salad with every green in season. Dessert was usually Tillamook Mudslide ice cream.

Evan messaged that he was minutes away as Rowan opened her parents' front door and let Thor inside. Her smile from Evan's text faded as she stepped inside the house and felt the heavy atmosphere. Her dad was speaking in hushed tones to Ivy on the couch while West was curled up in an easy chair across the room, completely focused on his tablet. Ivy had already been furious about Adam when Rowan called. She'd made a hotel reservation far outside of town even though her parents and sisters had offered their homes. "I won't let Adam affect your lives too," she'd said.

It already has.

"Hi, honey." Her mom took the bag of ice cream from Rowan's hand and kissed her on the cheek. Thor had already made a beeline for West. He adored the boy.

"Is Ivy okay?" asked Rowan.

"She will be," said Miriam. "She's frustrated." She glanced at the pair on the couch. "And your father is ready to skin the man if he ever sets eyes on him."

"Me too. Where's Iris?"

"She texted. She'll be here in a few minutes. Turn on some music. This house feels like a funeral parlor."

Rowan agreed. She used an app to start some Fitz and the Tantrums on her parents' sound system, knowing West would immediately react. Moments later West set aside his tablet, popped out of the chair, and started spinning while clapping his hands as commanded by the song. Everyone stopped to watch. It was impossible to not smile at the energetic performance. By the time the next song started, the mood was lighter, and smiles were everywhere.

That song always works.

Iris strode into the house and set two bags of potato chips on the kitchen counter. She frowned at the sight of West teaching a line dance to his mom and grandfather. She jerked her head at her mom and Rowan, and the three of them moved into the foyer.

"What's wrong?" Rowan immediately asked.

"When I was driving down this street, some guy darted from the sidewalk behind some rhododendrons three houses down. As I drove by, I spotted him peeking at me." She looked at her mom. "Whose house is that?"

Her mother already had her phone out. "Linda's. I'm texting to ask if she sees someone in her front yard."

Iris met Rowan's eyes, and she knew her sister shared her concern.

Is it Adam again?

"This is ridiculous," said Rowan in a low voice. "We can't jump every time we see a stranger on the street."

"This is a close neighborhood," said her mother. "Everyone knows everybody. I rarely see anyone I don't know." Alarm crossed her face as she read a text. "Linda says someone is deliberately hiding in her bushes. A man she doesn't know."

"Have her call the police right now. Have her tell them we've had problems with a . . . stalker," said Rowan, hesitant to use the word but knowing it was accurate. "If that's Adam causing problems, I want him taken back to jail. Lock the back door," she ordered Iris as she grabbed the handle of the front door.

"Where are you going?" asked Miriam.

"I want to know if it's Adam," said Rowan. "I won't scare him off. I want him arrested when the police get here."

"Do you think that's smart?"

"I'll keep my distance. I just need a glimpse."

"We need to tell your father."

Rowan paused, agreeing that her father should know what was going on, but also knowing that her father would probably try to catch the guy before the police arrived. "It could be no one," she said. "I don't think he and Ivy need to know yet."

Iris caught her words as she returned from locking the back door. She'd joined the line dance lesson for a few seconds on her way back, acting as if nothing were going on three houses down. "I agree with Rowan. They'll go ballistic. Let the police handle it first."

Rowan opened the front door and found herself staring at Evan. His eyes narrowed as he studied her face.

"What's wrong?" he asked.

Rowan stepped through the door and closed it before her mother or Iris could say a word. "Come with me for a minute." She led him to the driveway and peered up the street. A county deputy's car was slowly coming their way. "That was fast! There must have been a unit nearby."

"Rowan," Evan said, impatience in his tone.

She faced him. "Sorry. Iris saw a guy dash off the sidewalk three houses down when he saw her car, and then the neighbor spotted him hiding in her front yard's bushes. We told her to call the police since Adam is out of jail and who knows what he'll try."

"Adam?" Evan took a few steps to get a better look down the street. The cruiser had parked three houses down and two deputies had gotten out and were scanning the area.

Rowan saw a movement from the corner of her eye. Turning her head, she saw a man duck behind a vehicle two houses away but across the street.

Did he see me spot him?

"Evan," she said in a low voice. "A man is hiding behind that little silver sedan in the second driveway."

He immediately looked.

"You can't see him. He dropped down when I looked at him. It was deliberate."

"Was it Adam?"

"I don't know."

"I'll go talk to the deputies." Evan handed her his jacket, exposing his shoulder holster, and walked to the county cruiser.

Rowan kept her gaze glued on the silver car across the street, waiting for more movement. She heard voices and turned to see that the rest of her family had come out of the house. Her father had West by the hand, and she could tell by the look on his face that he knew exactly why she was standing outside. Ivy's eyes were hard as she approached Rowan.

Rowan knew to stay put. The situation had suddenly become a police action.

"You think Adam is in the neighborhood?" Ivy asked Rowan. She looked ready to go Adam hunting and rip his limbs off with her bare hands.

"There's a man hiding behind a car down the street," said Rowan, gently taking her sister's arm to keep her in place. "Evan and the deputies will check it out. We need to stay here."

The rest of her group moved to watch. "Maybe we should go inside," said Rowan. "We don't know—"

A shout cut her off, and the three men broke into a run. The man behind the silver car had sprinted up the street with Evan and the two deputies tearing after him.

"Was that Adam?" Ivy asked, pulling against Rowan's hold.

"I couldn't tell."

The man vanished around the corner of another house, and the three law enforcement officers went after him.

39

My heart pounds and my lungs beg for air. I can't run much farther.

I dart between two homes and glance back.

Now there are four men after me. Three of them cops.

If they catch me, they'll eventually find out about the bodies.

I should have left as soon as I saw the police car. But I couldn't bring myself to leave.

"Deschutes County sheriff! Stop!"

I pour on more speed, but I know my reserves are almost gone. I turn and run across the wide yard of a home. I risk another look back.

A man in jeans is right behind me, his eyes intense.

I take two more running strides, and his weight hits my back. I go down and land on my chest with him on top of me. Air is forced out of my chest, and suddenly the other cops are there. They grab my arms, wrenching them back, and handcuffs clank, digging into my wrists.

The man pushes himself off me, and I gasp for breath.

I bury my face in the grass. It's over.

I'm going to prison.

Hands dig in all the pockets of my jeans. "Where's your ID?"

I don't answer. I know men carry wallets, but I've never needed one. I don't have credit cards or a license. They toss my cash on the grass near my face.

The folded bundle seems so small. Besides the clothes I'm wearing, it's all I have in the entire world.

I was so close.

The men haul me up to a sitting position, and the one without a uniform squats in front of me. "What's your name?"

I say nothing and stare at the grass.

"What were you doing behind that car?"

I say nothing.

"Why'd you run when you saw us?"

I shrug and keep my gaze down.

"Do you know Adam Thornton?"

I glance up and shake my head, wondering who that is.

"You sure?" The man's voice is rough, and he's still breathing hard.

"Don't know him," I mutter.

"How about Ivy Wolff?"

I straighten and meet his gaze.

"That got your attention," says the brown-eyed man.

I realize he must be a cop too. He has a shoulder holster with a gun, and the other police stand back, letting him speak. Maybe he's their boss.

"What's your name?" he asks again.

I want to tell him, but I've had a new name for a long time, and I've been warned to never tell my old name. I always say Tim.

But part of me doesn't care if I go to prison.

At least I'll be away from Liam.

"My name is Tim Smith."

The man scowls. "Bullshit."

He doesn't believe me.

Liam told me no one will believe anything I say.

I shut my eyes. I was so close.

I've been stupid to think I could walk up and talk to them. My family doesn't want me back. They never even looked for me. That must have been the one thing Liam told me the truth about.

"Get to your feet, Tim *Smith*." They grab me by the upper arms and easily lift me.

"Dude doesn't weigh anything," says one of the cops.

"Didn't anyone tell you to never run from cops, Tim Smith?" asks the man in the shoulder holster.

I shake my head and they all snicker. "Right," says one.

I glance at them. I've always been told to stay away from police at all costs and don't understand why they laughed.

They walk me across the yard toward where I ran between the homes.

"Where's your car?" asks the cop on my left.

"Don't have one."

"Then how'd you get here?"

"Walked."

"From where?"

I'm not going to tell them that I walked for hours from the outskirts on one side of Bend to this little neighborhood on the other. And there's no way I'll tell them where I live.

"Run all the plates of the vehicles parked on the streets nearby," says the shoulder-holster man. "We'll figure out where he's from . . . and his name."

"No car. I walked."

"Right."

We reach the street and move toward the house. There is still a group of people in front, watching me be escorted in handcuffs. I lower my head, unable to meet their eyes, and my feet are suddenly heavy. The cop on my left pulls harder on my arm as I slow.

This isn't how I dreamed this would go.

I risk a glance up as we get closer. All are staring—no, glaring—at me. Each one is angry.

"Is he with Adam?"

The speaker is a young woman with dark hair. Her arm is entwined tightly with the arm of another young woman with the same face. Twins.

They're beautiful.

I drop my gaze, realizing I stared too long.

"He says he doesn't know Adam," says the shoulder-holster man. "And claims his name is Tim Smith."

"I don't know him," a man with silver hair says.

They don't see who I am.

I don't know whether to be relieved or sad.

The twin in the black dress steps closer, and I meet her gaze. "Did Adam send you?"

I don't know her name.

Pain shows in her eyes, and I ache to take it away. I shake my head and try to project truth in my gaze. I don't want her to think I'm a liar.

One of the cops pulls my arm, trying to turn me away. "We'll get him out of here and question him some more."

I clench my teeth and hold my ground, facing the group. It's my last chance for a memory, and I soak in their faces one by one, my gaze memorizing them all.

I meet the older woman's eyes and see a flicker of confused recognition. Her mouth opens but she closes it, giving a tiny shake of her head.

She can't place me.

I let the officers turn me around and walk away. This is how it ends. At least I have new memories to haunt my dreams at night.

"Malcolm?"

It's my mother's voice behind me. Uncertain and quiet. I haven't heard her say my name in decades.

I stop but can't turn in the officers' firm grips.

"What are you doing, Miriam?" asks my dad.

My mother comes around and steps in front of the three of us, her hand thrust in a halt command. She is wide-eyed as she stares at me. "Malcolm."

This time it isn't a question. I give a tiny nod.

She knows me.

She lunges forward and wraps her arms around me. Caught by surprise, the officers are too late to block her and try to pull her away.

She hangs on. *"Malcolm!"*

I lower my head against hers, and her scent opens an assault of memories in my head.

I am home.

40

"Mom!" Rowan shouted as her mom hugged the handcuffed stranger with the long hair.

She's lost her mind.

Her dad was beside her mom, trying to unwind her arms from the man.

"Stop it!" Miriam told him, pushing him away. "Can't you see it's Malcolm!"

Her dad froze, staring at the stranger.

Malcolm?

Impossible. Mom's overwrought.

Her heart in her throat, Rowan strode around to see the stranger's face, her sisters on her tail.

Her dad pushed the man's hair out of his face, and Rowan knew instantly it was her brother.

He looks like Dad.

"Malcolm?" she choked out as familiar brown eyes met hers. He immediately dropped his gaze, his head down. "Look at me!"

Evan touched her arm. "What's going on?"

Rowan couldn't look away from her brother. His hair was long and greasy, half falling out of a low ponytail. He wore battered jeans and tennis shoes that looked decades old. He was impossibly thin, his clothes hanging on him. Tears ran down his face as he lifted his head and made eye contact again.

It's him.

It made no sense. Jerry Chiavo had confessed to Malcolm's death.

Her dad hugged him. "Get the fucking cuffs off of him! It's my *son*!"

"It's Malcolm," she whispered to Evan. "He's *alive*."

"Are you sure it's him?" Evan frowned.

"I'm positive!" Rowan watched, drinking in the sight of her ecstatic parents.

No one expected this day.

Her father was crying now, and her mother hugged him from behind. The deputies holding Malcolm looked to Evan for guidance.

The twins hung back, confusion on their faces. "It can't be," said Iris, gripping Ivy's hand.

"Uncuff him?" Evan asked Rowan. "He ran away from us and won't answer our questions."

"Clearly he's scared of something," Rowan said, her gaze locked on her brother. He still hadn't said anything and struggled to hold eye contact with either parent for more than a second.

"Then I'll leave them on until we have some answers. But I'll link another pair to make it more comfortable."

"He's too thin to have much strength," argued Rowan.

"Trust me when I say you should never judge a suspect's strength by how they look." He asked an officer for another set of cuffs, then went behind Malcolm to remove a cuff from one wrist, replace it with the new one, and then link the old and new together. "Do you want to talk with him inside?" Evan asked Rowan's parents. Neighbors were coming out of their homes to stare.

"Yes!" said her mother. "Please bring him in."

Rowan was suddenly struck dumb, unable to take her gaze from her brother.

Malcolm is home.

41

I'm overwhelmed and exhausted. Feeling paralyzed.

There are too many faces, too many eyes, and too many people speaking. I struggle to look people in the eye, but it's too hard. Eye contact was considered confrontational and rarely allowed. Every time I realize I'm staring at my shoes, I force myself to look up.

And get overwhelmed again.

I walked inside my parents' home with my hands cuffed behind me, and the setting was unfamiliar. The house was the same on the outside, although it seemed smaller than I remembered. Inside I stopped before entering the huge family room with all the tall windows, stunned because I didn't remember it being this big. Then I realized the kitchen used to be separated from the big room by a wall, but now everything is in one giant space.

I didn't know where to sit. Everything was too nice. I wanted to sit on the floor, but the deputy guided me to the couch. I sat carefully on the edge, terrified I'd get it dirty, and instinctively waiting for someone to yell at me to get down.

My parents sit on either side of me as a deputy watches us from the kitchen. He can relax; I'm not going anywhere, but I can see in his face it's useless to tell him that. My parents keep touching me. A hand on my arm. A touch to my face. A hug. I want to tell them to stop, but

I also want them to never stop. No one has physically touched me in years . . . decades.

It feels wrong, yet I also crave it.

The twins pace the room, stealing glances at me and tapping on their phones. The boy, West, sits in an easy chair in the corner, staring at me. Squeezed into the chair with him is a black dog. I know it's Rowan's dog, Thor. I memorized his face and name from the newspaper.

Rowan crosses the room and sits in a big soft chair directly in front of me. She has a subtle limp, and I remember how badly her leg was broken. Is that why she limps? She has cried and smiled and laughed since seeing me. Sometimes all at one time. My parents have done the same.

I'm uncomfortable with the emotions zinging through the room. I feel like a giant spotlight is on me, and I want to hide in the cool, welcoming dark.

My gaze goes to the fireplace, and from deep inside my memories, I feel a little thrill as I recognize it. It still stretches to the high ceiling, covered in smooth, large, irregular rocks that I remember tracing with my hands, searching for the most unusual one. The jagged wood mantel is different, but I can't remember what it looked like before.

Then I see the school portrait on the mantel. I get to my feet and move closer as the room goes silent. I study the young boy in the picture. It's me. I was innocent. So unaware of the evil in the world. But I don't remember this particular photo. I turn to my mother and find her watching me, happiness radiating from her eyes. And it hits me.

They never forgot me.

My knees shake and my vision narrows. I feel strong hands guide me back to the couch. My father's hands. I hear Liam's hated voice in my head, stating over and over that my family didn't want me.

"How old am I?" I blurt. I haven't really spoken. I was bombarded with questions at first, but they stopped after I put my head on my knees, wanting to cover my ears.

My mother's eyes fill. "You're thirty-two."

I'm shocked. "I'm old."

I've lost so many years.

The twins tentatively sit on a large stuffed square beside the couch. I have seen both of them cry, but they have also held something back. I felt their hugs, but something was missing. They are as unfamiliar to me as this room, and I suspect I feel the same to them. Mentally I know they're my family, but the emotional connection isn't there yet. Not like I feel with my parents and Rowan. I look from one to the other, still searching their faces for something I recognize, and I see hints of my father around their eyes and mouths. "Which of you . . . who is who?" I bungle the question.

"I'm Ivy," says the one in the black dress.

"West is your son?" The boy was clinging to her earlier.

"Yes."

I memorize her face, repeating her name in my head. I look at Iris and do the same. "The two of you were so tiny, Iris." Her dark hair is long and wavy, a contrast to her twin's perfectly shaped hairstyle.

I can't get out of my mind how beautiful all three of my sisters are. I feel like a filthy dog next to them.

I stare at my shoes again.

"Your birthday was just the other day," said my mother. "We had a party for you. We hold one every year."

I missed twenty-five birthdays with them.

I look at her and immediately drop my gaze. "Did you look for me?"

My mother clutches my arm. "Oh, honey. We searched hard for you for years. We never gave up hope."

"I still go search every year," Rowan says quietly.

I glance at her. "I thought you were dead. Killed by wild animals."

She catches a breath. "I was found by a search dog and handler. They kept looking for you too."

247

I shudder and lower my head. "I thought I caused your death by leaving you alone."

She's suddenly kneeling before me, lifting my chin, making me look at her. Her face is wet with tears. "You were a seven-year-old child trying to save your little sister who had a broken leg. You tried *so* hard, Malcolm. You carried me so far. But you were right to hide me and go find help. It was the logical thing to do," she says forcefully. "You were so brave for a child. It boggles my mind what you did for me."

I screw my eyes shut, remembering how terrified I was that day when I realized I'd lost the path back to her. "I'm so sorry."

"What are you sorry for?" She shakes her head. "You did nothing wrong."

She's right. But I'm accustomed to apologizing for every little thing even when it's not my fault.

"Malcolm." Rowan moves her hands to my knees. My hands are still cuffed behind my back, making me lean forward at an awkward angle. "Look at me."

I try. I drop her gaze and then try again. It's almost physically impossible for me.

"Where have you been all this time, Malcolm?" she asks softly.

I can't speak and I close my eyes. Shudders rack my body. It's too hard. I want this moment with my family to stretch on and on, but if I tell them where I've been, they'll find out about the bodies. And I'll be taken away again. This time to prison.

"Did he find you that day in the woods?" It's a whisper, and her voice shakes.

He was so mean to her. She was just a little girl. I want to cry for the time she suffered with him. I'd go back if it meant her memories of that time would be erased.

I give a small nod. My eyes still closed.

My parents suck in breaths, and my father utters a long curse.

"What happened to you after Jerry was caught?" she asked.

I don't want to tell her about Liam, so I say nothing. I open my eyes. I'm miserable and long to share everything but know it will end this amazing day.

A day I dreamed about for twenty-five years.

Rowan must sense my reluctance, so she asks a different question. "Malcolm, why didn't you come before now?"

I take a deep breath. "I couldn't escape until today."

I swear the air is sucked from the room. The silence is deafening.

"You were held captive all that time?" my father asks, his voice tight.

I can't look him in the eye, but I nod.

"That's why you didn't know your age." My mother sobs, burying her face in her hands.

"Who kept you?" Rowan asks.

My pulse pounds in my head, and I'm suddenly dizzy, but I force myself to look at her and decide to tell the truth. "There were two of them, Rowan," I whisper. "Two men played those torture games with us. Jerry and Liam. Only one of them got caught."

"Take his cuffs off," Rowan says in a teary voice, looking at the deputy. The deputy glances at the man she called Evan, and he gives a small nod. I can tell there is something between Evan and Rowan. They look at each other as if they can read each other's thoughts.

The cuffs click a few times, and my arms are stiff as I rub my wrists.

"You are safe and home now," Dad tells me. "You will always have a place here."

I'm touched and tears well in my eyes.

How many times have I dreamed of this moment?

Home. *Real* family. Safety.

Thor comes and shoves his nose in my hand. I'm surprised, and I hesitantly touch the dog's head.

"He likes you," Rowan says. "He's very gentle."

The dog sets his head on my leg, and I run my hands over Thor's back, sinking my hands into the fur. I can't hold back my smile. I slide off the sofa onto the floor, and Thor tries to sit in my lap.

I wrap my arms around the dog, close my eyes, and I finally can relax.

"Wow," Rowan said. "I've only seen Thor do that with kids."

"I know he's a search dog," I tell her. "I read it in the newspaper. There was a picture of you and Thor. That's how I discovered you weren't dead and decided to escape."

Her mouth hangs open in a large O.

"Knowing you were alive gave me a reason to leave. I hated it there."

"I know," she whispers. "It was hell on earth."

"You have no idea."

42

Hours later the twins had gone home, Evan and the deputies had left, and Rowan's parents had gone to bed. Everyone was exhausted both mentally and emotionally. She and Malcolm had continued to talk as the people disappeared one by one.

"Do you want me to leave so you can go to bed?" she asked him, worried she was keeping him from getting much-needed rest. Thor had fallen asleep, curled up at their feet.

Malcolm glanced in the direction of the stairs. "Can you come up with me for a few minutes?"

"Of course."

Upstairs he hesitantly walked down the hall, pausing at a bathroom and nodding as if acknowledging that was where it should be. He moved past the bedroom that had belonged to the girls and stopped at his old room, pushing the door fully open. Thor entered ahead of them, sniffing at the floor.

Rowan bit her lip, wondering what was going through Malcolm's head. "It's a guest room now. Mom and Dad put all your things in storage." She gave a nervous laugh. "They did the same with our stuff when me and the twins moved out. Our room is full of exercise equipment, though." She spotted a small pile of men's clothing on the bed that her mother must have left for him.

The room was decorated in relaxing green and blue shades. A queen-size bed with a quilt a friend of their mom's had sewn. A few nature prints on the wall. A tall dresser and a chair.

The colorful boy's room with Teenage Mutant Ninja Turtles posters and sheets was long gone.

"Want me to go now?" Rowan asked.

"No. Stay for a bit, please." Malcolm sat on the bed, looking haunted as he gazed about the room. "It's changed a lot. So many times I thought about how much I missed my bed."

Her heart cracking, Rowan sat beside her brother and wrapped both arms around him, leaning heavily into his side, her head on his shoulder.

How many times did we sit like this in the shed to keep warm and fight off our fears?

He set a hand gently on her arm that was clasped across his chest, and she felt a faint quake go through his body.

"It's over, Malcolm. You're safe."

"I was remembering how we sat like this . . . there . . ." His voice was almost too quiet for her to hear. He'd been stiff when she first hugged him, but now he relaxed. "It was so weird seeing the twins," he said. "I've never been able to imagine them as grown. In my dreams they were faceless adults or still toddlers."

Rowan squeezed him harder. "They're fantastic women. Strong and smart."

"And seeing Dad so old. Is that how I'll look in thirty years?"

She laughed. "Probably. Trust me, it could be a lot worse. He looks great for his age. Both him and Mom. We've inherited good genes."

They sat silently for a long while as Thor lay on the floor, watching them with attentive eyes.

"Do you want to talk about . . . them?" Rowan asked. "Jerry was arrested five years later. No one knew there had been two men."

"Looking back, I realized there had been two men with us while we were blindfolded," Malcolm said. "Liam wore red laces in his hiking boots. Jerry did not. I'd see the boots below the blindfold sometimes."

Rowan sucked in a breath. "I remember."

"Liam got Jerry arrested. He bragged about it." His body started to violently shake, and he covered his face with his hands.

"What is it?" Rowan asked, aching to take away his fear and hurt.

"They made me do awful things, Rowan. If the police ever find out, I'll go to prison."

She sucked in a breath. "What did they make you do?"

He wiped tears from his face. "Liam killed two women while I was there. I don't know how or why he did it. I knew better than to ask questions, but he made me dig a grave and help him bury them. I'm an accomplice, Rowan. There's no getting around that."

Rowan straightened. "You said 'a grave' but two women. They were in one?"

He nodded. "Two women in the same grave a couple years apart. I must have been eighteen or so. Liam made me help him take them through the forest in a wheelbarrow. It was so hard. It'd take all day." He took a long breath. "The second time, he made me dig up the grave of the first woman, saying it'd be easier to put the second there since the dirt would be looser. Oh my God, Rowan. The smell of that old grave . . ."

"He forced you, Malcolm. You had no say in the matter. No district attorney would dream of bringing charges against you. You don't need to worry about that."

"That's not all," he whispered.

She waited a long moment as Malcolm struggled to form words to continue his story.

"There was a boy. Elijah," he finally said. "He was ten like me. They made us fight like they did with you and me." He cried, tears dripping on her arm across his chest.

She squeezed tighter, knowing the story wouldn't end well.

"They killed him and made me help bury him, Rowan. I never even got to know him. All I knew was his name and age. They kept us apart. I wanted so bad to have someone else there with me." He shook his head. "But why would I wish that hell on someone else? I'm a horrible person."

"No!" She took his head in her hands, turning it toward her. The pain in his eyes broke her heart. "You were a lonely and abused child. It's normal to feel that way. There was nothing wrong with you."

"I see his face every day, Rowan. It's my fault he's dead. I don't know what I did to make them choose me over him." He took a shuddering breath. "But there were many days I wished I had been killed instead."

"It's not your fault, Malcolm. Those men are responsible for their own actions. *They* killed him, not you. And I'm so glad you're alive. You made it out of there and back to us." She wiped his tears, crushed that he'd been consumed with such dark thoughts. "Were the two women buried near Elijah?"

He nodded.

She hugged him again. "We found their bodies, Malcolm. I thought the boy might be you, but now because you know his name and age, we'll be able to tell his family and give them some closure. Not knowing if someone is dead or alive is torture."

Malcolm exhaled heavily. "I've carried the image of his dead body with me for years. I thought I was digging my own grave at first."

"Oh, Malcolm." Rage flashed and hatred for his captors filled her. She continued to hold him, and they sat like that for a long time. "It's over," she'd occasionally whisper.

His head started to droop, and she encouraged him to go to bed.

She slowly moved down the stairs, her heart heavy, Thor beside her. *Will he ever be able to heal?*

43

The next morning, Rowan was playing fetch with Thor in her backyard, unable to get her conversation with Malcolm the night before out of her mind.

He was back. That was all that mattered.

Today the FBI would debrief Malcolm so they could find Liam, who'd held Malcolm captive. Rowan wanted him arrested too. And then tortured the way he'd tortured her and Malcolm.

She wanted him to pay. In pain.

Rowan had promised to be at Malcolm's side for the interview and hoped he could handle the stressful discussion. He seemed so fragile.

Rowan hurled the ball as far as she could with the launcher as her phone rang. She checked her screen and saw the call was from her mother.

"Hey, Mom." She watched Thor rocket across the grass. A black blur.

"*I can't find West!* I went inside for a minute and—"

"Wait!" Rowan clenched the phone, her nerves hitting high alert. "He's gone? What happened? Are you sure?"

"Your father is looking for him, but he was in the backyard on the swing set, and when I went back out he was gone! I called and called." Tears were in her mother's voice.

"Crap! And it's not like him to hide," said Rowan, her throat constricting.

Adam.

"I only left West for a minute to use the bathroom! He was in our own fenced backyard!"

"Hang up and call the police, Mom. *Now.*"

"I don't want to bother them if—"

"*Bother them!* You can cancel the call if Dad finds him. And give them Adam's address too and explain what happened the other night. Does Ivy know?" Thor returned with the ball in his mouth, dropped it at Rowan's feet, and then sat, his ears and eyes stating he expected another throw.

"No. I called you first." Her mom's voice cracked. "I couldn't tell her! She warned us—"

"I'll call her." Sweat beaded on the back of Rowan's neck. "Is she at work?"

"Yes. Both she and Iris are at the salon today. Your father is furious. He said he's going to kill Adam if he doesn't find West."

"Hide his keys—and yours too. *Do not* let him go to Adam's house. That asshole has a gun. Let the police handle it. Hang up and call them *now*," she repeated. Rowan ended the call. She hurled Thor's ball again and then shakily called Iris, knowing her sister was the best person to tell Ivy.

"Hi, Rowan."

Rowan heard the salon's music and chatter in the background. "Iris, it's important that you don't look at Ivy during this call, and I need you to find a quiet place to talk."

Her sister was silent for a second. "Okay. I'll go to the break room." Ten seconds later a door closed, and the salon sounds vanished. "What happened?" she asked sharply.

"West is missing. Mom just called me. Police should be on the way there by now."

"*West?* Shit!" Iris's voice rose. "I'm going to kill that fucking Adam!"

"We need to tell Ivy, but I know her first reaction will be to go to Adam's."

"Yeah, it will be. She'll go skin him alive, the bastard. He's only doing this to upset her."

"You need to get Ivy's keys. *Do not* let her go there. Can you take her to Mom's? She shouldn't drive anywhere right now."

"I'm already in her locker and digging through her purse," Iris said grimly. "I won't let her get near Adam, but I can't promise I won't castrate him first."

"Can the two of you leave the salon?"

"We'll make it happen. Our clients will understand."

"I'll meet you at Mom's."

"Rowan . . . if something happens to West . . . Ivy will never be the same," Iris whispered hesitantly.

"Nothing will happen. Adam won't hurt his son." Rowan swallowed hard as she remembered how she'd scoffed at Evan's similar comment. She ended the call and knelt next to Thor, who was waiting for another throw. She gave him a big hug, imagining how she'd feel if someone took him away.

"Hey, boy. Let's go look for our favorite nephew, okay?"

She strongly suspected Adam had taken West, but Thor could confirm that West hadn't wandered somewhere in the neighborhood.

Adam won't hurt West, right?

Twenty minutes later she arrived at her parents' home as Evan pulled up. She'd called him on the way over, and he'd promised to be there as soon as possible. Two sheriff's cruisers were parked on the street, and one deputy was talking to her parents in front of their home. She spotted two other deputies at the front door of a house farther down the street.

But deep inside, Rowan knew West wasn't in the neighborhood; Adam had taken him.

Iris's car wasn't there, but Rowan knew the twins would arrive soon. Her house was closer to their parents' home than the salon was.

"How are you?" Evan pulled her into his arms for a hug before they walked up the drive, then gave Thor a pat.

"I'm angry," said Rowan. He smelled good, and she relaxed into him, resting her overactive brain for a few seconds. "I'm going to kill him."

"You'll have to wait in line," said Evan. "I would like a few minutes alone with him too."

"Ivy will take care of it before either of us. She may be small, but she's a mama bear when it comes to West."

"As she should be." Evan looked up the driveway at her parents and a deputy. Malcolm was keeping his distance from the group, hovering near the garage, watching the deputy with a suspicious gaze. "Let's find out what they know so far." He took her hand, and they went to join the group.

Her mom's eyes were red and her lashes wet. Restrained fury showed in her father's gaze. "Little bastard," he said. "I never liked him."

Evan asked if a description of Adam and West had been put out yet.

"Yes," said the deputy. "I got a recent photo of West from the Wolffs and they described what he is wearing. We sent a unit to knock on the father's door, but no one is there. No car either. We put out a BOLO on the make, model, and color of Adam Thornton's vehicle, and the FBI is sending over an agent."

Iris's Jeep parked at the curb, and Ivy was out the door before the vehicle was turned off. The deputy blinked as Ivy ran up the driveway in a navy dress with a full skirt, looking like a movie star from the 1950s with her hair perfectly coiffed. Her red lipstick was half-gone, and mascara was smeared under her eyes.

Her angry gaze was focused on Rowan. "How dare you tell Iris to steal my keys! I have every right to go confront that bastard and get my boy back!"

Rowan held up a hand. "The police already went to Adam's house. He's not there."

Ivy opened and closed her mouth, frustration in her eyes. "But still—"

"I knew you'd be in no condition to drive and would try to go there anyway. I'd tell Iris to do it again too."

Her sister pressed her lips together, but her eyes still snapped with anger.

"Rowan told your mom to take my keys too," said her dad. He snorted. "It actually was a good thing. I was ready to go confront the asshole."

Malcolm had moved closer to the group when Ivy arrived. His hands were thrust in his pockets, and a haunted look was in his eyes. Rowan met his gaze, seeing he was uncomfortable and worried but clearly had some desire to connect with the family. She took his hand and squeezed.

"I'm sorry, Ivy," he said quietly.

"Thanks, Malcolm," Ivy said. "You're lucky you've never met the jerk."

Their mom hugged Ivy. "I'm so sorry, honey. It's all my fault. You warned me, and I thought I was being so careful."

"It's not your fault," Ivy and her dad said at the same time. Harrison put a hand on his wife's shoulder and squeezed.

"We'll find him," her dad promised.

"Did you come from work?" the deputy asked Ivy, who nodded. "Could West be at your house? Sometimes kids get it in their heads that they want to be somewhere else and just go."

"Only if he had wings," Ivy snapped. "I live on the other side of town."

"Your parents said he doesn't have a close friend in this neighborhood, correct?"

"Yes. There are very few kids here."

Rowan checked the deputies knocking on doors. They'd moved down two more houses. "I'd like to start a search with Thor now," she told the deputy.

He nodded. "I've seen you and your dog work before."

"Do you have something of West's?" she asked her mother.

"Yes, I haven't done his laundry from when he stayed the other day." Her mother dashed into the house.

Rowan looked at her family. "I'd like everyone to move inside to give Thor room to work without distractions. We'll start in the backyard since that's where Mom said West was last." They went into the house, and Miriam appeared with a small pair of tan shorts. Evan went with her as Rowan led Thor out back onto the deck and showed him the shorts. Thor sniffed them several times.

"Find it."

The dog went a few yards and scented the air. He leaped down over the deck's steps and zigzagged through the fenced yard. The fence was about six feet tall, and to see into the yard, someone would have to peer through a narrow space between the boards. Almost immediately Thor trotted to the swing set and circled a swing and then the slide. Then he lowered his nose and went to the tall gate on the west side of the house. He sat and looked over his shoulder at Rowan, his dark eyes begging.

/open/

"Looks like West went out the gate. Not surprised," said Rowan. She led Evan to the gate and praised Thor. The gate's latch was low enough for a child. Fingerprint dust covered part of its metal.

"Was the gate secured when they first searched for West?" asked Evan.

"Mom said it was. He could have gotten out by himself, but there's no way he could have latched it. From the outside, only an adult could have reached over the gate's top to fasten it."

Rowan opened the gate, and Thor went through at a slow trot. They followed the dog along the side of the house until he paused as he reached the driveway and lifted his nose. The dog went down the driveway and turned left on the sidewalk. He followed the sidewalk for several dozen yards and then stopped. He sniffed the air again and started to circle, clearly trying to pick up the scent again.

West isn't in the neighborhood.

"Most likely he got in a car at this spot. The scent is gone." She tried to feel encouraged. West was most likely with his father and hopefully safe.

They just need to find the bastard.

44

Evan was pleased to see Special Agent Eddie Peterson show up a few minutes later. The FBI had immediately jumped on the case, and Ivy and her parents talked with the agent as he took rapid notes. The family was stuck in place, waiting for news of West, hoping for a sighting of Adam or his vehicle.

Malcolm stood at the fireplace, touching several of the chimney facade's rocks, studying them with a faraway look in his eyes. He looked out of place in the nice home. He had showered and was wearing his father's shorts and shirt today. Both were way too large, and Evan suspected a belt was the only thing holding up the shorts.

His legs are impossibly thin.

Next to him on the sofa, Rowan rubbed her forehead. "It bothered me all night that Malcolm only escaped because he found out I was alive. What if he hadn't seen that newspaper article? He might have stayed forever."

"I can't imagine," Evan said.

She clapped her hands, and Thor darted to her side and sat. "I can't believe Jerry Chiavo had an accomplice and he held Malcolm prisoner all this time." Her voice was ragged with emotion. "I can't imagine what Malcolm put up with. I only experienced a few weeks of the cruelty, and it's affected me all my life. He's broken, Evan. He was tortured and isolated. I don't know if he'll ever fully recover." She wiped her eyes. "He didn't even know how old he was."

Evan hesitated, not ready to share that he suspected that, in the past, one of Jerry's accomplices had been Ken Steward.

But if Ken is dead, who is this Liam that Malcolm escaped from?

A question for the FBI to solve.

"I'm sorry, Rowan. At least he's here now and can recover. Your family has a lot of love to give." He embraced her as she shook with sobs.

Malcolm might know if Ken also spent time with Jerry.

Evan looked over Rowan's shoulder. Malcolm stood alone, staring at them, but rapidly dropped his gaze as their eyes met. A chill ran up Evan's spine.

I don't trust him. Something's not right with his story.

He wondered if Malcolm would tell him the truth about Ken or if he would cover things up as Jerry had.

I need to carefully consider how to ask him.

He suspected the wrong approach would make the man clam up forever.

Questions flared in Evan's mind.

If Ken Steward had been an accomplice of Jerry's, had he deliberately rescued Rowan twenty-five years earlier? Was it something Jerry had approved? Or had Ken acted on his own to get her out of the situation since her leg was broken?

Why not rescue Malcolm too?

Evan's gut told him Malcolm was holding something back. Something he would lie to protect.

Who is he protecting?

Evan and Noelle hadn't found solid evidence to link Ken to the recent murders of the three women. Yet. But he hadn't been ruled out either. Evan knew he couldn't tell Rowan that Ken was a suspect until he had concrete evidence. Noelle was working to discover where Ken might have met each of the three women. Ken's cell phone records—which they already had from his murder investigation—did place him in the very general location of where the first woman had last been seen and where the second woman's body was dumped.

It was weak evidence. Evan hesitated to even call it evidence.

Focus. West is the current priority.

"Let's go outside," said Rowan. "I can't just sit here doing nothing."

Evan led her out front, and she took several deep breaths. "I feel like I need to be doing more to find West."

Evan scanned the nearby homes. "I talked to the sergeant whose deputies did the initial search of the neighborhood. A lot of neighbors weren't home. They checked a few camera views of those that were, but none of them showed a vehicle on the street in our window of time. They can check more cameras as neighbors come home. We'll spot the vehicle," he said with a confidence he didn't feel.

"It was Adam," Rowan stated firmly. "Find him and we'll find West."

The boy had been missing for two hours, but it felt like much longer. Evan was pleased with the law enforcement response. The neighborhood had been partially searched, Adam Thornton's home had been visited, a BOLO was out for his vehicle, and the FBI had arrived.

"I saw a big green space with a lot of trees and brush about a quarter mile from here," Evan said. "I'll get a couple deputies to go through it."

"I can take Thor down there. He'll be faster and more thorough, and I'll feel like we're doing something."

"Good point. I'll go let the others know what we're going to do." Evan headed up the driveway.

"That bastard!"

Evan spun around at Rowan's curse. She was striding toward a silver Chevy pickup coming down the road. Evan's gaze dropped to the license plate.

That's Adam Thornton's truck.

Evan gestured at two deputies. "There's your BOLO!" The men immediately jogged toward the truck, and Evan followed.

The truck parked behind a deputy's cruiser, and Rowan yanked on the driver's door handle.

"Unlock it, Adam!" she shouted. Beside her Thor paced back and forth, picking up on Rowan's emotions. The driver said something to Rowan, but Evan couldn't hear it.

"*How could you do that to Ivy?* West is probably scared to death!"

The deputies positioned themselves to cover both sides of the truck, their hands on their weapons but not drawing them.

"Rowan, let the deputies handle it." Evan touched her shoulder, but she ignored him.

"Where is West?" she yelled at the driver. She put her face against her hands on the glass to peer into the back of the king cab. Inside the truck, Adam looked from deputy to deputy, clearly conflicted about what to do.

"Step back from the truck, ma'am," the closest deputy told Rowan.

She turned toward him. "That's him! That's Adam Thornton. He took West."

"Get back, ma'am. We'll take care of it."

Evan remembered that Adam had threatened Ivy with a gun. "He could be armed," he said in a low voice to Rowan.

Her face cleared. She grabbed Thor's harness and jogged to the driveway. Evan was right behind her.

She's more worried about Thor getting hurt than herself.

Her family, more deputies, and the FBI agent came out of the house to find the source of the shouts. Ivy immediately tried to dart toward the truck, but her father stopped her. She turned an angry face his way and tried to break free. Rowan rushed to help him contain her.

"West isn't in the truck," she told Ivy. "I already looked."

Ivy froze and searched Rowan's face. "Where is he?"

Evan's heart cracked at the sorrow and confusion in her tone. He glanced at Malcolm standing slightly removed from the family, watching the scene, confusion in his eyes.

"I don't know. The deputies will get him out and ask." Rowan put an arm around Ivy, and together the family watched as Adam got out of the truck with his hands on his head. Now there were four deputies around Adam. They ordered him to the ground.

"Ivy! Tell them I didn't do anything!" Adam yelled at their group as he got to his knees.

"Where is West, you fucking asshole!" she shouted back.

"I don't have him! I'm here because you left that screaming message about him on my voice mail. If my son is missing, I want to know what happened!"

"I don't believe him," muttered Ivy. "He hid him somewhere. Probably at a new girlfriend's house."

"If he's hiding West, why would he come here, where there are a bunch of police vehicles? He's too spineless to do that," Iris said, disgust in her voice.

"True," admitted Ivy.

"That's Adam Thornton?" Special Agent Peterson asked Evan.

"Yes. That's him."

Special Agent Peterson looked at Ivy. "Before we heard the shouting, you'd started to tell me about a recent incident with your ex. What happened?"

Ivy launched into a description of how a drunk Adam had broken West's window and then tried to stop the car as they left. The agent made more notes.

"Wait a minute." Malcolm's voice was quiet but caught everyone's attention. His haunted eyes looked at Ivy. "Did he break West's window two nights ago?"

"Yes." She frowned. "How did you know that?"

Malcolm ran his hands along his scalp and pulled on two fistfuls of his hair as he turned away. "No," he mumbled. "No, no, no."

But not before Evan spotted a flash of horror and comprehension on his face. "Malcolm. What's wrong?" he asked sharply.

Facing away from the group, the man shook his head, his hair still grasped in his hands.

His mother touched his back and walked around to face him. "What's wrong, Mal?"

He continued to shake his head. "I can't. I can't say it."

"What can't you say?" she asked in a tender voice, her gaze worried. "You're safe here."

"No. No, I'm not. Liam will find me. You'll find out what happened. I'll have to leave."

Evan exchanged a glance with Rowan. She looked as confused as he felt.

Malcolm knows something about the night Adam tried to break in.

The additional footprints.

Evan's breath hitched as he recalled the forensic tech pointing out where someone had stood in the dirt bed.

Was it Malcolm?

"Who will find you, Mal?" asked his mother. "We won't let anyone hurt you."

"*Liam* will." Malcolm turned away, pulling on handfuls of hair. "He'll put me in the box. He won't give me food for days," he muttered.

Malcolm suddenly whirled and pointed at Ivy. "You're my *sister*! That's why he thought it was a perfect plan! I'd do anything he ordered to protect your son. He knows that. He was counting on that connection to control me." His eyes were wide and his back stiff and straight, no hiding, no hunching over. Suddenly his face crumpled, and he covered it with his hands. "I'm sorry, Ivy. I didn't know. I had no idea that was your house that night or that he wanted your boy."

He knows who took West.

Evan's vision went red. Everyone seemed to fade away but Malcolm. He went to grab Malcolm's arm and order him to tell where West was, but Rowan gently caught his hand.

"You'll scare him," she said, holding his gaze.

She's right.

He took several calming breaths as Rowan turned to Malcolm.

"Can you tell us how to find West?"

Malcolm panted like a dog, hyperventilating. "I can't. I can't."

Thor suddenly appeared, pressing hard against Malcolm's leg. Evan glanced at Rowan, who looked surprised. Malcolm squatted next to the dog, sinking his hands into the fur as he had earlier. Then he pressed his face against Thor's neck, and the heaving of his chest slowed a fraction.

"I can't tell you how to get there," Malcolm said, his voice muffled against Thor. "But I can show you the way."

45

"Absolutely not!"

Outside the sheriff's department, Rowan watched Evan speak rapidly with SWAT team leader Vargas, his eyes hard, his posture stiff. Captain Vargas looked just as stubborn. Malcolm had stated he would only take them to where West was being held if Rowan and Thor also went. Then he'd shut down, burying his head in his knees and refusing to speak.

Vargas had an issue with a civilian and her dog on his scene. He'd already had a problem with Malcolm showing them the way instead of giving directions. He hadn't believed her brother didn't know street names and couldn't estimate miles.

The more Rowan had talked with her brother, the more she'd learned about the huge gaps in his knowledge and social skills. He could read but could barely carry on a conversation. He knew little of current events or how to use the internet. The man who'd imprisoned him hadn't allowed him in public until a few years before, and that had been so he could learn an electrician's trade because they needed the money, but Malcolm had been forbidden to leave his sight or speak with anyone.

Remembering how isolated they had been for weeks after their kidnapping, Rowan wasn't surprised at his lack of socialization or education.

Evan was arguing that she, Malcolm, and Thor would all stay far away from the action once they arrived.

"This man might be a killer," the captain told him. "This isn't an operation where a civilian's dog goes looking for a missing child. We will address the threat first. Then look for the boy. Understood?" He glanced Rowan's way and she gave a short nod.

Vargas was right. Thor wasn't a police search dog who knew how to take down criminals. She needed to let the SWAT team do what it was trained to do.

He acknowledged Rowan's agreement and strode away to his men.

Evan gave her a thumbs-up, a drawn expression on his face. They'd won, but there was a long, stressful day ahead of them.

Rowan glanced at Malcolm, who was sitting on a low brick wall, deliberately apart from everyone, Thor at his side. Her dog had stuck close to Malcolm for the past two hours, knowing he was needed. Rowan was surprised that Thor would leave her side for so long, but she was also very proud.

We'll find him his own dog when this is over.

Malcolm had a lot to learn and experience. Rowan was overwhelmed when she thought about his future. But the important part was that he was here. They'd tackle each challenge as it came.

"Let's go!" Captain Vargas hollered at his men, who loaded into the SWAT vehicle. A command center the size of a motor home was ready to follow.

The captain, Evan, Malcolm, Rowan, and Thor were to ride in a Suburban, Malcolm giving directions. Once the captain knew the location of the building in the forest, he'd pull back and formalize a plan with his men.

The group loaded into the Suburban, Malcolm in front with the captain, and set off.

Rowan blew out a breath, trying to slow her pounding heart.

Hang on, West.

"Turn left onto the highway," I tell the captain.

He is angry, his jaw tight. He's told me to speak up three times. I feel as if I'm back with Liam.

It is familiar, and I relax a fraction.

I find assholes comforting?

Even I know there is something twisted in that logic.

My stomach churns, and I taste acid on the back of my tongue. I'm sweating, and I dab at my temples with the hem of my shirt. I risk a glance back at Rowan and make eye contact with Thor. The dog sits on the bench seat between Rowan and Evan, his ears turned toward me. Something eases in my chest. Thor doesn't ask me questions, doesn't have expectations, doesn't look at me with confusion in his eyes.

But all the people do.

No wonder I'm drawn to him. He brings peace in this noisy new world.

I turn my attention to the road. "We'll drive this for quite a while."

"How long is 'quite a while'?" the captain snaps.

I cringe, instinctively ducking my head. I inhale deeply and remind myself he is trying to help. "I'm not sure. We'll pass an odd lava rock formation on the left and take the next turn. I don't know its name. Might just have a number."

The captain checks the position of the SWAT vehicle in his mirrors and repeats what I said over a radio.

"Copy." The response crackles loudly in the vehicle.

I close my eyes and fight against waves of nausea.

I don't want to go back.

Rowan and Evan swear I'll be safe. That they won't let him near me, but my anxiety tells me a different story. It says I'll soon be back in the box with Liam yelling what an idiot I am for thinking I could escape.

Shudders shake me in my seat. I open my eyes and suck in a breath.

Out of the corner of my eye, I see the captain frown at me. I know he hates me and thinks I'm stupid.

I'm not doing this for him; I'm doing it for three boys.

West, Elijah, and me.

Rowan wasn't surprised at how fast the SWAT team had set up its command center and put its members into action. She'd witnessed it before.

Malcolm had led everyone to a road near where Liam had kept him captive.

Rowan gripped Evan's hand as they watched the SWAT operation on video screens in the command center. It was crowded in the large motor home, and Malcolm had taken one look and said he'd wait outside. Thor was with him.

After scouting and checking maps and aerial views of the area, the team put together a plan. The target was a portable. One of those prebuilt rectangular buildings that businesses used for temporary on-site offices or when they simply needed a bit more space.

The team's snipers, who also functioned as scouts, had spotted a white truck parked near the portable, and the aerial photos showed a small structure two hundred yards away. Rowan stared at the small square, nearly hidden by large trees, and knew that was where she and Malcolm had been held. When Malcolm had first mentioned being held in a box, she'd assumed it was that structure. He'd later clarified he'd been in a small wooden box, showing the size with his arms. During his demonstration, his mom had left the room, her face pale, and Rowan had had to turn away, feeling ill.

Evan gave her hand a double squeeze, and she met his gaze, seeing concern for her in his eyes. She must have done something odd while remembering the box explanation. She smiled and mouthed, "I'm fine."

They both turned their attention back to the screens, which showed choppy views from the team's helmet cams. Two snipers had set up positions, relaying what they spotted through their sights to team members in the command center.

They reported no movement through the two small windows of the portable, and there was only one entrance.

The rest of the team set up closer to the structure, using the huge pine tree trunks for cover. Their brief statements and replies were broadcast into the command center. Rowan held her breath, knowing the team had decided to immediately enter the structure out of concern that a hostage situation could develop.

This is taking forever.

She understood the delicacy of the situation and had complete trust that the team knew what it was doing. But waiting for news of her nephew seemed to drag on forever.

West's face had been haunting her, his brown eyes and happy smile. She'd been in constant text contact with Ivy, who was going insane while waiting at home with the rest of the family.

There was a sharp command and movement on every screen as the men moved into place. One moved directly to the door, and another's view showed a small battering ram in the first man's hands. He swung it and the flimsy door flew open. Men streamed in behind him, shouts filled the command center, the screen views disorienting from the jostling, and Rowan had to look away to avoid getting dizzy.

"Clear!"

"Clear!"

More shouts.

"The structure is empty," came the captain's voice through the speakers.

"He's here."

Rowan spun around at Malcolm's voice. He had silently entered the command center and was staring at the screens. "His truck is parked out front. That means he's here. The only way to leave is on foot, and there's nothing within walking distance."

His voice was strained, his eyes full of torment.

"Could he get a ride with a neighbor?" asked one of the lieutenants monitoring the screens.

"No. There is no one. It was just Liam and me." He paused. "Just our family."

Rowan almost missed the last bit. Malcolm had whispered it. He'd referred to himself and his captor as a family a few times. He always said the word with a flat tone. It made her skin crawl.

The lieutenant relayed Malcolm's information to the team, which started a new search of the area outside the structure. It'd been cleared by the snipers when they moved into position, but now the men would fan out farther.

"What about the other building?" asked Rowan. She pointed at the small square on the aerial photo.

"He still uses that shed," said Malcolm. He met Rowan's gaze as they shared a painful memory.

"Soon as they clear the area outside this building a little more," said the lieutenant. "That's next."

"I need to step out," said Rowan. The jumping videos were too much. Evan and Malcolm went with her, and she took a seat on one of the several stools outside the mobile command center. Thor pressed his nose against her pocket and then walked back a few steps, his eyes and ears alert.

/play/

Rowan pulled a small collapsible Frisbee from the pocket. "You knew the Frisbee was in there, didn't you?" she said to the dog. She flung it, and Thor tore away.

"I need to look inside," said Malcolm, watching Thor.

Evan and Rowan exchanged a glance. "Inside the building they just cleared?" Rowan asked.

"Yes."

"Why?" asked Evan.

"I just need to. I need to get it out of my system. See it empty."

"I'll ask if we can do that now." Evan vanished into the command center.

As she threw the Frisbee again, Rowan studied Malcolm, noting the determination in his eyes. She understood the need for closure. It was why she'd searched in the woods for years.

And now he's here in front of me.

She'd immediately adjusted to his presence. Almost as if he'd never left. The twins had reacted more slowly, uncertain about the stranger before them. But Rowan had felt a piece click into place in her heart when she saw his face.

"We can go," said Evan. "The lieutenant is alerting everyone that we're approaching the house."

Rowan stood and brushed off the seat of her pants. She took the slobbery Frisbee from Thor and shoved it back in her pocket. Dog drool didn't bother her; pants could be washed. Malcolm immediately started in the direction of the house, and the others sped up to accompany him.

It was a long, silent walk. Pressure seemed to build in the air as they moved closer to the place where Malcolm had been mentally, emotionally, and physically tortured for decades. Even Thor was subdued. Rowan wondered what they'd see inside. Ropes. Restraints. Blindfolds.

She shook her arms, trying to rid herself of the crawling sensation under her skin, drawing a questioning look from Evan.

"I'm good."

They approached the little building. Its door was completely off its hinges and had been tossed aside. From top to bottom, it was splintered and cracked. Malcolm stopped and looked at the door for a long second and then kicked it. Without saying a word, he went up the three steps into the rectangular structure.

He has a lot of buried anger.

As he should.

Inside, it was hard to see, and Malcolm flipped a switch, lighting a dim bulb in the center of the main space. There was a small seating area, a table with two chairs, and a tiny kitchen along a wall across from the table. An open door to their left gave a glimpse of a bedroom.

One bedroom.

Graphic images assaulted her. Malcolm had never mentioned sexual abuse. Rowan took three steps toward the bedroom door and then turned back to find Malcolm watching her, an understanding in his eyes.

"It wasn't like that," he said. "He never touched me in that way."

Cooling relief flowed through her.

He walked past and shoved the bedroom door the rest of the way open. He paused and then deliberately stepped into the space. "I was never allowed in here." He moved to one side of the bed, where there was a tall stack of books on a nightstand. "But I risked it for books." He took the top one off the pile. "I haven't read this yet." He flipped a few pages and then set it back exactly how it'd been found. He squatted in front of the nightstand and ran a hand over a plastic box on the lowest shelf. He shrugged and stood, giving the room a last scan, and then passed Rowan and Evan, heading back to the main area.

Malcolm knelt and crawled under the table, which was shoved against one wall. He slid his fingers behind a loose wall panel near the floor and opened a tiny space. Rowan was surprised to see him remove a book. Her gaze slid to the folded blanket and extremely flat pillow in a corner under the table, and pain blossomed in her heart.

"Malcolm . . . is that where you slept?" She barely got the words out.

He stood up. "Yes." He looked down at the blanket as if seeing it through new eyes. "It wasn't bad. I could hide books."

Captain Vargas stuck his head in the door at that moment. "Y'all done in here? We're headed to the other structure."

"In a minute," said Evan.

Rowan eyed her brother. He'd been different since they'd stepped into the small building. More assured. More confident.

Getting closure was the right thing for him.

46

The building where Malcolm and his captor had lived smelled bad.

Evan had been breathing through his mouth since they entered. A combination of body odor, mildew, and urine. It was strongest near the small bathroom, which Evan refused to look inside. When Malcolm admitted to sleeping under the table, his heart had contracted in sympathy, but then he'd realized that it was all Malcolm knew. And Malcolm hadn't hated it.

"Done?" Evan asked after the captain left.

"Yes." Malcolm stepped outside.

Rowan sighed.

"You okay?" Evan asked her.

"As good as I can be. He lived in squalor while I grew up in a middle-class home."

"It's not your fault."

"I know. But the guilt drowns me sometimes." She exited the building with Evan right behind her, and he took several deep breaths of the clean forest air.

Malcolm turned a corner around the side of the house and disappeared, Thor at his heels. Evan and Rowan ran after him. "Keep him in sight," muttered Evan.

"Why? Where's he going to go?" asked Rowan. "You can't think he still wants to be involved with the man who took West?" she asked incredulously, shooting him a side-eye.

"I don't think that. Not at all," said Evan. He might have wondered that at first, suspicious of the way Malcolm had shown up at his parents'. But now he'd seen enough of Malcolm's pain to know the man wasn't acting. He was a victim.

They found Malcolm behind the house, staring at a large wooden box.

"Oh God." Rowan slammed to a halt.

That's the box he was held in.

Evan looked away from the box, but what he saw increased his sympathy. They were standing in the middle of a gorgeous, healthy forest with a bright-blue sky, nature's paradise. And in front of them was a weapon of abuse.

A small child would easily fit. Even a preteen. But a teenager or adult would have to lie on their side and pull up their knees to fit inside. Sitting up would be impossible for a person of any age. A rusty, unlocked padlock dangled from its black metal clasp. No doubt the SWAT team had looked inside.

Did they guess how it was used?

Malcolm threw the padlock to one side and flung open the lid, a ferocious look on his face. Evan peered inside. Empty. The bottom was made from heavy wooden slats, the walls thick and reinforced like the lid. Malcolm spun around and strode to the side of the house, where he grabbed a sledgehammer that leaned against the wall next to an axe and huge branch trimmers.

His gaze locked on the box, Malcolm swung the sledgehammer at the lid and knocked it off one hinge. Another swing detached it from the second hinge, and it fell to the ground. He lowered the sledgehammer, leaning on the handle, panting hard.

He's too weak to destroy it all.

Evan stepped to his side, placed a hand on his shoulder, and held out the other toward the sledgehammer. "Let me do it."

"No." Malcolm shook his head. "I can do it." He lifted the hammer again and let the heavy head slam into the side of the box. Boards cracked but stayed in place. Malcolm rested again.

"Please," said Evan. "Let me destroy the fucking thing."

Malcolm held his gaze for a long moment and then handed Evan the long-handled hammer.

Evan hefted it. It wasn't a wimpy ten-pound head. It had to be closer to twenty. He wondered how Malcolm had used it, weak as he was.

He's fueled by rage.

Evan clenched his jaw and swung, letting his body weight carry through the swing. One side splintered, and the impact rattled up every bone in his arms. He swung again. And again, feeding on Malcolm's anger and hate.

Minutes later, the box was in pieces.

Breathing hard, Evan lowered the handle and rested on it as Malcolm had. A sense of accomplishment and satisfying revenge filled him as he met Malcolm's gaze.

"Thank you," Malcolm said, sincerity in his tone.

"Anytime," answered Evan.

Rowan put her arms around Malcolm, and he tensed but then softened into her hug. "I'm so sorry, Mal."

He slowly shook his head. "I was always thankful that it was me instead of you."

Rowan shook with quiet sobs, and Evan struggled to stay back and let the two of them have the emotional moment.

After a moment Malcolm moved out of her arms. "There's something I want inside the house. Be right back."

"How are you doing?" Evan asked as she wiped her eyes.

"Why are people so horrible to each other?" she pleaded. "What kind of person does that to a child? Or even an adult? What are they getting out of it?"

"Power. Control," said Evan. "They feed on it. It's an addiction."

"I hate him," said Rowan. "I hate Liam *and* Jerry for what they did to us. Especially to Malcolm." Thor circled her, occasionally pawing at the ground, her emotions upsetting him. She pulled out the floppy Frisbee and threw it hard, and Thor rocketed after it. "Fetch therapy," she said.

"For you or him?"

"Both of us." Thor returned, and she hurled it again.

Evan took a few seconds to appreciate the simple happiness of the sprinting dog performing fetch therapy in the calm forest. "It's been quiet since the team headed to that other building."

"I think we would have heard a racket if they found Liam and West," said Rowan. "But it's a few hundred yards away. The trees could block the noise." Her face darkened, and her next toss of the Frisbee lacked the effort of the others.

"That's the building where the two of you were held, isn't it?" Evan asked.

"Yes."

Evan waited, but she didn't have more to say. Her time here was imprinted on her brain in a horrible way. And in the scars on her leg. He'd glimpsed them a couple of times. Silver and pink lines and splotches. She'd never lose them or the limp. Permanent reminders.

He suspected Malcolm's scars were much worse.

Frowning, Evan listened for movement inside the house. "Malcolm's been gone awhile."

Rowan's head turned sharply as she studied the building. Then she darted around toward the front, Thor on her heels and Evan right behind her. She leaped over the stairs. *"Malcolm?"*

Evan entered and followed her down the short hall. He pushed the bathroom door farther open this time. Empty.

And filthy.

In the bedroom, Rowan knelt to check under the bed. "He's not here." She started to stand and then caught her breath.

"What is it?" Evan moved behind her in the tiny room.

"That's a case for a gun."

He looked over her shoulder. The plastic box on the nightstand shelf that Malcolm had brushed a hand over was now open, and its inner dark egg crate foam was empty.

Malcolm took a gun.

"He's gone after Liam and West on his own," said Rowan. "We need to get to that other structure *now*."

The two of them dashed out of the stinking building.

47

Once I had the gun in hand, I ran in the opposite direction from the SWAT team.

I was always too scared to touch the tiny gun safe. I knew where the key was; I'd seen Liam hide it several times. Many nights I dreamed of taking the gun and shooting Liam as he slept. Sometimes I shot him in his sleep. Other times I woke him so he would know it was me.

But I never had the guts to do it. I had nowhere to run to if I killed him. He made the money and supported us. He always said I was too stupid to survive on my own, and I agreed. I also knew the police would eventually figure out who killed him, and then I'd go to prison.

So I did nothing.

Until today. Now I have a place to land and family to help me.

Although family will no longer matter if I kill him. I'll be in prison for his murder. I've decided I don't care because I will not let him torture West.

No one should suffer the way I did. Or Rowan or Elijah did.

My sacrifice is worth it.

There is one other place I know where he might have taken West. I run through the woods, breathing hard, the gun clasped in my hand. Its solid weight empowers me, and I feel a confidence I've never experienced before.

I've never fired a gun. Never even held one. But I've read about firing them in books. I know to release the safety. I know to aim for the largest mass. I know I will probably miss the first time. I wish I could take a practice shot now, but I don't want to give away my location.

I want him.

I told Rowan I needed closure. Killing Liam will give me more peace than watching Detective Bolton destroy that box.

It's a long way through the woods. I alternate between jogging and walking. When I ran from the work site yesterday seems so long ago. I swore to never return to this place, but here I am the next damned day.

I will stop Liam. I will put an end to this "family" legacy that he is so driven to continue. He will pay for what he did to me and Rowan. For what he did to those two women and Elijah. I suspect there are more recent victims. His odd behavior the last few weeks was identical to how he acted when he murdered the people I buried.

Did the SWAT team find more bodies in the shed?

I push on, stepping over tree roots and tripping over my own aching feet. The air smells like sun-warmed pine needles and sagebrush, and it's quiet except for the sound of my breathing. I listen hard for the sound of water. I'll know I'm close when I hear the river. I stop, resting my hands on my thighs. I'm light-headed and sweating.

The book I took from my hiding spot is tucked in the waistband of my jeans and slick with sweat. I didn't want to leave without it. It was one more *fuck you* to Liam that I stole a book he refused to let me read.

And I wanted to finish the story about the odd Los Angeles private investigator and his big, tough, silent sidekick.

I hear them before I hear the water.

Liam is yelling at West, telling him he must work hard and be good.

My skin crawls at the words I've heard so many times. It is odd to not be on the receiving end for once. I slowly sneak closer, moving from tree trunk to tree trunk until I can see them next to the river. It is Liam's favorite spot. Near where we buried the bodies.

West is carrying rocks. Liam has him moving big river rocks from one pile to another, and the boy is blindfolded. The water is halfway to his knees, and he trips. I wince as he falls and cries out as he smashes his fingers under the rock he's carrying.

My fingers ache in sympathy. This is a favorite task of Liam's. I think I've moved every rock along the river that I was strong enough to lift. I touch the skin next to my eyes, remembering the disorientation of the blindfold.

"No sniffling! And if you complain one more time, no dinner."

"I want my mom!"

"No dinner," Liam says in a disappointed voice. "Why did you make me say it? I don't want to see you go hungry, but you broke the rule. I have no choice but to punish you for it."

I close my eyes, despair drowning me at the familiar phrases. I tighten my grip on the gun.

I'm okay. He can't hurt me again.

West stops, a large rock braced in both his hands, his mouth open as he breathes hard. The moment Liam's message registers in his brain, his back stiffens. He's realized that he'll have to follow all Liam's rules if he wants to eat.

How will he act the first time he goes in the box?

But the box is gone. Destroyed. I imagine Liam staring at its ruins, and happiness warms me.

Because of me, no other child will suffer in that box.

"Not like that! Set them down gently! Don't make me punish you for not doing it right."

My stomach heaves, and I clench my teeth together.

I can't listen anymore.

I step around the tree, my heart in my throat, my hands shaking. I move the gun from hand to hand and wipe my sweaty palms on my jeans, not wanting the weapon to slip. I walk closer to the river, the gun in front of me. I grip with both hands and my arms instantly ache because I swung the sledgehammer.

The sun touches my hair and shoulders. "Stop!" My voice is louder than I expected, and adrenaline races through my veins. I halt several yards away.

I can do this.

Liam turns. Surprise flashes in his eyes for a split second, but then a wide smile crosses his face. "I knew you'd come back. Especially once you realized the boy was missing."

Acid builds in the back of my throat.

"I had no doubts. I'm your family and we are committed." Liam points at West. "And now there are three of us."

West is frozen in place, the water rushing around his ankles, unable to see me because of his blindfold.

"But since you ran away, I'll have to punish the new boy. That's how it works now. Listen up, boy, this is your uncle. When he disobeys me, I have to punish you."

West's shoulders heave as he holds back sobs.

Liam smiles. "You should tell your uncle to be good."

"Be good!" West shrieks. Tears stain his blindfold.

I see red. My vision tunnels on Liam and anger burns hot through me. But I am in control.

"You stole my gun," Liam states, gesturing at me. "That means I have to punish the boy."

"No!" West cries.

"Not sure what you think you can do with that," Liam drawls. "You've never fired a gun. Did you even check to see if it's loaded?"

I didn't. I'm not sure how.

But I don't think he'd lock up an unloaded gun by his bed. "I checked," I lie.

He smirks, and I fear I'm holding an empty weapon.

"I know she's alive," I tell Liam in a calm voice.

"Who?"

"Rowan. She wasn't killed by animals." I catch my breath and breathe deep. "You lied to me for twenty-five years! *I'm thirty-two years old and I never knew my age!* Why do you do this? Why did Jerry start this . . . this family?"

Liam rests a foot on a rock and shoves his hands in his pockets. "Looks like a gun in your hand gives you a big mouth. You're racking up hours in the box."

Instant fear makes my temples sweat. Then I remember the box is gone.

Gone like his power; I hold the power now.

The power is in my clasped hands, black and heavy. "What was Jerry to you? You call him family, but you got him sent to prison. The rule was to never betray the family!"

"Jerry was the closest thing I ever had to a father, and I was committed to this family. I'd do anything for the family. Jerry, Ken, and I were a solid unit!"

"Yet you got Jerry arrested."

"Jerry went against the family first! He let Ken leave after the first girl died. Just walk away. That wasn't right! No one walks away from us!"

I have no idea who he's talking about.

"Jerry said Ken agreed to stay silent if he was allowed to leave. That's not how we were brought up! Jerry changed the rules for him." He slapped a hand on his thigh, anger in his face.

"Sending Jerry to prison was payback for letting another guy leave?"

Liam looks away, and I know I've struck a chord.

He was jealous because Jerry let someone walk away from their twisted little family.

"Then you thought you could just walk away too." Anger infuses his tone. "That's not how it works. *We stay together.*"

That phrase has been pounded into my head nearly all my life.

"It didn't work out so well for Ken," Liam sneers. "He visited Jerry in prison and asked if I was involved in . . . something. Next thing I know, Ken wants to meet with me. Claimed Jerry was pissed about some women who'd recently died." He raised a brow. "Ken thought he could enforce Jerry's orders? I don't think so. Cocky idiot. I took care of him."

"I don't know who Ken is," I finally say. But Liam is talking about things I've wanted to know for decades. I'm not ready for him to stop.

Liam makes a sound of disgust. "When your babysitter turned up dead, Ken figured that Jerry probably had the two of you. He'd left the family several years before, but he recognized Jerry's work when he read about the babysitter in the paper . . . just as some dead women recently made him suspicious again.

"It was supposed to be a game that night I let you and your sister out of the shed." Liam's gaze became distant as he remembered. "A hunt."

I'd been so nervous when he unlocked the shed door and told us to leave.

"But you got further away than we expected. By the time we picked up your trail, we couldn't find your sister. We didn't care. We figured she'd find her end in the forest. She was deadweight and didn't fit in the family." He looks at me. "You fit. A docile idiot. You were perfect for our needs."

I shudder. They kept me drugged for years to feed their need for power and control.

At least Rowan got away.

"Ken found your sister. People were still searching for you two. He knew the general area to look and got lucky she wasn't dead yet. A few days later he came to the house looking for you, and we told him you were dead. An accident. Ken had to keep his mouth shut about your death because if he turned me in, I'd report him as an accomplice."

"Accomplice?" I've hated the word ever since he emotionally branded me with it.

"Ken knew Jerry and I killed women years ago. The wimp said he couldn't stomach it. Jerry let him go because Ken threatened to go to the police if he didn't."

My mind is spinning trying to keep up.

So many murders. First Jerry and Liam worked together, and then Liam continued on his own.

"Jerry must have been annoyed that Ken contacted him after all these years, because he told Ken you were still alive," Liam goes on. "Ken flipped out. He'd stayed in touch with your family, and seeing what they unnecessarily went through swamped him with guilt.

"You're a part of this," he says in a soft voice. "You can't just walk away. I know you don't want to. You belong with us. We'll work together and train this boy. You'll get to be a leader . . . It's a rush like you can't understand." He takes two steps toward me. "Give me the gun."

From several yards away, I fire at the ground in front of him, and West screams, terrified and slapping his hands over his ears. The boy drops to his knees in the shallow water, crying.

The noise and kick of the gun startled me, and I nearly dropped it. But at least I got my practice shot. Now I know what to expect. I aim at Liam's chest, barely aware of West's cries of fear. All I see is Liam. The man who abused me.

My finger plays with the trigger. I could fire several times and hope one hits him. But I don't know how many bullets I have.

Do I truly want him dead?

Years in prison like Jerry would be better. Let him experience being locked up and having all his freedoms taken away. I'm a better person than him and Jerry.

They are killers; I am not.

Liam should go to prison.

I instantly feel lighter and more confident, a burden lifted. I've made the right decision.

Liam gestures at West. "You scared the boy. Let me take his blindfold off so he can see what's happening."

I nod, understanding the terror of not being able to see. My weapon tracks him as he moves to the boy and gently unties the blindfold. His touch is tender. I want to vomit.

"That's better," he tells West. "Now you can see. Give me your hand." He helps West stand, the boy unsteady as the water speeds around his feet. Then he loops the blindfold around one of West's wrists, pulls it behind his back, and ties it to the other wrist.

"What are you doing?" I shout at him. He stands with the boy between him and me. I have no shot. I might hit West.

He knew that.

I am angry at myself for allowing him to use the boy as a shield.

Then I remember.

He threw me in the river with my hands tied, laughing and yelling at me to swim. I swallowed many mouthfuls of water and got water up my nose, terrified and scrambling to find a purchase for my feet.

I believed I'd drown.

The river isn't that deep at the edge, but it is fast and strong, and along the sides the bottom is uneven with drop-offs.

I know what he's going to do.

I freeze as he lifts West and hurls him toward the water.

I feel it is me being thrown in. I am the one fighting to breathe. To survive.

The boy's screams are cut off as his head goes underwater.

Save him.

"Put the gun down, and I'll help him out," Liam yells at me.

My gaze locks on Liam, but I'm fully aware of West's struggles. "I'll shoot you and help him out."

"You've never fired a gun until a minute ago, chances are you'll miss." Liam is jumping and shuffling from right to left, keeping his side toward me. A smaller target.

"Get away from him!" I snarl, moving forward.

Liam backs away as I get closer to the river. West has been pushed downstream by the water, being dragged over the rocks at the edge. The river's force is just rough and strong enough to keep him from getting his footing, his hands useless behind him. His head has popped up a few times, and I hope he caught his breath.

Keeping one eye on Liam and the other on West, I stumble on the slick rocks and scramble toward the boy, moving deeper into the water. After two misses I grab his upper arm and lift his head out of the water. He breathes deep and relief swamps me. But he's too heavy for me to haul out of the water with one hand. I shove the gun in the waist of my jeans at my stomach.

A force plows into my back, and I'm thrust face-first into deeper water, losing my grip on West.

"No!" My mouth fills with water at my shout, and my chest slams riverbed rocks.

Liam.

He lands on my back, keeping my head and torso under the water, and his hand searches around my stomach for the gun. My arms flail as I try to reach back to push him off.

His hand continues to dig, scratching my ribs.

I can't let him have the gun.

Where is West?

Water goes up my nose, and I open my eyes underwater. Bubbles from the thrashing water cross my vision. My lungs hurt, and my brain screams for oxygen. But I'm pinned.

I need air.

48

On their dash to the shed, Rowan and Evan encountered the returning SWAT team. Rowan panicked when she didn't see Malcolm among them. "Sit," she told Thor, knowing he'd want to greet each man.

"It's empty," Captain Vargas told them. "We're going—"

"Malcolm is gone," she gasped, catching her breath. "He's armed, and I think he's gone after West on his own. We thought he was headed to the shed, but he must have known another place Liam would take the boy."

Captain Vargas turned to his men. "Pair off. We'll set up a search grid."

"That'll take too long. We have to use Thor," Rowan said in a low voice to Evan. "There's no way Malcolm knows how to use that gun. Liam would never allow him to handle one. Someone is going to end up dead. Especially if Liam is armed too."

Her mind sped ahead, already planning. "Captain! Thor can search. He can follow Malcolm's trail from the other building."

Captain Vargas frowned. "You sure? I don't know if that would turn out to be faster. The guy used to live here. His scent will be everywhere."

"Thor can pinpoint the most recent."

"Okay . . . but I'm still going to have my guys work a grid." He turned back to his men.

Rowan ignored him. She'd encountered plenty of distrust on searches. The best plan was simply to get to work and let the naysayers go their own way. Evan looked about ready to argue with the captain, and she touched his arm. "It's okay. Less distraction for Thor." Evan was armed, and Rowan had her little backpack of supplies she always took when she and Thor went into the woods.

"We'll use the pillow from that place as a scent article." She rubbed Thor's head. "Ready to work?"

His tail swept a V in the dirt, his eyes eager.

/play/

Rowan watched her dog. He knew what they were about to do, and he loved the hunt. It was his favorite game. "Let's go." She started to jog back to the little house.

It's not really a house. I don't know what to call it.

"That *place*," she mumbled.

"What?" asked Evan, running beside her.

"Nothing."

Minutes later Thor sniffed the pillow and turned his excited gaze on Rowan. She'd decided to start at the destroyed front door, knowing Malcolm had been there recently. "Find it," she ordered. He spun and started to smell along the ground, moving at a slow trot, his tail slightly raised. He stopped and lifted his head, his mouth opening the slightest bit to get more scent. Then he took off, headed in the opposite direction from the shed.

Rowan and Evan followed.

Thor moved at a confident pace, clearly in work mode. Rowan spotted an occasional footprint in the dry, dusty dirt and darker spots where pine needles had been recently disturbed.

"We're going the right way," she said to Evan.

"That's a damn fine dog you have."

She nodded. "I agree."

Thor never stopped and searched for the scent, which told Rowan the trail was very recent. She wiped the sweat from her forehead.

Don't do anything stupid, Malcolm.

She hoped her brother wouldn't get hurt. A gun in the hands of a person with little experience was a dangerous thing. He could be quickly disarmed unless he was committed to shooting someone.

He hates Liam with all his being.

Rowan quickened her pace to catch up with Thor. She suspected Malcolm would fire if given the chance, no matter the consequences.

The crack of gunfire filled the forest.

Thor halted and looked back at Rowan. "Find it," she told him as alarm shot through her limbs. She'd hesitated to give the command, not wanting to send her dog into a dangerous situation.

But West is out there.

"That shot wasn't far off," said Evan. He'd drawn his weapon, his gaze scanning the woods around them.

"But was it Malcolm or Liam?"

A minute later she recognized the rushing sound of a river. "I think I know approximately where we are," she said.

Near Liam's dumping ground.

Shouts reached their ears, and she commanded Thor to return. She hooked the leash to his harness and got a reproachful look for it. He wanted to finish the search.

"We'll celebrate later, boy," she whispered.

Evan moved in front, weapon leading, and she followed.

"Holy shit!" Evan started to run.

Rowan tried to see past him as she ran too. They broke out of the forest onto the flat banks of the river. Two people were fighting in the water, but she could only see the back of one man's head as he held the other underwater. He had short hair.

That must be Liam.

He's drowning Malcolm.

Cries drew her gaze farther downriver, and she saw West struggling. He came up for air but was flipped and dragged by the water hitting the rocks.

"Get West!" Evan shouted at her. He had his gun trained on the men in the water.

"That's got to be Liam!" she yelled back, already running with Thor toward the boy. Rowan's bad leg struggled with the big, slick rocks, unable to get a purchase. Thor pulled, and she let go of his leash.

He was a black blur, leaping over rocks, an arrow headed straight for his target. Thor crashed into the water and grabbed West's shirt in his mouth. The water was too deep for Thor to stand, so he swam, pulling the boy to shallower water.

Got him!

West was crying and sputtering, and Rowan was furious when she realized his hands were tied behind his back. She planted both feet and scooped him up in her arms. "I've got you, West." She sat on one of the bigger rocks and pulled at the fabric on his wrists. It came loose, and West lunged to wrap his arms around her neck, wailing.

"You're safe now," she said. "No one is going to hurt you." Thor shook, showering them both with water, and then sat, his gaze meeting Rowan's.

"Good boy, Thor. Best job ever."

"Get off him! I will shoot!"

Rowan looked upriver. Evan stood in a foot of water; his weapon was trained on Liam, who was flailing in the water two yards away.

He's still holding Malcolm underwater.

Evan yelled his warning two more times.

Clutching West, she got to her feet and carefully stepped from rock to rock, putting more distance between them and the struggling men. She reached the river's bank and turned to watch.

Liam abruptly sat up and swung his arm toward Evan. Rowan saw the blur of black in Liam's hand.

A gun.

He's going to shoot Evan.

The crack of a shot filled the forest as Evan fired.

Liam jerked and fell to one side with a splash. Malcolm shot up from the water, coughing and gasping for air.

Thank God.

For a split second she'd believed she'd lose both Evan and Malcolm.

Evan grabbed one of Liam's feet as he started to float downstream.

"Show me your hands!" Evan yelled at the man. *"Show me your hands!"*

Liam didn't move.

"Stay back, Rowan!" Evan shouted. "He could still be armed."

She stayed in place, balanced on two rocks. West was quiet but clung to her like a koala.

Malcolm pushed through the thigh-deep water toward Evan. He was dripping, his long hair plastered to his shoulders.

"Stay back," Evan told him.

Malcolm ignored him. He stopped next to Liam and stared down at his face. He met Evan's gaze and shook his head. Malcolm turned around and studied the water, as if trying to see into it. He took a couple of steps, lowered himself into the water, and came up with a gun.

"Thanks, Malcolm." Evan holstered his weapon and dragged Liam to the shore by his feet. Malcolm grabbed Liam's shoulders, and they moved him to a flat area.

Rowan stepped off the rocks and set West down on one. "Don't move," she told him. He nodded, his eyes wide.

He'll remember this for the rest of his life.

She joined the others. Evan sat on the ground near the man's feet, resting his arms on his legs. Liam had a large wound in the side of his chest.

"There's no pulse," Evan told her.

"I'm sorry, Evan," Rowan said. It didn't matter that Evan had fired in self-defense; he'd killed someone, and it would forever weigh on him.

Malcolm stood silently at Liam's head, staring down at the body. Rowan moved beside him and wrapped an arm around him. "It's over."

"Yes."

Evan joined them. "Why do I feel like I recognize this guy?"

Rowan finally looked at the dead man's face and then gasped. "That's Eric Steward. Ken's cousin."

49

Three days later

Evan grabbed another beer at the birthday party. He was quickly becoming a fan of Rowan's family. They were a lot of fun and clearly cared deeply about each other. He twisted the top off as he watched Malcolm happily eat a second helping of strawberry shortcake.

The three sisters had decorated their parents' house for Malcolm's party. Someone had plastered banners all over the great room that said HAPPY 8TH BIRTHDAY! and HAPPY 9TH BIRTHDAY! all the way up to HAPPY 32ND BIRTHDAY! The enormous stack of gifts by the fireplace was clearly intended to make up for twenty-five missed parties.

They had served hamburgers, Tater Tots, orange soda, and strawberry shortcake. Prosecco had been added to the soda, but Evan had seen Malcolm take a sip and make a face. Iris had laughed and poured him straight orange soda.

Evan sipped his beer, stuffed from the big meal. He couldn't remember the last time he'd had Tater Tots. Malcolm's eyes had lit up at the hamburger patties on the grill. He'd eaten his burger with just ketchup. Rowan had whispered that that was how he'd eaten them when he was a kid.

Her brother had lost so much time.

Liam, a.k.a. Eric Steward, had controlled Malcolm for the last two decades, and Jerry had controlled both of them before that. Eric and Ken had been Jerry's apprentice electricians. Eric had changed his last name to Steward at the same time that Ken changed his. Evan had spoken to another electrician who had worked with Jerry and been told that the two young men had been very close. Called themselves blood brothers and had even lived with Jerry off and on.

A family of three. Jerry controlled Eric and Ken.

And then Jerry controlled Eric and Malcolm.

Then for many years, it was just Eric controlling Malcolm, until he decided to add West.

When Eric Steward's photo hit the media as that of the killer of the three recently murdered young women, a waitress from a truck stop half an hour south of Bend had come forward and said Eric had been a regular in the restaurant. She'd seen him eat with many young women over the years but hadn't thought anything of it. She couldn't confirm that she'd seen him with those particular three women, but that was enough that Evan figured the truck stop had probably been where Eric found his victims.

Elijah had vanished from the same truck stop. After decades of wondering, his parents now knew that their son had ended up in a forest grave.

There wasn't anyone to ask if the truck stop had been Eric's hunting ground. Everyone who would know was dead. Except Jerry Chiavo, who refused to speak when Evan tried to interview him again.

Malcolm had spoken of a weird family commitment among all the men. Something about never betraying one another.

It appeared Jerry was sticking to the rule.

Ivy stopped beside Evan and clinked her half-empty flute against his beer. "It's a good party, isn't it?" She beamed as she looked over to where Malcolm sat at the table, talking to West.

"It's probably the happiest I've ever been to," Evan truthfully admitted. He was still dealing with the shock of shooting Eric in the river and was on paid leave while the incident was under review. He had no doubts he'd be in the clear; Eric had been about to shoot him.

"West seems to be doing well," Evan said, considering the child had been kidnapped and had witnessed a shooting.

"He is," agreed Ivy. "He's had his upset moments, of course, but I think knowing that Eric died has helped him feel safe. The bad man is gone for good. I hate that he saw him get shot, but I think it might help psychologically in the long run."

"I see the logic in that," said Evan. "What about your ex, Adam? Have you heard from him?"

"I did." She narrowed her brows. "He blamed his behavior on being drunk. Believes he broke West's window because some drunken part of him thought if he took West away, it'd be the ultimate revenge for me divorcing him. Now that Adam is sober, he told me that he had no idea what he would do with a kid and was actually alarmed at the thought of having to care for West by himself."

Evan snorted. "You married *that guy*?"

"I admit to being young and in love—for a very short period of time. I got smart after two months and the first black eye." She took a long drink from her glass. "I'm thankful every day that I left him. But I don't regret that I married him because if I hadn't, I wouldn't have West."

"He's a great kid."

"Absolutely." She followed Evan's gaze to Rowan, who was talking to Iris near the fireplace. "You know," she said with a conspiring tone in her voice, "Iris and I think you might be the first guy in Rowan's life that holds a higher place in her heart than Thor."

Evan grinned. "We both know that's not true." He sipped his beer. "But I plan to change that."

"Good," said Ivy. "Now go talk to her."

That sounds like good advice.

Rowan watched Evan cross the room with her in his sights. Iris saw him too, made an excuse about helping their mom, and left. He stopped in front of her, placed a hand at the back of her neck, pulled her close, and kissed her. She melted into him, a little dizzy and happy from the drinks and the joy in the room.

After a long moment he pulled back. "Good party," he said with a gleam in his eye, and he gave her a quick peck on the lips.

He's not talking about the party.

"This has been the best day ever," Rowan said, looking him right in the eye so he knew she considered him one of the reasons. Then she looked at Malcolm, who was quietly listening to West enthusiastically tell a story about a goat.

It's so good to have him home.

Malcolm had spent the last few days adapting to his new world. The first day he'd shaken and cried as he confessed to his role in burying the bodies of two women and a boy. It'd taken hours to assure him that he was not in trouble and that their murders were all on Eric. He'd been convinced he'd go straight to prison for being an accomplice.

He'd been brainwashed about several things.

It'd taken some clarification from Malcolm, but Rowan had figured out that Ken had worried she'd never forgive him after Jerry Chiavo had told him two weeks before his death that Malcolm was alive. All those years ago, Jerry had convinced him that Malcolm was dead. Rowan couldn't imagine Ken's thoughts when he'd realized that Malcolm had been kept by Jerry and then Eric for decades. He must have felt incredibly guilty knowing Rowan's family had mourned him for so long.

If only Ken had gone to the police with what he knew about Jerry and Eric killing women before we were even kidnapped.

Malcolm would have lived a normal life.

She would have too.

No memories of torture for either of them.

Malcolm had been staying at her parents', but Rowan had extended an offer to stay with her. She hoped he'd take her up on it in the near future. They'd already put things in motion to get him identification. It sounded as if he was a skilled electrician. She had no doubt they could figure out how to get him a real job in the field.

At first Rowan had enjoyed watching him have new experiences such as simply taking a walk down the street alone or sleeping in a big bed. Using a shower whenever he wished. Opening a cupboard and pulling out a box of crackers. But then she'd grown angry about all he'd missed, hating the men who had done this to Malcolm and her family.

Her brother had a long road ahead.

But lots of support.

"Malcolm's going to do great," Evan whispered to her. "Your family is fantastic."

She looked him in the eye again, his face close to hers. "Thank you." She lifted a hand to his cheek, running her fingers over the faint stubble. "I think you're fantastic too."

His eyes lit up. "You do?"

"Yes." Evan was a good, trustworthy man, and she couldn't wait to spend more time with him. Lots of time.

We waited a long time to get to this point.

"Ivy told me you might like me more than Thor," he said with a knowing smile.

Rowan chuckled. "Ivy is deranged."

"I told her it wasn't true," Evan said. "But then I told her I planned on changing that."

She caught her breath at his serious gaze.

That might be easier than he realizes.

"How about we both work on it?"

His smile warmed her heart. "I've already started."

Acknowledgments

Rowan Wolff first appeared in *A Merciful Promise*. She intrigued me, and I knew I'd write about her in depth one day. Her relationship with her dog was fascinating, and I wanted to know why she limped. Evan Bolton has been a fan favorite since he first appeared in the Mercy Kilpatrick series. Many readers asked me to write his book and help him move past his unrequited interest in Mercy. It felt very natural to have him and Rowan come together.

If you're wondering when the next Mercy Kilpatrick book is coming, I plan for it to be one of the next two books I write. It was definitely to be next, but Detective Noelle Marshall is stuck in my brain, and I'm vacillating between writing her and writing Mercy. Either way, I love to have previous characters pop up in the middles of my stories, and according to my email, my readers love it too.

Montlake has always let me decide what I wish to write. It is an amazing publisher, and I'm thankful every day that it's published all my work. Charlotte has been my dev editor for more than ten years; she is simply the best and keeps my stories on track. My acquisitions editor, Anh, gives me and my books amazing support. My agent, Meg, always wants to know what I need and then immediately makes it happen.

On to the next.

ABOUT THE AUTHOR

Photo © 2016 Rebekah Jule Photography

Kendra Elliot has landed on the *Wall Street Journal* bestseller list multiple times and is the award-winning author of the Bone Secrets and Callahan & McLane series, the Mercy Kilpatrick novels, and the Columbia River novels. She's a three-time winner of the Daphne du Maurier Award, an International Thriller Writers Award finalist, and an RT Award finalist. She has always been a voracious reader, cutting her teeth on classic female heroines such as Nancy Drew, Trixie Belden, and Laura Ingalls. She was born and raised in the rainy Pacific Northwest but now lives in flip-flops. Visit her at www.kendraelliot.com.